I0654944

RALPH GRECO & LISA GRECO

Ralph Greco has taught middle school English for 45 years at the Palm Beach Day Academy. As an educator, coach and mentor he has influenced generations of young people in his community and continues to this day. A lifelong athlete, Ralph played football and basketball before switching to running and tennis. His many hours on the court preparing his daughter, Lisa, for tournament play provided the inspiration for this book. He lives in Palm Beach, Florida with his wife Dolly.

Lisa Greco played competitive tennis on the USTA Junior Circuit in Florida and at the college level before becoming a recreational player who still enjoys a weekly match with her father, Ralph. A former magazine editor and counselor, she is currently working on several writing projects and volunteers as a Guardian ad Litem, advocating for abused and neglected children in the dependency system. She lives in West Palm Beach, Florida with her husband, Richard, and their dogkids, Lady and Django.

Published by Principio Books, LLC.
14525 SW Millikan Way, #75822
Beaverton, Oregon 97005
info@principiobooks.com
www.principiobooks.com
ISBN: 1-62908-002-0
ISBN-13: 978-1-62908-002-4

NO TEARS TO WIMBLEDON

Ralph Greco and Lisa Greco

 **1**

One day in January...

"Terry, this is your last wake-up call. I need to see some movement so I know you're alive."

The figure in bed slowly stirred then rolled over and faced the wall.

"Come on, sweetheart, right *now* and I mean it. If you're late again, you'll have to stay after school and you won't be able to help Papi on Thursday."

The figure lay motionless amidst the wreckage of her bed.

"Terry!!!"

"OK, OK, I'm not deaf!"

Maria Gomez paused in the doorway, torn between wanting to give her granddaughter a good morning kiss the way she used to, or dragging her out of bed and into the bathroom. Instead she ignored the bratty reply and walked back down the hall to the kitchen.

Waiting until she was sure her grandmother was gone, Terry slowly sat up and began disengaging herself from the sheets and blanket tangled around her. After a short struggle, she threw off the last restraint, sending the whole pile flying off the bed with a violent kick.

Finally, she swung her legs across the bed, planted her feet on the floor and just sat for a moment, letting her body get used to the idea of being awake. She stared at her mattress with its sole surviving fitted sheet, damp with sweat and pulling away at the top. Her nights were getting worse and worse. She used to crawl into bed, fall asleep immediately, sleep solidly through the night and simply straighten the pillows and bedspread in the morning. Now the mess on the floor spoke louder than any words about the nights she was having.

Heaving herself off the bed, she plodded across the hall to the bathroom where she rinsed her face with cold water until her eyelids finally became unglued and she was forced to look up and face the first bummer in the string of bummers punctuating every day. Glaring at her reflection in the dreaded surface covering the front of the medicine cabinet, she listened to the soundtrack in her head playing her favorite early Pink song:

> *Every day I fight a war against the mirror.*
> *I can't take the person staring back at me.*
> *I'm a hazard to myself. Don't let me get me.*
> *I'm my own worst enemy.*
> *It's bad when you annoy yourself. So irritating.*
> *Don't want to be my friend no more.*
> *I want to be somebody else.*

Exactly. Pink had this one nailed. Somebody else. *Anybody* other than Terry Gomez with her banana nose and clown mouth outlined by lips that looked like the wax ones people wore on Halloween. Her mustache was filling in nicely, too. Combine these assets with an absurdly long neck and a gigantic body and you had the next star of the freak show at the South Florida Fair. Really, how many 5′11″ seventh graders were there, girls *or* boys? Answer: one. How special. When she was forced into a group activity with girls her age—during every excruciating minute at school, for instance—she felt like a Clydesdale horse stuck in the middle of a bunch of ponies. And her sorry looks weren't the worst part. She identified even more strongly with being her own worst enemy. Terry Gomez kept getting her into trouble, but she couldn't seem to stay away from her.

Arrgghhh!! Terry turned her back on the offending mirror and stomped back to her room. If only she could glance back and catch a glimpse of her true reflection she'd be pleasantly surprised by the stranger staring back. Thick, shiny hair the color of freshly ground coffee streaked with copper highlights from the sun framed a triangular-shaped face—high, wide cheekbones slanting to meet a pointed chin. Eyes so dark they flashed black were almost hidden by lavish curly lashes. When she smiled, which wasn't often, her generous mouth revealed a perfect set of dazzling white teeth made even brighter by the light olive tint of a complexion remarkably unblemished for an adolescent. And tall, yes, but beautifully proportioned with the beginning of curves in all the right places hinting at the knockout body of the future.

This was the Terry Gomez seen by everyone except Terry Gomez. The Terry who grudgingly woke up on this chilly January morning and glowered into this mirror wasn't capable of recognizing her.

Terry shuffled into the tiny, immaculate kitchen, dropped heavily into a chair and drained the glass of orange juice sitting at her place in three noisy gulps.

"One of these days you're going to choke, drinking like that," Maria said, setting a plate in front of Terry. "I don't know if the Heimlich maneuver works with liquid, and I don't want to find out."

Terry eyed the plate of bacon and eggs with distaste and shoved it away. "I'm not hungry."

"But you need a good breakfast. You can't go all morning on just a glass of juice."

"Stop hassling me! I said I'm not hungry!"

Maria stepped back as if she'd been slapped. Her first reaction was to slap back, though she didn't. She'd never hit Terry, or anyone else, for that matter. The mouthing off had been going on for awhile now, but this tone was new—different, harsh and mean. Blinking back tears of frustration, she grabbed Terry's plate and started over to the sink.

"I'm sorry Bria." Terry caught the hem of Maria's blouse and gently pulled her back. "It's just that my stomach feels a little weird, but I know you're right. I'll try to eat a little, OK?"

Terry felt so guilty she'd gag on those eggs to make it up to her grandmother.

"Your stomach? What's wrong? Are you sick?" Maria fretted, immediately forgetting her anger and placing the back of her hand against Terry's forehead.

Now look what she started! "It's nothing, a little grumbly, that's all," Terry said, shifting away from Maria and psyching herself to take the first bite.

"Because it's empty," Maria snorted. "What do you think "breakfast" means? Break your fast."

"I can't wait to break my fast!" boomed a voice from the hall followed by the appearance of Terry's grandfather, who burst into the kitchen with his usual surplus of energy, kissed his wife and granddaughter and settled at the table. "Good morning, lovely ladies of mine! What a glorious morning! Hey, Terry, aren't you glad to be alive on a day like this?"

"Sure Papi. It's the best ever," Terry remarked, her words drenched in enough sarcasm to narrow Maria's eyes in anger all over again.

Alberto didn't hear. Or didn't care. "And being healthy and beautiful, too…" he continued, pouring cream into his coffee with a flourish, "…now *there*, my darling granddaughter, is something to be thankful for."

Terry cringed each time he called her beautiful. She knew he meant it with all his heart, but it was embarrassing, especially when he said it in front of other people, who probably felt sorry for him because he was going blind, or senile. OK, so 54 wasn't old enough to be senile, what other explanation could there be when they heard him say the word beautiful then saw the fright mask that passed for her face? Maybe poor Papi had Terry confused with *her*. This thought made Terry stop pushing the food around her plate in a weak attempt to pretend she was eating and drove her to her feet.

"I gotta go," she announced, heading for the kitchen door where her knapsack lay exactly as she'd thrown it yesterday.

"Terry, you didn't eat a thing. At least take…" Maria protested.

"I'll get something at school, I promise. See you later Bria. Bye, Papi."

"Be good, corazon, and remember…what day is it?"

Terry rolled her eyes. "It's the start of the most wonderful day of my life." She walked out the door then poked her head back in. "I'll try to remember that in English class," she said with a laugh so false and empty it sent a shiver down her grandmother's spine.

"What are we going to do with her?" Maria asked once she knew Terry was truly gone. She sat down and fiddled with a piece of toast much the way Terry was playing with her eggs. "You should have heard the way she spoke to me earlier! And did you notice her school sack was right where she left it yesterday? How could she not have any homework? I'll tell you how, because she's not doing it, that's how. You know how terrible her last report card was, and the reports we've been getting from her teachers. She's getting worse, Berto, I'm so worried. What if…"

"I know. I know. Mira, querida." Alberto put his cup down and took his wife's hand.

"This year's been hard on all of us, but especially on her. She loves to put up the tough front, and lately I agree it's been tougher than usual, but behind all that she's still our same Terry."

"Is she?" Maria asked. "I'm not so sure, anymore. She's so negative about everything, and so secretive, the way she shuts herself in her room for hours. And angrier now than she was last winter."

"You can't blame her for being angry."

"Of course she has the right to be mad. But it's been a year and she hasn't made any effort to at least try. Have you forgotten about Christmas already?"

Alberto shook his head slowly, his earlier cheeriness clearly dampened.

"And she's smoking, you know that, right? All the Tic Tacs in the world aren't going to hide it, despite what she thinks. This is how it starts, Berto, I'm so scared…"

"Querida," Alberto said, rising and pulling Maria up to hug her.

"Don't be afraid. Terry's not Isabel. She's so much stronger. She'll bounce back, you'll see. I'll talk to her when we go to the Shaver's on Thursday, OK? I've got to get going now, so promise you won't sit here and shoot your blood pressure through the roof."

"Promise," she lied.

Maria waved as Alberto backed the truck down the driveway then began watering the amaryllis, the bromeliads, the orchids and all the other lovely flowers making their little yard a miniature paradise. Alberto Gomez's yard wouldn't, couldn't, be anything less than spectacular. After all, he was a master gardener, specializing in tropical and exotic flowers and plants. He always joked that his sunny disposition was responsible for his magical green thumb. Maria smiled thinking how Alberto's good mood had been restored in the ten minutes it took to get ready and leave the house. He was the eternal optimist, always seeing the silver lining, the glass half full, the golden pot at the end of the rainbow.

And why shouldn't he be happy? Life had treated them well, especially since emigrating here from Cuba 22 years ago. It was hard at first, arriving in Miami with thousands of others desperate for a fresh chance at a life with choices. There were problems with language, discrimination, crime, and money, of course—never enough of it. Moving here to West Palm Beach was the second-best decision they'd ever made. Alberto got a job with a large landscape business while slowly building his own clientele to the point where he could be his own boss. This house, though small, was in a safe neighborhood "in transition" as the real estate people described it to young couples searching for their first home. They could still use more money, but they certainly didn't want for anything, especially when compared to what they left behind in Cuba.

No, there'd been only one fly in the ointment. These days, make that two.

Their daughter Isabel had been 13, Terry's age, when they left Miami, with Isabel kicking and screaming the whole way. She hadn't wanted to leave her friends, her school, their neighborhood.

After a few weeks she'd calmed down and suffered in sullen silence until she started her new school, made friends and announced one fine day that she was glad they moved to West Palm and why didn't they think of it sooner? Maria and Alberto had breathed a sigh of relief and enjoyed the relative peace of the next few years. Until Isabel's junior year in high school. Then it had started. The backtalk, the lying, the many hours shut in her room with music blaring, the cigarettes, the drugs, the boys.

The one boy in particular.

When they'd finally met Manuel Reyes, the young man Isabel declared herself to be madly in love with, it didn't take but five minutes for Maria to realize he was every mother's nightmare. Handsome and wild with a charm too slick for his 18 years. Isabel gazed at him adoringly, clutching his hand like a lifeline. Here's trouble, Maria had thought. So she hadn't been surprised when Isabel snuck out of the house almost every night to be with him. And she hadn't been surprised when Isabel calmly informed them that she and Manny wanted to get married because she was going to have a baby. And, tragically, she hadn't even been surprised when Manny flipped his motorcycle speeding on the Interstate and was killed instantly two months before Terry was born.

Isabel had plunged into a depression she couldn't pull out of for five years. Finally, when Terry turned six, Isabel had suddenly woken up to the fact that she had a daughter who needed her to be a mother instead of a sad and distant older sister. She'd gotten busy, found a job in cosmetics at Macy's and was promoted quickly to management. After moving to a nearby apartment complex with Terry, she'd eventually started dating again. Maria and Alberto had been ecstatic to see their little girl getting on with her life. And proud! She was a successful single mother with a promising career and a beautiful daughter who adored her. The only thing she'd complained about was her love life, how she was afraid she'd never love anyone again the way she'd loved Manny. Some of her dates had turned into boyfriends, but nothing serious until an art dealer named Jack Price swept into town from Los Angeles then swept Isabel right off her feet. Isabel had brought him over to the house about midway through his month long stay. She had found her Manny once more in another time and place.

After Jack returned to L.A., they'd continued their romance long-distance, but Maria had known it was only a matter of time before Isabel took Terry and moved west. But Isabel had a slightly different plan. She said she needed to be with Jack on her own, first, to make sure it would work before she uprooted Terry and forced a ready-made family on Jack so soon. You'll see, she'd assured Maria and Alberto, Terry will be fine with it. She'll understand.

If only they had known just how wrong Isabel would be.

2

As soon as Terry turned the corner at the end of the street she stopped and dug in her knapsack for a crumpled pack of Newports and a green mini BIC. She had to settle for an inferior nicotine high this morning since she was out of pot and couldn't meet up with Justin until later this afternoon. What a drag. She could really use it right now, lousy as she felt about being so mean to her grandmother. Bria—a shortened combination of abuela, Spanish for grandmother, and Maria—loved her so much, only wanted the best for her. Not like the other one, Her. Terry should be thanking Bria every day for being a *real* mother instead of treating her like she did this morning. She felt in the front pocket of her jeans, making sure the pitiful wad of bills was there. Twenty dollars— enough for a small quarter ounce bag she'd always suspected was more seeds and twigs than pot, but it gave her a buzz, took the edge off all the bad stuff and that's what counted.

Lighting the cigarette, she slung the knapsack over her shoulder and followed the sidewalk for another two blocks before crossing the street to Hillcrest Park, which wasn't so much a park as a bunch of overgrown trees, a few benches and some broken, rusty playground equipment. And it was flat. Not one hill. Or crest. How dumb was that? Her grandparents' neighborhood was called Hillcrest Heights. Again, no heights in sight. It was a ridiculously fancy name for block after block of dinky houses like theirs. Her hag of an English teacher might say Hillcrest Heights was ironically named.

Just thinking about English class made Terry shudder, imagining what was in store for her. She hadn't finished her History questions, had completely ignored the 15 Math problems and, as for the English homework, didn't even want to think about it. Besides all this, she couldn't find her gym clothes, which meant another zero in P.E., the sixth one of the marking period. Oh what the hell, she thought, might as well be consistent and fail every class instead of just three or four. She couldn't care less.

Right. Who was she kidding? She could pretend it didn't matter, but all the bravado in the world couldn't replace the gnawing, empty feeling in the pit of her stomach that threatened to swallow her the closer she got to school.

It hadn't always been this way. In fact, up until last year she'd been one of the best students in her class. But seventh grade was a disaster. She'd started poorly and had sunk deeper. She couldn't seem to concentrate on anything for too long, so she'd given up trying. Simply imagining the effort it would take to save herself at this point was enough to exhaust her. Her teachers and grandparents could lecture all they wanted. They didn't understand. She just wished everyone would back off and leave her alone.

Terry took the last drag from her cigarette, exhaling with a heavy sigh as she left the shady haven of the park and crossed the big athletic field which sat behind Agnes Quigley Middle School. She strolled slowly around to the front of the building and casually climbed the steps even though the second bell was ringing and the other kids who were late were hurrying to avoid detention. Entering her homeroom, she slid into a seat at the back of the class, relieved to see Ms. Meeks writing on the board, back turned.

"Hey Terry," Krystle Kessler whispered from across the aisle, "Can I see your Math? I need the last two problems."

Terry frowned and shook her head. "Didn't do them."

"How about English? I don't get the difference between direct objects and predicate nominations."

"Predicate nominatives, Einstein. I didn't do those either."

Krystle's pink, fleshy face creased with a smile in anticipation of the drama to come. "Adams is gonna get you, girl."

"Funny, I don't remember asking what you think." Terry turned in her seat so her back was facing Krystle. Exactly what she needed, a heads-up from that fat lamebrain. Terry had gotten used to floating through this early part of the day, wrapped in the comforting cocoon of being stoned. The homeroom routine of the pledge of allegiance, morning announcements and attendance usually occurred in a distant haze with minimal participation on her part. This morning, it all seemed to be happening at full volume, which didn't help her mood one bit.

When the bell rang for first period, Terry was heading for the door when Ms. Meeks called her name.

"Miss Gomez, may I have a word with you please?"

Josephine Meeks stood by her desk, tall and imposing as an African queen in her purple and green caftan, beaded braids springing crazily from her head. She watched over the rims of gold half glasses as Terry reluctantly approached, thinking what a shame. What a waste. Nothing disturbed her more than seeing a student like Terry self-destructing. She made a mental note to speak with Guidance about setting up a conference with Terry's grandparents.

"I don't want to keep you from Math class, so I won't ask why you were late. This is your fourth tardy already this marking period, so you realize what that means?"

"Yeah, detention," Terry mumbled.

"Right, but instead I was thinking of a more positive use of your time, like making an appointment with Dr. Felsen."

"No way," Terry said. Felsen was the school head-shrinker. "I don't need to talk to him. I'll take the detention."

"Then I'll expect you tomorrow after school. You can go now," Ms. Meeks said in a calm tone that belied her frustration. Sure, she could insist that Terry meet with the school counselor, but she couldn't make her open up to Dr. Felsen with any more success than she'd had herself, which was a dismal zero after numerous attempts. At this point, she didn't know who could penetrate the girl's armor, which seemed to grow thicker by the day. All she could do was try again tomorrow.

Terry headed to Math, simmering with resentment towards the teacher she liked most. She couldn't believe Ms. Meeks wanted her to see a psychiatrist, like she was crazy, or something! Just because she was late a few times and wasn't doing so great in her classes? She promised herself that tomorrow during detention, when Ms. Meeks talked to her the way she usually did, pretending she was actually interested in Terry's life, Terry would totally ignore her. That'll show her.

She felt a little better as she walked into her first period class and saw the TV and VCR sitting at the front of the room. Mrs. Connors announced that the video would last the full forty minutes, so homework would be postponed until tomorrow. Well, at least something was going her way today. As the room went dark and the music from the video began, Terry pulled out her History book and managed to finish her homework for the next class in sneaky spurts without being caught by Mrs. Connors, who was sitting at her desk, staring out the window, too preoccupied to notice anyway. Terry felt a little sorry for Mrs. Connors. Last week, right in the middle of explaining a pre-algebra word problem, she burst into tears and had to leave the room. It was weird to think of teachers having real lives and problems away from school, just like regular people.

The bell rang for second period. Since she'd finished her homework, Terry didn't care what kind of mood Mr. Pontifex was in and was more relaxed than usual as she took her hated assigned seat in the first row right in front of the podium where he always stood. If he was in a bad mood, he'd immediately ask them to lay their homework on their desks. Then, with grade book in one hand and red pen in the other, he'd stalk up and down each aisle checking each student's work with microscopic care, gleefully and generously dispensing red marks with a flourish. Almost like he *wanted* them to screw up. "Your reward for doing your job is not receiving a zero," he'd say to anyone who had the nerve to ask.

What a butt-head! She couldn't stand him, and she knew the feeling was mutual. He was an adult Boy Scout, boring them constantly with stories about his troop and their dorky adventures. That should tell you something right there. Today he asked for the homework, but didn't check it, just started discussing it until Jeff Chauncey managed once again to divert him to his favorite subject. How General Sherman's march to Atlanta related to Harold Pontifex's Eagle Scout merit badges, Terry couldn't guess. Nor would she ever know because she slept through the rest of the class with her eyes open, a useful talent she'd developed in the last few months as it became easier and easier for her mind to be a million miles away from her body.

Third period Science held no terrors. Mr. Whitefield was the kindest, friendliest, most patient teacher in the school. He was also the most clueless. His class seesawed between general disorder and complete chaos. He'd forget which chapter they were on. His experiments usually came to a premature end with the fire extinguisher. The floor of his lab was covered with little bits of broken glass because he constantly dropped tubes and beakers. Still, all the kids, Terry included, loved Mr. Whitefield and appreciated how lucky they were to have such an easy class.

Unlike the next class. As Terry watched Mr. Whitefield fumble his way through another experiment, the fast and ominous approach of fourth period made her seriously consider faking illness and asking to be sent to the school nurse. Then she remembered she did that just last Tuesday. The Abominable Adams was already suspicious. She couldn't pull it again so soon.

"OK, Gomez, suck it up," Terry muttered to herself as she made her way through the hall and up the stairs to her most dreaded destination.

"Ready to get thrashed on?" Krystle goaded as she followed Terry into the room.

Terry ignored her and took her customary seat in the back row next to the window, as far away as possible from the beautiful strawberry blond woman perched on the edge of her desk at the front of the class, talking and laughing with the kids sitting as close as they could get. What a bunch of suck-ups. They all thought Adams was so cool, the way she dressed and joked around and made class fun instead of so boring you wanted to smash your finger with a hammer to remind yourself that you were alive. All the boys drooled over her, and all the girls wished they looked like her. Terry had to admit she was pretty, but then, it was no big feat to look good when you had a rich husband and lived in Palm Beach and had the bucks to pamper yourself. What she hated to admit more, though, was that Adams was by far the best teacher at Quigley. Even though she was old, 30 at least, she talked to them on their level, like she was a really mature seventh-grader, and seemed to remember being 13 better than the other teachers. So what. Terry hated and envied Adams. And she admired her, which made the hatred stronger.

Chris Adams felt the coldness of Terry's stare from clear across the room and deeply resented it. She loved teaching and prided herself on being a professional. So it was extremely upsetting to have to admit to herself that she disliked a student. And she disliked Terry Gomez. The girl had begun the school year with a chip on her shoulder which Chris had tried to dislodge as gently as she could. Terry certainly wasn't the first angry adolescent she'd ever encountered in the classroom, but she was the most impenetrable. The surly attitude, the disrespect, the obvious contempt had worn her down to the point where she found it easier to ignore Terry unless she was directly challenged. A pity, too. Terry was a bright girl whom Chris would have enjoyed teaching if...well, if she was someone else.

After the tardy bell rang, Mrs. Adams stood, signaling that the small talk was over. "All right, let's pick up where we left off yesterday with pronouns. Most of you are still having trouble, especially with the predicate nominative. So before we go over homework, I want to review what we did near the end of class."

She began asking questions to which the students would raise their hands and answer. After seven or eight mostly correct answers, she nodded her head in approval.

"Good! Now which parts of speech do we use as predicate nominatives?"

No response. Finally, Gordon Skinner weakly raised a hand and answered tentatively, "Verbs and adjectives?"

Terry laughed.

Gordon blushed and stared down at his open grammar book.

"No, sorry Gordon, that's not correct, but thanks for trying," Mrs. Adams said, giving Gordon a reassuring squeeze on the shoulder as she walked past him towards Terry. "Since Terry seems to find your answer so hilarious, maybe she'll give us the answer."

"Nouns and pronouns," Terry replied in a bored tone and pointedly looked out the window.

Mrs. Adams fought to hide her annoyance at the right answer. Unwilling to let Terry off the hook so easily for her rudeness, however, she continued. "Suppose you tell us the three ways to recognize a predicate nominative?"

Terry continued to gaze out the window as if there was something more fascinating to see besides a row of portable classrooms.

"And since I'm speaking to you, I'd appreciate it if you'd have the common courtesy to look at me."

Terry narrowed her eyes and stared deliberately at her archenemy. "It follows a linking verb. It refers back to the subject, and it can be switched with the subject without changing the meaning of the sentence."

Mrs. Adams bristled inwardly at both the correctness of the answer and the tone of the girl's voice. She turned abruptly and walked back to the front. "Okay everyone, cough up the homework."

Notebooks snapped open. Papers rustled. Terry saw she was the only one without a paper.

Mrs. Adams started at the opposite end of the room, walking up and down the rows of desks with her grade book, checking and marking until she reached Terry.

"Where's your homework?"

"I didn't do it."

"May I ask why?"

Terry shrugged her shoulders. "I forgot."

Mrs. Adams examined her grade book. "Let's see, this is the seventh time you've forgotten this marking period, which means seven zeros."

Again Terry shrugged her shoulders and this time added a smirk and an exaggerated eye roll, red flags to the bull.

"Are you so special that you feel homework is beneath you?" Mrs. Adams asked, eliciting nervous giggling from the rest of the class, which she immediately silenced by holding up her hand.

Terry shifted in her seat and frowned. "I don't think I'm special. I just didn't do it."

Mrs. Adams closed her grade book slowly and took a deep breath, trying to remain calm, telling herself to remember that she was the adult, Terry the child, miserable though she was. "You recall what I told you the last time this happened. I won't have you sitting here pouting and doing nothing, putting a damper on the rest of the class. Gather your things and report to Mr. Dillard, *now.*"

The class watched, enthralled, as Terry roughly stuffed her book in her knapsack and walked to the door, slamming it behind her.

"Come back here!"

Terry heard the teacher shout so loudly she could have been standing right in front of her. She considered pretending she didn't hear, but opened the door instead and stepped back inside the classroom.

"Don't you dare slam a door on me!" Mrs. Adams said in a soft, low voice that was somehow scarier than more yelling would have been. "Now try it again, the right way."

Terry set her jaw and glared at her nemesis, hatred churning, threatening to spill over and make her do something she knew she'd regret. Like leaving and slamming the door so hard it would shake in the frame.

Mrs. Adams stared back, her pretty face a mask of false tranquility.

The class held its breath, hoping to see some blood drawn.

Terry broke first. She backed out the door and closed it softly behind her.

✎ 3

Terry sat under the banyan tree at the edge of the patio outside the cafeteria, picking at a chicken salad sandwich, wishing she was anywhere else but here. Mr. Dillard, the vice-principal, had kept her imprisoned for the rest of English period, lecturing in his phony-friendly voice, as if he and Terry were a couple of buddies just hanging out, which she guessed was supposed to make her "let her guard down". Though she'd heard it all before, having been a guest of Mr. Dillard's many times this year, a few words stuck out from the otherwise meaningless noise pouring from his mouth.

Detention. Probation. Suspension. Whatever. She almost hoped he *would* suspend her, then she'd at least get a break from this zoo. She looked over at the patio, picnic tables full of kids talking, laughing, joking with their friends. A little over a year ago, she'd been there, too, with Margie, Tia and Irene—her girls. They were their own little group, not part of the Barbies, or the Poindexters, or the Gangstas, or the Stoners, or any of the other cliques that claimed every student at Quigley. Terry couldn't point to the exact moment she and her friends lost each other. There'd been fights and tears and makeups for a long time and then, one day, she was alone.

Fine. That's how she wanted it. She didn't need anyone, and she certainly didn't have to belong to some stupid group to feel accepted. A few of the Stoners actually had the nerve to approach her, like she had anything in common with those losers! Sure, she liked to catch a buzz, but she wasn't like them. She didn't need to get high constantly. She could stop anytime she wanted. But what she wanted right now was for 3:30 to hurry up and get here so she could keep her appointment with Justin.

Music, then P.E., then home free. Physical Education was usually a joke. Today, though, Terry kicked herself for not having her gym clothes. It wasn't that she cared about getting a zero. The way she was going, what was one more? No, today they were doing time trials for track while she was stuck picking up trash on the field. It figured. If there was one thing she could do, it was run fast, faster than any of these dweebs.

The girls and boys normally had P.E. separately, but this afternoon, Ms. Rondowski and the boys' teacher, Mr. Ackerman, stood together in front of the bleachers, taking roll and explaining how the trials would work. As everybody else fanned out on the field, Terry conducted her own time trial, picking up the few soda cans and stray potato chip bags so quickly that she was seated back on the bleachers before the first race began. She watched as her classmates streaked, plodded and waddled up and down the track. Some, like scrawny Stacie Drexel and Howard Reese, the School Jock/ Jerk, were pretty fast. Others, like porky Ronda Singletary, barely made the finish line before collapsing in a heap. Pathetic. Worst of all for the slow ones, Mr. Ackerman loudly called out each time to Ms. Rondowski, so everyone could hear and either laugh or cringe over the differences. With all races run, Stacie was the fastest of the girls. Howard's time, predictably, was the overall best.

Terry thought it was lucky for Howard she wasn't out there today. He would have been embarrassed to have his time beaten by a girl's. Too bad. It would have been fun to see him squirm. Howard was a mean bully who picked on kids smaller and weaker than he was. Terry couldn't stand him. She fought the urge to smash him in the face whenever she heard him ragging on one of his victims, or saw him pushing someone out of his way. In other words, all the time.

Climbing down from the bleachers, she started back to the gymnasium when the irritating voice struck a nerve at the back of her neck and made her turn around. Howard always sounded like he had to blow his nose, yet never did.

"Hey, Gomez, how come you chickened out today? I thought you were the Speed Queen around here!" He was directly behind her, surrounded by his usual fawning gang of goons.

"Figure it out, Brainiac. Do you see me dressed out?" Terry replied and resumed walking.

Howard followed closely behind, making clucking noises and flapping his arms, much to the delight of his asinine audience. "You're not fooling anyone, Godzilla. Nothing like forgetting your clothes on purpose. You just know you can't beat Stacie, so you bailed."

More clucking. More laughter.

Terry felt her face getting hot. "I don't need a stopwatch to tell me what I already know."

"What's the matter Ganja Gomez," Howard hissed, pretending to take a toke off a joint, inhaling loudly, eyes crossing, "A little too much weed stuck in the old gears today?"

Terry clenched her fists. With a superhuman effort, as well as Mr. Dillard's warnings ringing in her ears, she managed to keep from hitting him. Shaking with anger and struggling to maintain control, she jammed her hands in her pockets and came up with the small wad of bills. Unfolding them, she fanned them out, waved them under Howard's nose, then slapped them lightly across his face.

"Twenty bucks says I can beat her right now," she said, looking over at Stacie in direct challenge.

Stacie saved Reese from replying. "I'm not running again today," she announced and headed quickly back to the gym.

"Yeah, now you want to race her after she's already run," Howard snorted. "That wouldn't prove squat, Ga-ga-ga-ganja Girl."

Terry poked his chest hard with her index finger, which made Howard step back and bring his hands up defensively. Gomez was a girl, but she was a little taller and maybe heavier than he was. He wasn't taking any chances.

"How about you, then, Asswipe. You're so great, you shouldn't have any trouble making an easy twenty bucks. I'll race you." Terry waved the bills in front of him again. She was beginning to enjoy this.

The rest of the class was enjoying it too. They were hooraying, goading them on.

The first bell for dismissal rang, saving Howard. Or so he thought. "You? A girl? Race me!" he laughed. "You gotta be kidding. What kind of ganja you been smokin' there, Gomez?"

"Who's the chicken, now?" Terry taunted. "No, not a chicken. You're more of a pussy."

Reese swallowed hard. Glancing around the crowd he couldn't sense any support, even from his friends. In fact, some of the guys looked positively stoked by his predicament. "Man, if you weren't a girl..." he floundered, his voice cracking, wishing he'd never started this.

Terry was relentless now. "If I weren't a girl, what? You'd hit me? Go ahead. Oh, wait," She smacked the side of her own head, "I remember! You're a pussy! If you don't wanna race, you sure as hell don't wanna fight, right, Pussy Boy?"

The chanting began. Fight. Fight. Fight.

Howard picked the lesser of two evils. "Okay, we meet here after homeroom. To race. But I've only got nine bucks on me."

"Done," Terry grinned. Nine bucks meant a bigger buy this afternoon.

News of the challenge had raced around the school during homeroom, so that by the time Terry arrived back at the field, there was quite a sizable group, all of whom, she was certain, would be rooting for Howard.

As if she cared.

Howard was already on the track, running in place. She sauntered up to him, fanning herself with the bills in her hand. "Let's see your money, Reese."

Howard produced a pile even more crumpled than hers along with a handful of change.

"It's all here. You wanna count it?"

"No, but I want someone else to hold it."

After some bickering they agreed to let Bonnie Keller hold the money and judge the race. Bonnie's father was a minister, and she was regarded as the angel of their class. After Sammy Menendez was approved as the official starter, Terry and Howard lined up at the starting line.

Howard got down in a four point sprinter's stance, the one taught by Mr. Ackerman.

Terry merely crouched low, her hands held close to her body.

"On your mark. Get set. Go!"

Reese exploded out of his starting position, leaving Terry almost two feet behind. At the fifty-yard mark he had increased his lead by another foot. As they approached the last twenty-five yards, Terry had settled into her rhythm. Long legs churning, arms pumping smoothly in unison, she blew by him and crossed the finish line a good two feet ahead.

The cheering which had started at the beginning of the race when Howard was winning turned to booing. Terry went over to Bonnie and took the money. Without a word to Howard or any of her classmates, she picked up her knapsack and walked across the field towards the park.

She didn't want to keep Justin waiting.

4

Two days later...

Terry slumped against the passenger door of her grandfather's truck, halfway listening to him droning on about her detention yesterday, the phone call from Guidance, her rotten grades, her mouthing off to Bria, her cigarette smoking (luckily he didn't know about the *other* smoking), her general bad attitude. The soft and understanding tone of his voice didn't cancel the fact that he was chewing her out, which made the always humiliating experience of riding in the truck even more unbearable. Sure, it was a huge, shiny, practically new pearl white truck, not a rattling heap of junk belching clouds of exhaust. But the large green letters on both sides—GOMEZ HORTICULTURAL DESIGN—ruined everything. Just because it said horticultural design instead of yard service didn't make it any less embarrassing.

Poor Papi. He just didn't realize what a cliché he was. It was practically a rule that you had to be Hispanic to be a gardener in South Florida. Bria could talk all she wanted about how Papi was a specialist, a master, an artist! Blahblahblah. He still made his living being some rich person's servant. If they had a family crest it would be a golden leaf blower surrounded by a border of intertwined silver hedge clippers (never mind that Papi didn't use either one of these tools except at home). She especially hated it when the bridge was up going into Palm Beach, where most of Papi's clients lived, and they were stopped next to another lawn truck. While they waited, Papi would talk and laugh in the loudest possible voice with the men in the other truck. For some reason, everyone sounded louder in Spanish than in English. Then all the other people in the other cars would look over, frowning at the noise. It made Terry cringe.

"…And I know you're still very angry with your mother," Alberto said, finally gaining Terry's full attention, "but it's time we all stopped using that as an excuse for your behavior."

"What are you talking about?" Terry asked innocently. "I'm not mad at Bria."

Alberto looked over at Terry and shook his head sadly. "You know who I mean," he said, his voice heavy with disappointment.

"Oh, I get it. You're talking about your daughter. It confused me when you said 'your mother' because we both know it's not *her.*"

Alberto didn't reply. He set his jaw and stared straight through the windshield, turning up the volume on the radio to let Terry know further conversation wasn't advisable.

Terry could tell Papi was really mad because it looked as if there was a little worm wriggling in his jaw. She slouched further against the door, trying to put more distance between them. She didn't know why he was so upset. It was the truth after all. His daughter had more important things to do, like hang out in L.A. and be her boyfriend's love slave, than play mother to a kid she probably wished she'd never had in the first place. Maybe it would have been different if her father had lived. They could've been a normal family, with a mom and dad who loved each other, and at least one brother or sister, and maybe a dog. Nah, they'd probably be divorced by now anyway. It happened to almost everyone's parents. But not everyone had a mother who bailed on her because of some guy and moved clear across the country. Oh sure, she made a show of coming back every few months, and constantly asked Terry to visit (like it's normal to visit your own mother, not that Terry thought of her that way anymore), but Terry knew the truth, that *she* just wanted to stay solid with Papi and Bria so they'd take care of the kid she didn't want anymore.

The last time Terry saw her was Christmas. She and good old Jack (Gack, to Terry) had been staying at a hotel and came over to

Papi and Bria's for Medianoche. Cubans celebrated on Christmas Eve rather than Christmas Day, which, of course meant opening presents. Except for a few one-word replies, Terry had managed to stay otherwise silent during the whole meal, making zero eye contact with her and Gack and willing the miserable ordeal to be over. It wasn't until she'd grudgingly unwrapped her gifts from them that she lost it completely. Lots of clothes, earrings, gift cards—and her big gift, a huge caramel-colored, buttery-soft leather suitcase. It pushed her right over the edge. Kicking the suitcase across the room, Terry screamed at her that she never wanted to see her again, let alone visit, then ran out of the house, ran until she was sucking wind and clutching at the pain in her side.

Remembering Christmas made Terry furious all over again. And the fact that she still cared so much made her even more furious. If only she could banish her from her thoughts forever. She could do it temporarily when she was stoned, but the minute she came down, she was there again. If only she'd had time to get high earlier. But Papi picked her up right after school (*in front* of school, *in the truck!!*) so she had to resign herself to spending the rest of the afternoon stone cold straight, earning her measly $5 an hour and feeling resentful that she didn't live in a mansion on the beach.

Alberto punched in a series of numbers on a keypad set into the massive gray stone wall stretching endlessly from opposite sides of the towering wrought iron gates, which swept aside slowly to let them enter. When Terry was little, these gates used to scare her, so tall and black and forbidding, and they weren't nearly as big as the gates at the main entrance. As they continued up the winding driveway towards the parking area in front of the garage, which was five times bigger than Papi and Bria's house, Terry tried to swallow the gush of envy that crept up her throat each time she came here. The Shavers had been Papi's clients for as long as she could remember. In fact, they'd been his first clients when he started his own business and had given him lots of referrals to their friends.

Papi loved the Shavers, and they loved him, especially Mrs. Shaver. If she was in town, she'd usually meet Papi at the gazebo by the gardens, dressed in white with a huge straw hat and hang with him the whole time, chattering, asking questions, helping him. Terry usually didn't come here during the winter, because Papi had his special assistant. But she came a lot during the summer, when the Shavers went to Maine and stayed until November. What a life! Here they had this fantastic house, and they used it for only half the year. Actually "house" wasn't the word to describe the place. "Estate" was more like it.

The main house was a giant rectangle of dazzling white brick set in the middle of a lush green lawn rolling down to the ocean. Between the house and the beach were the pool and pool house (again, twice the size of the Gomez hacienda), a tennis court and cabana, a two-story guest house, the gazebo and the formal gardens, where Alberto and Terry headed as soon as they parked the truck. Terry wondered if the house in Maine was like this. No doubt. She gritted her teeth and followed her grandfather, cursing the bad luck of her birth into, well, not poverty, but sure as hell not wealth.

"All right, corazon, enough for you for today. I can take it from here," Alberto said, removing his hat and wiping his face with a towel. "I need about 20 minutes or so. Why don't you go over to the tennis court and see who's playing?"

The sound of tennis balls being hit and female laughter had been floating over from the court for the last hour. Might as well, Terry thought, piling her damp hair on top of her head in a messy pony tail. It was warmer than usual this afternoon, especially for winter, but it would be nice and cool under the cabana. Years ago, Mrs. Shaver had said she should bring a bathing suit and use the pool whenever she wanted, but Terry never did. It wasn't like she was some kind of charity case. Too bad, because she had to admit it would feel great right now.

As Terry approached the tennis court she could see two women on opposite sides of the net, smacking balls harder than you'd think to look at them. They were both so thin it was hard to imagine either having the strength to get the ball over the net at all. Terry didn't know much about tennis, but she could tell that they must be pretty decent. She'd watched a little on TV, the US Open and Wimbledon, but only if there wasn't anything else on. It didn't seem too hard. Get the ball over the net. Keep it within the lines. Big deal.

The taller, skinnier one hit a ball that caught the top of the net and dribbled onto the other side. "Sorry," she laughed, "But I'll take it. I need all the help I can get." She turned to walk back to the baseline when she noticed Terry sitting in a chair under the cabana. Lifting her sunglasses, she squinted for a moment then smiled and jogged over.

"Oh my God, is this who I think it is? You're Alberto's grand-daughter, aren't you?" she exclaimed, extending her hand to Terry. "I'm Libby and I'm sure you don't remember me. I used to tag along after your grandfather about a thousand years ago."

"Yeah, hi," Terry mumbled, rising to take Libby's hand without a clue as to just who this Libby was.

"Jen," Libby said to the other woman coming over. "This is...I'm sorry sweetheart," she apologized to Terry, "I don't remember your name."

"Terry."

"Terry, this is my friend Jen. Jen, Terry's grandfather is the wonderful flower wizard who makes it possible for my mom to win all those Garden Club awards she's so proud of."

"Hi, Terry. Nice meeting you," said Jen, collapsing in a chair and taking a long drink from her water bottle. "And thanks for giving me an excuse to rest."

"Well look at you!" Libby exclaimed. "So tall and gorgeous! The last time I saw you, maybe five, six years ago, you were so small."

"Kids tend to grow if you keep feeding them, Lib," said Jen, fanning herself with a tennis racket cover.

"You're in, what, high-school, now, right?"

"Seventh grade," Terry replied, embarrassed once again to be mistaken for older because she was so ridiculously huge. But *gorgeous!* Libby was yanking her chain. Or else she was suffering from the same vision problem as Papi.

"Seventh? So you're…"

"Thirteen." Terry wished she would let it go and move on.

Libby shook her head. "It's strange to think so many years have gone by. So, where's your grandfather?"

"He's still in the gardens, but he should be over in a little bit. I just came over to wait. You guys keep playing."

"Do I have to?" Jen whined.

"Come on," Libby laughed, "Let's finish the set. One more game and you've got it wrapped."

Terry watched as Libby and Jen resumed their game. At least now she knew that Libby lived here, or used to at least, though she still didn't recall seeing her. She was pretty if you went for the sort of blond, thin, model look, which everyone, apparently, did. If Terry saw Libby as a stranger walking down the street, she'd have guessed she was rich. She seemed OK, nice, but she was probably nice to all the servants.

Libby's prediction proved correct. Jen won the game, raised her arms and did a little victory dance as the women walked back over to the cabana.

"Gotta run, hon," Jen said, gathering up her racket, towel and tennis bag and giving Libby a kiss on the cheek. "Good workout. Same time tomorrow?"

"Can we make it four instead?"

"Sure, see you then. Bye, girls." Jen hurried off.

"Bye," Libby called after her. She took off her sunglasses and cleaned them with the hem of her skirt. "So Terry, what are you up to these days?"

Libby's direct gaze made Terry uncomfortable. She had the same eyes as the Siberian husky that belonged to their neighbor, Mr. Manso. Icy light blue with glittery black marbles in the center. "Not much," she muttered. She popped out of her chair and started backing away. "Anyway, I should see if my grandfather needs me. Nice to meet you and all, but..."

"You play tennis?" Libby asked, totally ignoring Terry's attempt to escape.

Terry shook her head. "Nahh..." she said in a tone implying that tennis is the last thing she'd be interested in playing.

"Ever?"

"Nope."

"Well then," Libby said, picking up a second racket that was sitting on the table and handing it to Terry. "There's a first time for everything."

Terry reluctantly took the racket, her face screwed up into a *Whattayounuts?* expression.

"One word of advice," Libby called over her shoulder as she walked to the baseline.

"Keep your eye on the ball."

Ten minutes later Libby couldn't decide whether to be amused or annoyed. After spraying the first few balls way wide, and two over the fence, Terry had managed to keep the majority of the balls Libby fed her within the lines, netting several, but not many. Though she held the racket like a club and swung it like a baseball bat, the kid had obviously played before. Someone had shown her basic movement—the short little steps to approach the ball while taking the racket back, the follow through, the return to the ready position. She hit the ball hard and moved extremely well, especially for such a big girl whom Libby estimated to be almost six feet tall and perhaps 140 pounds. Not that she was heavy by any means. The weight was distributed perfectly on a medium, long-limbed frame.

Libby hit the ball further and further from her, forcing her to run from side to side, forward and backward. Terry returned every-thing. The returns, which weren't in the net or out, landed deep in the court with enough pace to force Libby far behind the baseline in chasing them down.

Enough was enough.

"OK, you got me," Libby said, leaning against the net after putting away a volley winner on one of Terry's short returns. "Had your fun for the day?"

"What?" Terry walked toward the net, genuinely perplexed.

This kid should be an actor, Libby thought. "Come on, joke over. Really, how long have you been playing?"

Terry grinned in spite of herself. This rich bitch was calling her a liar, but it was sort of a compliment in a weird way. "This IS the first time. I swear."

"Right, and I'm Nikki Minaj"

Though she was getting angry Terry still had to laugh. This tall, blond, skinny glass of white milk was the exact opposite of the curvy black hip-hop star. "I swear on my grandfather," she said loudly.

"Hey, no swearing, especially on me," Alberto said as he walked onto the court. "Do my old eyes deceive me, or am I seeing Miss Libby Shaver?"

"Alberto," Libby cried with genuine delight. She threw her arms around him after kissing him on the cheek with a resounding smack.

"Look at you," Alberto said, holding Libby at arms length and examining her. "Even more beautiful, but too skinny. How long has it been?"

"Oh, years! Maybe four or five? I've been home most Christ-mases, but I haven't stayed more than a few days so it's no wonder I've missed seeing you."

"So what brings you here now?" Alberto asked. "They told me up at the house that your parents are in London."

"Oh, they'll be back in a few weeks," Libby said. "Actually I'm home for awhile, definitely until summer, so you'll have to choose between me and Mom whom you'd rather have as your assistant."

Alberto laughed and started to ask another question, but Libby beat him to the punch. "So how are you?"

"Couldn't be better. The family's healthy, business is good, all's right with the world if you can say that."

"Well, speaking of your family," Libby said, gesturing at Terry with her racket. "Not only has Miss Terry grown a foot and turned into a ravishing creature, but she was trying to run me into the ground out on the court."

"She was?" Alberto said, clearly surprised.

"Sure was. Where's she taking lessons?"

"She doesn't. I don't think she's ever been on a tennis court, have you, corazon?"

Terry gave Libby a look that said, "See, I *told* you!"

Libby glanced from granddaughter to grandfather, making sure they both weren't in on this little charade. But noting Alberto's genuine confusion, she had to admit the impossible.

"Unbelievable," she said, regarding Terry with amazement. "Terry told me she'd never played," she explained to Alberto, "but after these last ten minutes hitting and watching her move around the court, I thought for sure she was having some fun at my expense, you know? So..." she turned to Terry, "My deepest apologies. I have only two more words of advice for you. Start playing. If you do, some day you could give Shawn Chillingsworth and Jemma York and the rest of the crew a run for their money."

Terry erupted with the noise, a cross between a cough and a grunt, that she always made when someone said something ridiculous (or complimentary, or embarrassing to her. She made this noise a lot, far too often for Papi, who instantly glared at her). As if. Even she knew who Shawn Chillingsworth was, star of about a million commercials—for clothes and shoes and cameras and cars. Libby was making fun of her, and Terry didn't like it one bit.

"I'll be sure to do that," she said, injecting her voice with as much sarcasm as possible. "Maybe I'll join your club and just play all the time."

Libby raised her eyebrows over those icy eyes that gave nothing away, but didn't reply. Instead she started talking to Alberto again as if Terry wasn't there.

Terry walked to the cabana and sat, waiting for Papi to finish his conversation, feeling somewhat guilty after awhile because maybe Libby wasn't making fun of her after all. She seemed too nice. And she sure liked Papi. She was all smiles and laughing, like you'd talk to a friend not to the gardener.

"Come on, my tennis-playing granddaughter," Papi finally called over to her. "We need to get going. Your grandmother has commanded dinner out tonight."

"See you for our orchid lesson next week, then, Alberto," Libby said. "And Terry, if you feel like playing again, I'd love to. Think about it."

"Sure," Terry said insincerely, remembering at the last minute to add, "and thanks for hitting with me."

"My pleasure," Libby replied.

Libby watched Alberto and Terry walk across the lawn, still slightly in shock. How could it be? How could someone pick up a racket and hit and move as if they'd been playing for at least a year or more? The kid was a natural. She was also full of an attitude that went beyond the usual adolescent posing. Alberto's lovely granddaughter bristled with negativity and resentment, and Libby couldn't help but wonder why.

"I've known her since she was just a little older than you," Alberto was saying as Terry stared out the window, wishing Papi would let the subject drop already. Ever since they got back in the truck and started home, it was Libby this, and Libby that. Jeez.

"Just like her mother, that one, so in love with flowers, wanting to know all about them. Every holiday when she came home from her school up north, she'd be right back in the gardens. Such a lovely girl. It'll be a treat to have her around again. She said she's taking time off from tennis. She's a professional player, did she tell you? So you should take as a compliment what she said about your playing."

"I never heard of her," Terry said, which meant zip since she could name a grand total of maybe three or four pro tennis players. "She must not be very good."

"She's good enough to be traveling all over the world on the tour, so she must have *some* idea which end of the racket to use," Alberto said. Terry wasn't the only one in the family who could be sarcastic.

Terry made her noise again, the cough-grunt, because she wasn't willing to let Papi know how secretly psyched she was by what had happened on the court this afternoon.

Sure, at first it felt awkward and strange, same as the first time on a bike, or on roller blades, when your body wasn't quite sure what your brain wanted it to do. But after she'd managed to get a few balls in, she relaxed and stopped worrying about how klutzy she looked. Magically, more balls stayed in. The truth was, she'd been incredibly pleased when Libby accused her of lying about her experience. And disappointed that Papi showed up as soon as he did. She'd wanted to keep playing. It made her feel good, better than she had since…well, since her twelfth birthday.

The day her world had fallen apart.

⚲ 5

One week later...

Terry slammed her bedroom door shut and blasted Lady Gaga, hoping to drown out the sound of her grandmother's fury rolling down the hallway from the kitchen.

"Go ahead, hide in your room! And you may as well just stay there since you can't seem to behave like a decent person..."

It wasn't working. Terry cranked the volume a few levels higher and flopped on her bed, distressed that Bria's voice wasn't the only one jostling for space in her head. There was competition from two other sources, one angry and shrill, the other calm and dangerously quiet, like Robert De Niro always sounded in mobster movies.

"That's it. You've crossed the line. As of this minute, you're no longer welcome in my class. I want you out of my sight! Right now. Go!!" *Voice #1. Abominable Adams.*

"I'm very disappointed to see you so soon after our discussion last week, Terry. I thought we reached an understanding about modifying your behavior, but I was mistaken. Showing such disrespect towards Mrs. Adams is not a step in the right direction. I'm suspending you for the rest of the week, Thursday and Friday, which means you'll be unable to make up any work or tests you miss. I sincerely hope you use the time wisely to reflect on how to turn this year around for yourself." *Voice #2. Mr. Dillard.*

Terry was reflecting, all right...reflecting on how unfair everyone was being. For one thing, she couldn't understand why Adams flipped out the way she did. You'd think she'd get used to Terry not having her homework done. But no, she had to make a federal case out of it every time. This morning she had a total meltdown when Terry ever so gently suggested that PMS might be the cause of her teacher's crankiness. This is what she got for being honest. See? Unfair!

It was also incredibly unfair to get a two-day suspension for something so lame. You usually had to steal something, or make someone bleed or get busted with drugs to get suspended. Terry Gomez gets bounced for *allegedly* dissing a teacher. So unfair!

And speaking of absolutely, utterly unfair...Bria had gone ballistic on her in the car on the way home, refused to listen to Terry's side of it (the right side, by the way), just acted like Adams' and Dillard's version was The One and Only Truth. How unfair could you get?

Arrgghhh... Terry felt so angry, so frustrated, so much like, well...crying.

Crying, of course, wasn't going to happen. On January 6th, one year ago, Terry had made a promise to herself that it would never happen again. And it hadn't.

Who would have guessed that one of the best days she ever had would turn out to be the worst day of her life? For that matter, who would have imagined she'd end up hating the person she loved most, all in the space of twenty-four hours? Before that wonderful, horrible day, the day she turned 12, Papi and Bria's daughter, *her*, was Isabel. Beautiful, funny, crazy-in-a-good-way Isabel, who had taken Terry almost everywhere with her, treating her more like a little sister or a best friend than a daughter. Terry's friends had been jealous because her mom was so young and pretty and cool and let Terry call her Isabel instead of Mami, or Mom, while their moms were more like Bria (not that there was anything wrong with Bria. She was way cool, for a grandmother).

For Terry's birthday, Isabel had invited Irene, Margie and Tia for what she called "Terry's Girlie Birthday Blowout". Perfect. The Posse loved any excuse to hang out with Isabel. They'd spent the morning getting haircuts, manicures and pedicures at Karma, the salon where Isabel and all her friends went. Then, a raid on City-place, a food and shopping paradise. After getting free makeup "makeovers" at the Clinique counter at Macy's, Isabel treated all four of them to new outfits from their store of choice, insisting they wear them to The Cheesecake Factory, where they drank round after round of nonalcoholic strawberry and apricot daiquiris and ate only gooey desserts for lunch. When they'd gotten back to Isabel and Terry's apartment complex, they swam in the heated pool until Papi and Bria came over with Terry's birthday cake and three huge shopping bags full of presents. They ordered pizza, gorged on Bria's famous triple chocolate cake with dulce de leche icing, opened presents and listened to Terry's new CDs until the girls' various rides came to take them home.

Terry had been glad she hadn't asked them to spend the night. She was deliciously exhausted, stuffed and content to lie on the floor surrounded by her gifts, drifting off to sleep until Isabel shook her gently and said she'd be more comfortable in bed. She hugged her grandparents, hugged and kissed Isabel, thanking her for a terrific birthday and fell into bed without brushing her teeth or getting undressed.

It was the last time she had felt happy and normal.

She must not have slept too long before waking up and needing to pee because she heard her mother and grandparents talking in the living room as she padded down the carpeted hallway to the bathroom, still drowsy. She stopped, instantly awake, when she heard her name.

"...With Terry it might be too much at once, not just for me and Jack, but for Terry too," her mother had said.

Curious, Terry crept closer, very quietly. The dreadful overheard words ran together, forming a hard fist slammed into her stomach.

"ShecouldfinishschoolherewhileJackandIfigurethingsoutyouknowhowshelovesyoubothshe'llbefinebutIsabelshe'llmissyoutoomuchwhydon'tyouwaitbutIcan'tI'msoinlovewithhimit'smychanceTerrywillthinkyou'rechoosinghimoverhernoshe'llunderstandJackandIneedtimealonehardenoughmovingtoL.A.withoutworryingaboutTerryofcourseshecanstaywithusbut..."

Terry had made it to the bathroom just in time to lose it all—daiquiris, brownies, pizza, birthday cake—everything consumed throughout the awesome day she'd dumped into the toilet to be flushed away along with the way her life used to be. Back in her bedroom she'd put a pillow over her face and cried, sobbed, wailed, screamed until she was choking and gasping for air. She'd made a few decisions during that long, sleepless night. She no longer had a mother. The old Terry, the one who *did* have a mother, was dead. The new Terry wasn't going to get hurt again because she wasn't going to allow herself to care.

And the most important vow, symbol and motto of the new Terry she had carved deeply into the newly constructed wall around her heart.

SHE WOULD NEVER CRY AGAIN. Not for **ANYTHING.** Not for **ANYONE.**

Terry sat up on her bed, temples pounding from bad memory overload, not to mention the stress of her current predicament. She needed to get high, needed to get some distance and comfort. Smoking pot was like snuggling into a soft, puffy cotton ball. It absorbed and protected. She felt so terrible right now that she was willing to do something she'd never done, smoke right here with Bria a mere several yards away. Scrambling over to her dresser, she pulled the bottom drawer all the way out and snagged the plastic bag taped to the back. It was almost empty, much to her dismay. Though she'd bought close to half an ounce from Justin (seedier and twiggier than usual, in her defense) exactly a week ago, she had barely enough to scrape together one decently sized joint.

Sliding the drawer back, she settled herself on the floor in the small space between her desk and her bed so that if Bria decided to burst in uninvited (Papi took the lock off her door not long ago after Terry refused to open it during an argument) she could shove everything under the bed in one quick movement. Still, she was nervous and sweating in spite of the chill in the room. Plucking her pack of rolling papers from the baggie, she pulled one out and actually managed to roll a surprisingly plump little bone, if she did say so herself. Mission accomplished, she got up and sifted through her knapsack for the lighter. Convinced that Bria would appear brandishing the fire extinguisher at any moment, Terry nevertheless went over and opened the window wide, sat on the sill and lit up. Drawing the sweet, heavy smoke deep into her lungs, she held it for as long as she could before exhaling out the window. Waiting impatiently for the fog of relief to descend, she texted Justin on Papi's old Samsung phone she inherited when he got an iPhone.

She definitely needed more.

Things really couldn't get much worse, Terry thought as she crossed the street into the park. Meeting up with Justin would be the one bright spot in a truly awful 48 hours. After Papi had gotten home Wednesday and had a chat with Bria, they'd made Terry sit through the longest lecture ever delivered. It had gone on for hours. Luckily, she'd still been somewhat stoned from her afternoon medication, so it wasn't as unbearable as it could have been. She was grounded for two weeks, allowed to go to school only. Yesterday she had to help Bria give the house a cleaning "en todo", which meant scrubbing floors and walls, washing windows—everything. Fortunately the tiny house was built for hobbits. Unfortunately, it was much too small for two people who were fed up with each other.

All day the soundtrack of Bria's nagging had played, over and over, until Terry had been forced to ask (quite politely in her opinion) if she could please give it a break. Bria had gotten so upset the veins in her neck and the big one in her forehead popped out. Later that night, when Papi had taken over in the Tag Team Torture of Terry, he said he was worried about Bria's high blood pressure and that it wasn't good for her to get so stressed out. Well, what was she supposed to do? She didn't have control over Bria's emotional extremities.

She'd spent today in her room, listening to exactly *nothing* since Papi had decreed she couldn't listen to music during the suspension, and remembering that she had two tests today in math and history. Two more major zeros to factor in to her already failing average. Finally, miraculously, a break in the heavy weather. Bria had to go grocery shopping. The minute she'd left, Terry texted Justin. When he got back to her five minutes later they'd agreed to meet right after Justin's last class, twenty minutes. With luck, she could make it back well before Bria's return. Her buy from Justin was always fast, no small talk, strictly business. Truthfully, she wouldn't have minded hanging out some with Justin. He was really cute in a scraggly blond surfer way, but he was a senior at Hillcrest High and certainly wouldn't be interested in a seventh grader, especially a fat, ugly one as tall as he was.

As Terry approached the clump of trees marking their usual meeting place, she saw that there was someone else with Justin, a short guy wearing all black with a shaved head and multiple piercings—ears, eyebrows, lip.

"Hey," Terry said, walking up to them, suspicious because Justin had never brought anyone with him before. "Who's this?"

"Yo Terry, what's up?" Justin drawled, already digging in his knapsack. "This is Brad, he's cool."

"Sup, Terry?" said Brad, deliberately looking her up and down. "Haven't seen you around. Where you been hiding?"

"I don't go to Hillcrest," she said, wishing for once that Justin would hurry and get this over with. She didn't like this guy. He had a smirk on his face like he was enjoying some mean private joke.

"Oh yeah? Where then?"

"None of your business," she snapped.

"Whoaa," Brad staggered backwards in fake fright. "C'mon, bro," he said to Justin, "Let's motor before she takes a swing at me."

"We're on our way to Sebastian, so it's lucky you got me when you did," Justin said, referring to the classic road trip north the surfers took whenever they got the chance. He sorted through a bunch of baggies from his bottomless backpack. "You said you wanted a quarter, right?"

Before Terry could answer Brad reached over, snatched one of the baggies and held it up, examining it. "Making your quarters a little light, huh dude? How much you gonna charge her for this pitiful pile of dirt?"

Justin laughed and grabbed the baggie. "Don't be trying to make points with her now. Terry knows it's all good, right?" He smiled at Terry. "Twenty, same as usual."

Terry handed Justin a pile of ones and fives, ten of which she'd taken from Bria's wallet, a first that wouldn't be added to the list of Terry's Proudest Moments. She took the baggie and stuck it in the pocket of her hooded sweatshirt without looking at it.

"Well kids," Brad said, reaching under the neck of his shirt and pulling out a thick silver chain. "It looks like we've got a problem."

Dangling from the end of the necklace was a police badge.

"No way!" Justin cried, his mouth hanging open in disbelief.

"Way," Brad said. "You're both under arrest."

Terry had been so wrong. Things *could* get much, much worse.

🎾 6

Monday of the next week...

Libby Shaver stood on the ground floor terrace sipping coffee from the first in an endless series of cups she'd drink throughout the day. She watched the early morning sun brightening the ocean from grayish green to turquoise and wondered how she was going to fill the hours ahead.

"What's the plan, Pretty Boy?" she asked her companion, who took a break from chewing his tail to consider the question.

"You get back to me on it, OK?" she laughed, bending to scratch his head. Amazing how attached to this mutt she'd gotten in just a little over a week. Actually, it had been love at first sight in the parking lot of a Thai restaurant, as she stood by her car searching her purse for keys, when she'd felt something cold and wet swipe across her calf. She turned to see a bundle of filthy fur, tail wagging furiously, super skinny, dancing around her like he just recognized his long lost best friend. She'd taken one look into his sweet, smart, dirty face, black lips pulled back into a grin, and felt the same way.

No collar. No identification. No problem. Judging from his bony frame and soiled, matted coat, he'd obviously been on his own for awhile. Opening the passenger door of her BMW convertible she had ushered him in, confident that he was truly a stray and she wasn't snatching someone's dog. Once she'd gotten him home and bathed he was more identifiable as some type of Border Collie mix with calico markings, one pointy and one floppy ear and a crooked, bushy tail with a big bald spot in the middle. Just to be sure, she'd taken him by her beloved Animal Rescue League to get scanned for a microchip and was overjoyed that he didn't have one. Negative for heartworm. Clean bill of health according to the staff vet who saw him. Excellent! While he wasn't about to win any beauty contests, she'd been calling him Pretty Boy until she thought of a better name.

As if she didn't have great gobs of time to think of one! It was driving her crazy. Sure, she had group and individual therapy, and meetings whenever she felt the need. She volunteered at the ARL, played tennis and spent more time with her parents than she had since going away to boarding school in ninth grade. These last few months she'd felt like a kid again, relying on Mommy and Daddy to make it all better. And her parents were only too happy to play along, wrapping their little girl in a cocoon of love and protectiveness. They'd been upset when she bailed on going to London with them, worried about her being alone. They hadn't added "without supervision", but it was what they'd been thinking.

"It's just you and me, pal," she said to Pretty Boy, who rolled on his back, legs straight in the air, better access for further scratching.

"Whatta good boy! Whatta baby boy," she cooed, giving him a vigorous rub that carpeted the terrace floor with hair. She straightened up in time to see Alberto Gomez walking across the lawn toward the gardens.

"Alberto," she called, waving as she jogged over, coffee sloshing from her mug, Pretty Boy up and racing ahead of her in one fluid movement.

Alberto stopped and bent to pet the leaping, squirming, tail-wagging heap of fur.

"Who's this?" he asked, averting his face to avoid being drenched in a spray of dog saliva.

"Not too friendly, is he?" Libby laughed, grabbing the dog by his collar to give Alberto a break. "I found him last week in a parking lot. If you think he looks scruffy now, you should have seen him then. Meet Pretty Boy Shaver."

"Seems like you found a good one," Alberto said, though he didn't crack a smile at the name.

"Speaking of last week, I'm sorry I missed you," Libby said, falling into step with him as they continued toward the gardens. "I wanted to pot those new orchids with you, but you did them all, so I was thinking, depending on what your plan for the day was, maybe I could help with something else?"

Alberto shook his head. "Sorry, Libby, but I don't have much to do today except for some watering and pruning and a few odds and ends, nothing too exciting."

"Well, I can water while you do the rest and we can catch up," Libby persisted, wondering if Alberto had maybe gotten up on the wrong side of the bed this morning. That would be a first. She looked closely at his face, suddenly noticing the puffy bags under his eyes. "Alberto, you look exhausted. Is everything all right?"

Alberto sat heavily on one of the stone benches in front of the gazebo and put his head in his hands. "*Nothing's* right," he said, his voice thick with what Libby feared were tears. On no! Did someone die? Was someone sick? His wife? His granddaughter?

She sat next to him and gripped his shoulder. "Tell me."

He did.

It gushed from him in a torrent held back too long by a dam of pride and denial. His daughter leaving. Terry's year long slide. Her personality and behavior changes. His wife's worrying. The fights. The lies. The drugs. The arrest.

Alberto spoke, uninterrupted by Libby, until there was nothing else left to say except how sorry he was to burden her with his problems.

"My God, Alberto, there's no need to apologize!" Libby said, knowing how embarrassed and ashamed he probably felt about breaking down and divulging so much personal information. "You can keep things bottled up for only so long before you explode. It's a natural response to stress and it really helps to tell someone, to talk it through. Believe me, I know. Will you do me a favor, now, and let me tell *you* a few things?"

"Of course," Alberto sniffed, pulling a handkerchief from his pocket and noisily blowing his nose. He still looked absolutely mortified.

Fifteen minutes later he felt slightly less humiliated and not quite so hopeless and all alone.

While Alberto went about his gardening, Libby and Pretty Boy walked along the beach. Libby smiled thinking of the relief washing over Alberto's expression after hearing her story, his comfort in knowing that everyone had dirty laundry to air. Having spent the month of November in alcohol and drug rehab, and these past six weeks since in therapy and meetings, she was now an old hand at the tit-for-tat of recovery. You tell me yours and I'll tell you mine. She'd now spun her tale so often that the words fell matter-of-factly, almost casually, from her mouth, so different from the beginning, when each revelation had been coughed up by a sob. The short version, the one she just told Alberto, went like this.

Once upon a time, three years ago, when she was twenty-five, she'd been the number nine ranked women's professional tennis player in the world. Unlike most of the other top players, most of whom hadn't even attended high school, she'd graduated from Stanford University after a star college career and joined the professional tour at the advanced age of twenty-two. And also unlike the huge majority of the other players, she was already incredibly wealthy, so her slow climb up the rankings hadn't been nearly as nerve-wracking as it could have been. She didn't have to win matches to survive financially (In fact, every dollar she'd ever won playing tennis had gone to the foundation she established for mentoring and teaching tennis to under-privileged kids). She had worked hard because she loved tennis and wanted to accomplish something that couldn't be bought.

She had also *played* hard, which hadn't affected her tennis until she started playing *too* hard, until it couldn't be called "playing" anymore. Gradually her life had became more about drinking and coke and parties, about dating actors and rock stars and showing up regularly in *PEOPLE* and *US WEEKLY*, bleary-eyed and grinning sloppily—than about being a professional athlete. She'd fallen lower and lower in the rankings until she finally quit the tour and settled permanently into her Tribeca loft, the better to concentrate on her busy New York social life and time-consuming alcohol and cocaine addictions.

By the time a group of friends did an intervention and dragged her on a plane headed to the world-renowned Madison-Caplan Institute (MadCap for short, ha-ha), conveniently located mere miles from her parents' home in Palm Beach, she'd been ninety-five pounds of bone and nerves and very little sense of reality. That had been almost three months ago.

Libby bent to pick up a small coconut. "Yo, Pretty Boy," she called to the dog, who twirled and barked until she heaved it into the ocean. He plunged into the surf, grabbed his prize and took off down the beach.

"Hey, bring it back," she yelled. Clearly there wasn't a retriever in his genetic mix. Her recovery program strongly discouraged establishing new relationships right now, and apparently pets were up there with new boyfriends on the *do not get involved* list. Well, too bad. Pretty Boy was a done deal. She was following all the other really important rules, so she figured she could afford him. She needed the distraction he provided, the welcome pleasure of focusing on something other than herself. Recovery was turning out to be quite the ego project, so tapping into someone else's world, like listening to Alberto earlier, made her feel connected and—dare she say it—*excited*—about the seedling of an idea that had sprouted while he spoke.

As Libby followed Pretty Boy down the beach she nourished the seedling with a continuous stream of thought, pouring it on mile after mile. By the time she returned to the house, she was able to present Alberto with a magnificent flowering plant of a plan.

"Alberto," she said, coming up behind and tapping him on the shoulder. "I have a great idea!"

Four days later Terry studied the man seated behind a desk the size of a giant redwood and tried to guess just how painful the next few minutes were going to be. Judge Horace Walpole didn't match his name. He was pretty young, or at least younger than the old geezers Terry pictured, and handsome in a TV news guy way, dressed in a gray suit instead of a black robe. And sitting here in his office—or "chambers" to be official—was way different than what her imagination had conjured, seeing herself in an orange jump-suit and handcuffs, trembling in a drab courtroom in a scene right out of *Law & Order*.

Actually, from the time she'd been arrested, everything had been different than she'd assumed. She and Justin had ridden together to the police station along with their good buddy Brad, but once they'd arrived, Brad had taken Justin in one direction while a policewoman led her in another. After they'd taken her picture and fingerprints, she hadn't been placed in a cell. They'd just stuck her on a bench in the office until Papi and Bria had shown up. That had been the worst, looking at their faces. Terry could tell Bria had been crying. They hadn't even come over to her, but had headed straight to the policewoman's desk and spent forever talking. Terry couldn't hear what they were saying, which was just as well since she'd certainly gotten an earful the moment they climbed in the truck to go home. At some point during the Long Weekend From Hell, sandwiched between Papi's lectures and Bria's weeping, had come the information that she was supposed to have her case heard in juvenile court the following week. Until then, Terry hadn't known what would happen, just that she was under a type of house arrest, with her grandparents as her jailers.

Now here it was playing out, but not how she expected.

There were four leather chairs arranged in a semi-circle in front of the judge's desk. Bria sat next to Terry, and Papi next to Bria, and next to Papi sat the weirdest part of this whole scene.

What in the hell was Libby Shaver doing here? She had waltzed in a few minutes after they did, saying a simple hello to Terry, hugging Papi and Bria and shaking hands with Judge Walpole before planting herself in the chair farthest from Terry, all model-y in a fuzzy purple sweater, long black pencil skirt and pointy-toed black boots, streaky blond hair a shiny curtain brushing her shoulders. Terry glanced down at the long-sleeved white shirt, navy blue sweater vest and stupid plaid skirt Bria made her wear and cringed at the comparison. Libby smiled over at her but Terry couldn't bring herself to return it.

Libby sensed the hostility and confusion radiating from Terry. She didn't blame her one bit. The kid was totally in the dark about the phone calls and planning and negotiating which had brought them all to this room. After Libby had presented her proposal to Alberto, he'd gone home, talked it over with Maria and called Libby late that Monday afternoon to give her the go-ahead. Libby had immediately gotten in touch with close Shaver family friend Judge Janice Dickerson, who happened to be the Chief Judge of the Fifteenth Judicial Circuit of Palm Beach County. Judge Dickerson had spoken with Judge Walpole of the Juvenile Court. On Wednesday, Alberto, Maria and Libby had met with Judge Walpole and hammered out the agreement which Terry was about to hear.

"All right, folks, let's get started," Judge Walpole began. "I'm sure Miss Gomez wants to end the suspense as soon as possible, correct?"

"Uhh, yeah," Terry croaked. She suddenly had no saliva in her mouth.

"You were arrested for buying marijuana, which, as I'm certain you knew, is an illegal substance. This is a serious charge not to be taken lightly. I believe in imposing the maximum punishment, even for a first-time offense, in order to teach an important lesson. Drug abuse escalates. Using marijuana is the first step on the road to harder drugs, which ultimately leads to disaster. It's best to nip it in the bud now and that calls for a severe consequence."

Terry tried unsuccessfully to swallow the lump in her throat. This wasn't sounding good so far. The vision of orange jump-suit and handcuffs returned with a vengeance.

Judge Walpole removed his reading glasses, clasped his hands in front of him and stared hard at Terry. "Theresa Margarita Gomez," he boomed in a voice that kicked Terry's heartbeat into overdrive. "I sentence you to one year in the Juvenile Detention Center."

Whaaaat!!! Terry couldn't believe it! *One year* for a lousy quarter ounce of pot??

How could this be happening? Why were Papi and Bria just sitting there? Why weren't they saying anything? "But Judge," she stammered, "It isn't fair, it's…"

Judge Walpole held up a hand to stop her. "Quiet, please, young lady. I'm not finished. That is your sentence. However, I am suspending this sentence and placing you on indefinite probation instead."

"What does that mean?" Terry asked, sensing a glimmer of hope in his words. "I don't have to be locked up?"

"Correct. But don't think for one moment that probation means getting off the hook. The terms of your probation will be decided upon and enforced by Miss Shaver, who will report directly to me."

"Why *her*?" Terry practically spit the pronoun, refusing to look at the person it described.

"If I were you, Miss Gomez, I'd be showing more respect toward the person who has the power to send you to the Detention Center," Judge Walpole said. "Miss Shaver is, in effect, your Probation Officer. You must comply *exactly* with her guidelines. If you don't, she'll be forced to notify me. And make no mistake. There are no second chances. I will not hesitate to reinstate your sentence. Am I making myself clear?"

"Yes sir," Terry mumbled.

"Good. Now, as I said, the length of the probationary period is indefinite. Miss Shaver will report regularly on your status and progress. After one year I'll review your case and either end or extend it. Once you've satisfactorily completed your probation your juvenile record will be expunged. Do you know what that means?"

Terry shook her head. "No sir."

"It means that your arrest disappears as if it never happened. It can never have a negative effect on your future. It may not seem so important to you now, but, believe me, you'll appreciate it when you're older—and wiser." Judge Walpole pushed his chair back and stood, which automatically brought them all to their feet. "This hearing is concluded. Good luck to you Miss Gomez. I trust I won't be seeing you again until next year at your review."

Terry listened to her grandparents thanking the judge and wondered again why they were acting so calm, smiling, not asking any questions. She was beginning to smell a rat.

"Hey, Terry," Libby said, walking over to where Terry was standing by the door, ready to bolt. "It's almost noon. Your grandparents said it was OK for me to take you to lunch. We've got a lot to talk about. I'm sure you have a million questions."

"I'm not hungry," Terry snapped.

"Then drink something, I don't care. We just need a chance to chat, start getting to know each other a bit. I can't wait to tell you…"

"I *said* no thank you." Terry turned to open the door.

"It's not a request."

Terry turned back and searched Libby's smiling face, looking for an indication that she was joking. She didn't see one. "For real?"

"For real," Libby replied. "Let's go."

7

"I'll have the Salmon Caesar Salad and an iced tea, please," Libby told the waiter, handing him the menu and leaning back in her chair.

"Whatta shocker!" Terry gasped, widening her eyes for effect. Salad for lunch! No wonder Libby was such a stick. How skinny did she want to be? Though truly not hungry, she felt like getting lots of disgustingly fattening things if only to see the look on Libby's face. No, better not push it. She'd been pretty obnoxious already, not that Libby had seemed to notice, busy as she'd been, chattering away, driving her little sports car, rich and beautiful and not a care in the world except where to take her prisoner to lunch.

"Personal Cheese Pizza, please. Oh, and a Coke," she ordered then looked around the restaurant, at the other diners, at the boats in the Intracoastal on the other side of Flagler Drive, at the ceiling fans on the terrace where they were seated—everywhere but at the person sitting across from her.

Libby watched her with a mixture of amusement and pity tinged with growing annoyance. Terry was practically a parody of Miserable Female Adolescent, an irritating sub-species of homo sapiens. On the short ride over from the courthouse she'd responded with only three words—yeah, no, or whatever—to anything Libby had said. Crouched sideways, leaning over the door of the convertible with her back to Libby, she had occasionally supplemented her three word vocabulary with grunts, exaggerated sighs and elaborate hair tosses. Playing along, Libby had blithely continued asking questions, ignoring the bitchy tone and attitude, acting as if Terry's rudeness and disrespect were perfectly normal.

Time for both of them to stop the act.

"Here's another shocker," Libby said. "My order has way more fat and more calories than yours."

"So?"

"So I'm not dieting, as you seem to think."

"Good for you." Terry shrugged, slouching further in her chair. The Stick clearly had her confused with someone who cared.

"Suppose I told you I was so thin because I had cancer and lost a lot of weight during chemotherapy."

Terry was silent. No snappy comeback for this one. "Sorry," she said, straightening up and fiddling with her silverware. And she was. She felt terrible.

"I said *suppose.*" Libby thanked the waiter for bringing their drinks and emptied three sugar packets into her tea. "I don't have cancer, thank goodness, but what if I did? You'd have hurt my feelings and reminded me of how sick I was instead of just pissing me off."

"I said I was sorry," Terry repeated, though not as sincerely as before. Libby said she was mad but she didn't sound it. Her tone of voice hadn't changed at all.

"Making assumptions about people is a bad idea because they're usually wrong. Like all the assumptions you've made about me are wrong. You don't know the first thing about me, haven't asked me one personal question, yet think you can make remarks that imply you've got me all figured out."

Terry started to speak, but Libby cut her off.

"Just listen for a minute, OK? I know you're angry, confused, feeling shafted and ganged-up on by your grandparents and me—a total stranger, right? I don't blame you. I felt the same way when a bunch of my friends trapped me in my apartment in New York and blasted me for three solid hours about what a mess I was then forced me onto a plane headed for rehab. It's called an intervention, Terry, and it's the last desperate attempt for family and friends to get help for people they love who are in trouble. What happened today is basically an intervention for you."

"But I was just…"

"You were just smoking pot, right? Big deal. And if you hadn't gotten busted, no one would know. It's bullshit, Terry. There are things I know about you because Alberto and Maria told me...."

"What things?"

"Like why you've had such a terrible year and why they're so worried about you. But the other things I know, like that you're smoking more and more because it takes more to get high, and that you need to get high because it's the only way you feel better...I know because I'm an alcoholic and a drug addict. I wouldn't listen to anyone who told me I had a problem. I drank and did coke until it made me completely screwed-up and very sick."

Terry stared at Libby, mouth open in disbelief.

"You're looking at me, thinking, no way," Libby laughed. "You should have seen me three months ago, twenty-five pounds lighter, bad skin, greasy hair, 'cocaine eyes' like in that Rolling Stones song, vodka oozing from my pores. I was the Poster Girl for *'Don't Let This Happen to You'.*"

"It just seems weird to think of you that way, you know, the way you seem now and all." Terry was having a hard time picturing Libby as a scuzz rather than, say, on the cover of Vogue or Glamour. "And I believe you, but I still don't get why you're part of this, or what exactly 'this' is."

"For now, let's just say that I think we can help each other. Let me ask you this, how did you feel about playing tennis with me the other day?"

"What do you mean?"

"Did you enjoy it?"

"I guess."

"Do you think you'd like to play again?"

"Maybe."

The food arrived. Libby waited until the waiter left and continued in a casual tone meant to keep Terry from feeling any pressure. "Well, I'm involved with an organization that helps kids who want to learn tennis, especially kids who could be really good if they had the proper instruction and equipment and..."

"You mean a charity," Terry said, instantly defensive. "I don't need that."

Libby held back a smile. The kid was sharp. And proud. And so quick to rattle her armor. "Not charity. Opportunity. I meant it before when I said you could be an excellent player, but there are a lot of ifs, the biggest being IF you want to be. So if you didn't feel anything special about playing and couldn't care less about ever holding a tennis racket again, just say the word. I thought I saw a spark when you were out there running around, but maybe I was wrong."

Terry examined her pizza, struggling to appear nonchalant. The truth was she had loved being out on the court that day and couldn't wait to try it again. It was the one thing she'd done all year that made her feel better than getting high.

"I wouldn't mind trying it again. It's not like I have anything better to do."

"Good," Libby said. She picked up her fork and dug into her salad. "After lunch there's someone I want you to meet. I think you'll like him."

Terry had ridden by the Palm Club many times, or rather, ridden by the gated driveway and forty-foot hedges hiding the club from the road and from all the poor slobs who didn't have the piles of money it took to belong. She had never in a million years thought she'd find herself on the other side of that gate. Leave it to Libby to be a member. The whole way over she'd raved about this tennis pro she wanted Terry to meet.

"Pete May is awesome!" Libby had declared, thumping both hands on the steering wheel for emphasis. "I've known him forever. We used to play tennis together when we were kids. He's a little older than I am, but we hung out in the same group. I had such a crush on him when I was your age. All the girls did. He looks a little like Brad Pitt, only cuter, if you can believe it. Anyway, Pete was the top-ranked junior in the country when he was eighteen. He dropped out of college to turn pro and played on the tour for six years until he hurt his shoulder. After three surgeries he just couldn't be competitive at that level anymore, which was a shame because his ranking had been steadily climbing. He's still a great player, but an even better teacher. While I was on the tour, I'd always work out with Pete when I came home. He's fantastic, you'll see."

After Libby slid an ID card into a machine that lifted the gate, they drove down a narrow road lined with palm trees and turned right into a parking lot.

"The main clubhouse and pool are up there." Libby pointed ahead and to the left. "Tennis courts right here." She circled the lot crowded with other BMWs and Jaguars and other cars that Terry figured probably cost more than Papi and Bria's house until finally wedging into a space between a Mercedes convertible and a Hummer. They got out and headed towards the loud thwock-thwocking sound of multiple balls hitting multiple rackets.

Libby led Terry through the pro shop, emerging onto a long raised terrace filled with umbrella-covered tables and chairs looking out over twelve Har-Tru tennis courts, all but two being used. Must be nice, Terry thought, to be prancing around batting a ball back and forth in the middle of the afternoon on a weekday.

Libby waved at a man and woman standing at the net on the first court.

"Hey, Lib," the man called over, waving back with his racket. "Be with you in a sec, we're just finishing up."

"Take your time," Libby replied. "We'll see you in the shop. C'mon Terry, let's go look at some rackets."

Terry would have preferred staying right where she was, watching Pete. Libby was right. He *did* look like Brad Pitt, only better, at least from a distance. But she wasn't about to agree with Libby to her face.

One wall of the pro shop was filled entirely with rackets.

Libby lifted a ruby red racket from its hook and handed it to

Terry. "Go ahead, try it out. Try a bunch of them. Hold them, swing them, see what feels best to you."

Terry selected several different rackets and swung them around, but the only thing she felt was like an idiot. She had no idea what was supposed to feel right. They all seemed the same to her.

"Which one do you use?" she asked Libby.

Libby reached up, plucked a shiny black model with neon green stripes and cobalt blue letters that spelled Prince from the wall and handed it to Terry. "This one, but it might be a little heavy for you."

Terry swung it around. It felt just like the others, but she said, "It feels OK, but how much is it?" She was searching for the price tag when a voice right behind her made her jump.

"Excellent choice!" Pete May studied the tall striking girl awkwardly clutching the racket and recalled all the things Libby had told him about her when they spoke earlier. The kid looked pretty tightly wound, all right. "Terry? I'm Pete, and I'm a little sweaty at the moment, but I promise, I don't always smell this way."

"Don't lie to her," Libby said, hugging Pete and holding her nose. "It's your natural scent. Eau du Locker Room."

"I don't smell anything," Terry said, trying to crest the sudden wave of shyness threatening to swamp her. Pete was even hotter looking up close, without the straw hat he was wearing on the court. Deeply tanned with long, sun-streaked brown hair pulled back in a ponytail, he smiled at her with his whole handsome face, not with just his mouth the way most people did.

"So I hear you might be up for playing some tennis," Pete said. "Libby says you hit a mean ball, especially for not having played before."

Terry looked down at her feet, embarrassed as usual by any compliment.

"And she should know, as someone who hit a wicked ball herself back in the old days."

"Hey, it wasn't that long ago!" Libby protested. "If you want to talk old, let's strain our brains to remember your glory days, Old Man"

"Let me tell you about our friend Libby here," Pete continued. "Top Ten in the world for two years, only woman with the guts to serve and volley all the time, three-time semi-finalist, two-time finalist at the Slams…"

"Stop!" Libby cried. "Enough with the bio."

"Believe it, Terry. She knows tennis talent when she sees it, and apparently she sees it in you." Pete took the racket from Terry. "Should we string this baby up and give it a workout."

Terry looked at Libby who said to Pete, "You bet. Are you still clear for tomorrow?"

"Two, right?" Pete answered.

"Perfect. Terry, Pete's coming to my court tomorrow to hit with us, if that's okay with you."

"I've got to ask my grandparents…"

"Already done," Libby said "They're fine, so it's up to you."

"I guess."

"Great!" Pete said, looking at his watch and walking to the door. "I've got to get ready for my three o'clock. See you girls tomorrow. Good to meet you Terry."

"Me, too. I mean, good to meet you too…uhhh bye," Terry stuttered, angry at herself for being so tongue-tied.

"I told you," Libby chuckled. "He has that effect on all the girls, but it wears off eventually, don't worry."

The drive back to Terry's house wasn't much different from those to the restaurant and the club, with Libby carrying the burden of conversation and Terry grudgingly responding. Only this time Libby drew some small satisfaction from Terry's improved body language, no longer facing away from her, and the absence of blatant rudeness in her replies. Still, by the time she pulled in front of the Gomez' house, it was obvious that Terry couldn't wait to get away, leaping from the car before it came to a full stop.

"Uhh, thanks for lunch and the tennis stuff…and everything," Terry said, shutting the door and backing away.

"I thought I'd come in and see your grandparents for a minute."

"They're not home, see, the truck's gone."

"Well, okay then. Alberto knows to bring you over around 1:30 so we can hit before Pete comes. And remember, try to wear those shoes as often as you can to break them in. It'll be fun tomorrow, Terry. See ya."

Terry watched Libby drive off. Even her car looked out of place on this crappy street. She glanced down at the snazzy florescent yellow Adidas tennis shoes Libby had bought for her at the pro shop and wondered for the millionth time today why she was being so nice to her. Terry had done her best to be as unpleasant as possible, but Libby kept coming back for more. Why? What was in it for her?

She turned and started up the brick walk to the front door, uncomfortable in her new shoes, but looking forward to the next afternoon with more excitement than she would ever admit.

8

The next afternoon...

The egg and bacon sandwich she'd eaten earlier rolled around in her stomach like a loose ball on a shaky pool table. Chill out, Terry ordered her inner wimp, taking a few deep breaths while she waited for Libby and Pete to finish the conversation they were having on the other side of the court.

She couldn't figure out why she was so nervous. Last night she had slept even less than usual, thrashing around until finally dropping off early this morning. When she woke up she'd been shocked to see it was almost 11:00, later than Bria had ever let her sleep in on a Saturday. She hadn't been hungry for breakfast, as usual, but Bria had made her eat, As usual, which was now proving to be a colossal mistake. By the time they'd driven to Libby's house, she'd managed to convince Papi and Bria that if they stayed and watched like they wanted to, she'd die of humiliation. So after Papi had opened the service entrance gate for her, she bounded from the truck, waved goodbye over her shoulder and made a dash for the tennis court before they could change their minds.

As promised, Libby had been waiting for her, decked out in sleek hot pink warm-ups that made Terry feel like an elephant in her old gray sweats. She wished it wasn't still too chilly to strip down to the shorts and t-shirt she wore underneath. When Libby had handed Terry *two* black rackets, the one she'd picked out yesterday and its identical twin, Terry noticed that each had a small brass plate on one side with *"Terry Gomez"* engraved on it. Rubbing her finger over the nameplate she'd looked Libby straight in the eye for once and flashed her first genuine smile since they left Judge Walpole's office. Her second smile had followed immediately after, when she heard barking and turned around to see a dog rushing across the lawn towards them, dragging a palm frond twice his size. As Libby introduced her to Pretty Boy, who was anything but, the dog had leapt and slimed Terry's face with kisses, wagging his tail so hard his whole body vibrated. Terry had never seen a dog so cute and ugly at the same time. She'd also never met one so friendly and hyper. After they'd walked out on the court and closed the gate behind them, with Libby explaining that if they didn't Pretty Boy would chase the balls and jump at their rackets, he stood on his hind legs, front legs propped on the gate, barking furiously. Libby said he had doggie ADHD, so he'd get bored and run off to do something else, which sure enough, had happened in less than a minute.

When they started hitting, Terry sent the first ball over the fence, the second off to the side, the third into the bottom of the net. It's OK, she told herself. Last time she'd done the same thing. Watch the ball. Libby hadn't said anything, just kept feeding her balls. As Terry had loosened up, her shots started landing in and she began enjoying herself, temporarily forgetting the anxiety that kept her awake last night, that made her beg her grandparents to just leave her at the gate, that turned her feet to lead in her new tennis shoes and her arm to stone trying to swing her new racket.

But it had come back, full force, the minute Pete May appeared courtside.

Now, as she tried her best to settle her stomach she had to wonder why? Why was she so determined to impress Pete? Maybe she wanted to show him she could hit the ball just as well—if not better—than those rich brats he taught at the club. And if she was being totally honest with herself, she realized she wanted to impress Libby even more.

Get a grip, Gomez, you can do this, she whispered as Libby walked off the court, calling over to her.

"Go wide to his backhand. It's his weak spot."

"Don't listen to her, Terry," Pete said, making a fist and shaking it at Libby. "Even if I did have a weak spot, which I don't, forget it.

Just think about hitting the ball. Don't try to place it, and don't worry about getting it in, OK? Let's just smack these around and have some fun."

Watching them hit, Libby could tell Terry was tense. Good. It showed she cared about the impression she was making. Pete fed her balls, moving her back and forth, forward and backward, testing her the same way Libby herself had done that first time, when she immediately recognized Terry's pure, natural ability. It hadn't been a fluke. Terry moved smoothly around the court, instinctively approaching the ball with short steps, following through with her stroke and hustling back to the center of the baseline as if she'd been playing since she could hold a racket. Amazing. She could see Pete trying to contain his own amazement. At one point, when Terry was gathering balls at the back of the court, Pete looked over at Libby, widened his eyes, dropped his jaw and cupped his face with his hands in a comically exaggerated expression of disbelief.

Libby chuckled. "Told you so," she called to him.

No kidding Lib, Pete thought, growing more incredulous by the minute. Returning one of Terry's forehands, he was shocked by the power behind it. The kid hit the hell out of the ball. She hit harder than some men he could name. And the way she *moved*. Just like Libby, he'd have thought Terry was playing him by claiming she'd never been on a tennis court before. But there were things she did—clutching and swinging the racket like a baseball bat, bending to pick up balls by hand instead of using her racket, showing a total lack of form on the serve, misunderstanding court directions and tennis terms—which proved her inexperience. She wasn't a tennis player, but she was an athlete. Pete wanted to see more.

"Terry, come up here for a sec," he said, walking up to the net.

Terry jogged up to meet him, wondering if they were done already. It probably hadn't been an hour yet. Pete was saying all kinds of positive things this whole time, and joking around, but what if he'd already seen enough, decided she was bogus and was only going through the motions with her because he was tight with Libby and didn't want to hurt her feelings?

Pete leaned on the net with one hand and held his other out to her. "I want you to squeeze my hand as hard as you can. Give it all you've got and don't be afraid to hurt me. In fact, go ahead, *hurt me*, please hurt me!"

Terry laughed, grabbed his hand and squeeeeeezed.

"C'mon, I can barely feel that," Pete said, yawning and pretending to examine the fingernails of his other hand.

Terry squeezed harder.

Pete bent backwards at the knee and let out a yelp, "Lemme go! Lemme go!" he cried, pulling his hand from Terry's. He straightened up and took Terry's racket from her. "We don't need this for the next fun-filled activity. You want a break before we do some movement drills?"

"Nahhhh," Terry replied. Tired? She felt the opposite, so stoked she could probably run for miles without breaking a sweat.

"OK, why don't you go stand over there." Pete pointed with his racket at the service line in the middle of Terry's side of the court. When Terry turned to walk over, he glanced over at Libby, grimaced and shook his hand as if it really hurt. And it did!

"Now, this is what I'd like you to do," he said when Terry was in position facing him.

"Whichever direction I point to with my racket, I want you to get there as fast as you can, moving sideways and never crossing your feet, like this." He demonstrated, scuttling sideways and making Terry giggle. He looked like a huge, crazed crab.

"I know it looks funny, but no one's here but Libby, and you should see her doing it. So…go!" Pete pointed directly to Terry's left.

At his command Terry automatically dropped into a crouch, knees bent and body weight forward on her toes, then darted to her left, feet never crossing, body never rising from its coiled position, much more cat than crab.

Pete was so fascinated and Terry so quick that she almost reached the fence before he pointed his racket to her right. She seemed to change direction without stopping, yet maintained the same speed and balance as she scrambled to the other side of the court.

During the next twenty minutes, Pete put Terry through a series of drills involving running forward and backward, pivoting and jumping. Finally he asked her to go to the fence at the back of the court, and when he said GO, run as fast as she could to the fence at the opposite end.

Terry walked over to the fence, relieved at being asked, finally, to do something she understood. The other things Pete had her do seemed kind of pointless as far as this tennis stuff went. After all, she hadn't used a racket or ball the whole time. But this, this was her thing, flat-out running, speed. She'd show him fast, faster than anything he ever saw at his precious Palm Club.

When she reached the fence and Pete called "Ready...get set..." Terry dropped into her customary crouch. At "Go," she exploded, streaking to the far side of the court in such an impossibly short time that Pete was yelling for her to slow down at the same time she reached the fence, throwing up her hands to break the full-impact crash. The collision threw her a few feet backward, and she landed on her back, gasping to regain the breath she'd just had knocked out of her. Libby reached her before Pete, who seemed as stunned as Terry by what he'd just witnessed. "Just stay on the ground, sweetheart. Take a minute and catch your breath. Let's make sure you didn't..."

Terry sat up, elbowed her way past Libby and stood, biting her lip at the pain shooting through her elbows and knees. Her butt was numb too, but the embarrassment of looking like such a klutz bothered her much more. "I'm good," she said, pacing back and forth across the court to assure herself as well as Libby and Pete that nothing was broken.

"Well, that about wraps it up for today then," Libby said.

Pete was still shaking his head as he watched Terry try to walk with Pretty Boy dancing in maniacal circles around her. The dog had arrived at the court with perfect timing, dropping some unrecognizable, mangled object from his mouth to bark insistently. Libby had asked Terry if she minded taking Pretty Boy down to the beach to tire him out while she chatted with Pete for a few minutes. Terry had eyed them suspiciously, sensing a conspiracy. And, in a way, she'd been absolutely correct.

When he was certain Terry was out of earshot he turned to Libby, awe plain in his voice, "That is the fastest, quickest, strongest, best-co-ordinated girl—hell, woman—I've ever seen."

"I know." Libby smiled triumphantly at her old friend. "So what are we going to do about it?"

"Hey, come back here, ya crazy mutt," Terry yelled, her words torn away by the wind, which had kicked up strong and cold throughout the afternoon. She shivered, glad she'd put her sweats back on (ugly as they were) and wishing she was in a warm shower instead of banished to the beach with this nutty bouncing-off-the-walls ball of fur. She could imagine how Libby and Pete must be having a few good yuks at her expense. She couldn't keep the ball in, couldn't serve worth a damn, couldn't even stop herself from smashing into a fence! How lame could you get? They were probably trying to figure out a nice way to tell her she was hopeless. As if she cared. She wasn't asking to learn the stupid game. They were the ones who had forced her into that pitiful demonstration in the first place. She didn't need this. She didn't need them, their charity, their pity.

She didn't need anyone.

As Pretty Boy let loose a flurry of barking in the distance, Terry searched the beach and saw a pink figure jogging towards her. By now, she'd worked herself up into a nice, hot hate for the Tennis Twins and was looking forward to displaying her bitchiest behavior as she waited for Libby to approach.

She never got the chance.

"Having great potential doesn't give you a free pass to instant stardom, you know," Libby was saying, as Terry walked beside her, still absorbing the things she'd been hearing during their chilly trek down the beach. That Pete thought Terry could someday be a top-ranked professional player. That Libby hadn't been kidding when she said she could play with Shawn Chillingsworth and Jemma York—someday. That Libby and Pete both wanted to help Terry get to "someday" IF she wanted it.

"There would be years filled with hundreds of hours of practice and matches and hard physical workouts between now and standing on the same court with Jemma York," Libby said. "I can't mislead you here, Terry. Even for someone with your physical gifts, it would be hard to catch up. You're 13. Almost all the girls you'd play against have been playing since they were six or seven—or even younger. That's a huge head start and the only way you could make it up is practice, practice, and then some more practice. All the great players have three things in common—the willingness to work harder than anyone else, the refusal to get discouraged and the overwhelming desire to be the best."

Libby paused, took Terry's arm, turned her around and continued walking in one continuous motion. "Let's start back. I'm freezing." She chattered her teeth and pulled the hood of her warm-up jacket over her head. "Anyway, that brings us to more big *ifs*. First, *if* you're willing to put in the time and effort. I'm talking two hours a day after school, four or five hours a day in the summer. Working with Pete— but mostly with me—and following our instructions and suggestions without question. Running drills and practicing the same things over and over until you swear you can't do them one more time, but you do. Falling into bed at night exhausted then getting up and doing it all over again the next day. Playing in tournaments and getting badly beaten until you make up the time difference.

"I know it sounds extreme, but it's the only way. It's a big commitment Terry, which means the second big *if*, really the most important one. If you want this enough to bust your butt and make a lot of sacrifices. The road to the tour is hard, and once you get there, it's even harder. But the payoff can be huge in more ways than one."

Terry's initial excitement was being slowly swamped in the wake of Libby's warnings about hard work and endless practice, but now her ears perked up again at the word payoff.

"Let's see, there's the pride of achievement, the adrenaline rush of competition, the thrill of winning championships," Libby listed, counting off on her fingers. "Not to mention traveling all over the world, meeting tons of people, hanging out with celebrities, *being* a celebrity."

Terry licked her lips and grinned. This was more like it!

"Oh, yeah, and then there's the money," Libby added casually. "You know how much Keiko Tanaka made for *losing* the US Open final last year? Seven hundred and fifty thousand—three quarters of a million dollars. And Jemma pocketed a cool million for beating her. Granted, it's the richest tournament in the world, but it's *one* tournament. And it's not just the prize money. There are a lot of opportunities in tennis if you have the talent and the looks—product endorsements, exhibition appearances, broadcasting contracts."

"OK, sign me up!" Terry exclaimed, rubbing her hands together greedily.

Libby stopped and turned to face Terry. "Listen, this isn't a joke, kiddo. It's a major life change for you. I don't want you getting into this thinking it's a breeze then bailing when it starts getting tough."

"Or what? You tell the judge to send me to Detention?"

Hearing the anger and defiance in Terry's voice, Libby considered, for one brief moment, saving herself the trouble of taking on this troubled, angry, spiteful girl. Did she really need this? The moment passed. The answer was yes. And Terry needed her. She just didn't know it yet.

"Whether or not you play tennis has nothing to do with the terms of your probation, Terry. If you don't want to play, we'll think of some other project to help you stay off drugs, improve your school-work and adjust your attitude. Those are the important issues here, not tennis. I just thought it would be a fun way for you to reach the other goals."

Terry shook her head. "I still don't get why you're going to all this trouble for me. I'm nobody to you."

"To be perfectly honest, I'm doing it more for me than for you," Libby said. "So don't go thinking I'm some sort of saint, because, believe me, I'm not. I told you how sick I made myself, and I'm better now. But it's a struggle every day to stay better. This is where you come in. If I can focus on helping you feel better about yourself and your life, then that'll help me feel better about myself and my life. Quid pro quo. Know what it means?"

"No, what?"

"It's Latin and it means something given for something, an exchange. If you truly want to try the tennis, you promise to give me your best effort, on and off the court, especially in school, to take care of your body, which means no smoking of *any* kind, and to keep an open mind and trust me to steer you in the right direction. In exchange, I promise to give you every chance in the world to get where you want to go. I certainly don't need an answer this minute. Talk it over with your grandparents, sleep on it and let me know when you decide."

Terry could tell her right now there was no need to talk over or sleep on anything. Deep down, she'd realized from the first day hitting with Libby, from the minute she had connected solidly with the ball and sent it flying across the net, that she wanted to keep doing it and learn to do it better. What Libby and Pete believed about her "potential" merely confirmed what Terry knew in her gut. She could do it. And she'd do it better than anyone. All the other stuff—the money, the travel, the fame—would be fantastic, of course. But her greatest satisfaction would come from showing them all—the geeks at school, her ex-friends Tia, Irene and Margie, the Abominable Adams and Mr. Dillard, Papi and Bria, everyone who thought she was some juvenile delinquent loser—that they were dead wrong.

Most of all, she wanted to show *her* that throwing away her daughter hadn't been such a bright idea. When Terry was rich and famous and she came crawling back wanting to be her mother again, what would happen then? Terry's lips curled into a poisonous smile. "I don't need time. It's a deal. Let's do it."

"Are you sure, about the tennis, the practice, everything we talked about," Libby asked, though she wasn't surprised. This kid was aching to channel all those boiling emotions *somewhere*.

"Absolutely," Terry vowed. "I can't wait to start. The sooner the better."

It was true. The sooner she began her revenge, the better it would taste when she was ready to gorge on it.

 **9**

Three and a half months later...

"Hey, gimme that, ya mangy fleabag," Terry yelped at Pretty Boy, pulling her tennis shoe from his mouth and examining it for signs of damage. "If I find one tooth mark, just one, I'll tie that big pink tongue of yours in a knot."

Pretty Boy rolled over on his back, tail wagging, four legs pedaling madly in the air.

Terry laughed and rubbed his belly hard. He wasn't in the least flea-ridden or mangy. Since she first met him he'd gained weight and his fur, once thin and covered with bald spots, was now thick and shiny. Even the huge hole in the middle of his tail had filled in.

Pretty Boy sure wasn't the only thing that had changed since the end of January. Take this room for instance. Pale turquoise walls and plush, cream-colored carpet made it seem as if the ocean and beach outside flowed right over the balcony and through the French doors. There was a wrought iron bed almost the same color as the walls (Libby called it "verdigris"), a weird little couch (Libby called it a "chaise"), white wicker dressers, vanity and desk. It was the most beautiful room Terry had ever seen.

And it was all hers! At least it was every weekend from the time Libby picked her up from school Friday afternoon until Papi came to get her Sunday afternoon. At first she had felt like she was a guest in a luxury hotel and avoided exploring the rest of the house, even though Libby had said to make herself at home. She'd been uncomfortable with Lupe and Diego, the husband and wife "household management team" (as Libby called them) who lived in the apartment above the garage and insisted on speaking Spanish to her despite speaking perfect English themselves. And she'd been extremely shy around Libby's parents. They weren't around often, and when they were, they couldn't be nicer. But she was intimidated anyway. They were so *perfect*. Mr. Shaver looked like an old movie star, like Sean Connery or someone like that, and Mrs. Shaver was an older version of Libby, which was to say gorgeous, and spoke with an accent, being from England and all. Terry had tried to stay out of their way. But that was then.

Now, here it was the middle of May, and everything was different. Terry had wandered all over this enormous house and no longer thought of the huge room by the front door (Libby called it the "foyer") as the lobby. She loved Lupe and Diego and hung out with them in the kitchen all the time, talking and joking around—in Spanish. She even managed to have normal conversations with Mr. and Mrs. S without breaking into a sweat.

While school still sucked in general, her grades had improved almost 100% since she'd started doing her homework and actually studying for tests. It seemed even easier to score mostly A's now than back when she used to get them on a regular basis without really trying. In fact, this very afternoon before Papi picked her up for early dismissal, Mr. Dillard had called her to his office and given her the news she was dying to tell Libby. No summer school! No wasting hours in a classroom when she could be out on the tennis court.

She was getting along much better with Papi and Bria, who were so relieved to see her happier and not smoking pot or cigarettes or any of that stuff that they didn't mind her spending every weekend away. And this was about to change, too, because they'd all agreed that Terry would spend the summer living at Libby's to be able to devote as much time to tennis as possible.

Of all the changes in her life (except for one other pretty big one), tennis was the best. Terry had fallen in love with the game, pure and simple. She was so psyched about playing and improving that her lessons and workouts and conditioning (as Pete called them) routines were fun instead of hard work. During the week Libby picked her up after school and drove her to the Palm Club for an hour lesson with Pete, then usually hit with her on another court for awhile before taking her home. After dinner she did homework, read or fooled around on the iPad Libby had bought for her with Papi and Bria's permission.

On Friday afternoon, Pete came to Libby's for her lesson then spent another hour putting her through movement drills. Saturday morning she was up at seven for a five-mile run on the beach, then breakfast followed by two hours of hitting and drills with Libby. After lunch and a soak in the pool or a catnap on the terrace, Terry would play a match with either Pete's assistant,

Charlie (who was OK, but a bit of a Poindexter and not nearly as cute or funny as Pete), Libby or Libby's friend Jen, who Terry had met the same day she met Libby. Libby and Jen played on their college team together and were really tight, probably because they were a lot alike. So far, Terry had lost every single match, but she was slowly winning more games from all of them each time. Sunday was a repeat of Saturday except Papi would show up around three to take her home.

Instead of being exhausted by the tennis-intense weekend, Terry was exhilarated and couldn't wait to get back out on the court Monday afternoon. Libby had a video library of great matches going back years, classic battles which Terry watched over and over, studying and comparing. Who had the best forehand, backhand, serve, volley? She wanted to imitate the best and make them her own. She got a real kick out of watching Libby's matches, particularly her Wimbledon and Australian Open Finals and her three Semifinals, one at Wimbledon and two at the US Open. She looked like the same Libby only heavier. Terry loved the way she rushed to the net behind her killer serve and volleyed away her opponents' weak returns in a split second. And it was true, what Pete said. Libby had been the only one in her time period doing it, as opposed to earlier years when almost all of the great women players served and volleyed. Some of the men still did it. Terry promptly decided she wanted to play more like a man. Libby told her she was getting ahead of herself, to concentrate on grooving her groundstrokes and keeping the ball in play.

Libby. The Other Big Change. More specifically, the change in Terry's feelings about her. In the beginning, awkward around this rich and beautiful stranger, resentful of Libby's butting into her life and taking over, Terry had resisted liking her—for about a week. It had been too hard to keep it up. Libby was so nice and funny and fun to be around. They spent a lot of time together on and off the court, going shopping, eating out, seeing movies, and watching old and new tennis matches while Libby fed her gossip about the players and told her stories about the tour. Sure, the clothes and shoes and CDs, the iPad ,her weekend bedroom—were awesome, but they didn't have anything to do with why she liked Libby. She just enjoyed hanging out with her. They laughed and joked and teased, the same as she used to with…well, never mind.

Terry was shocked that LIBBY wanted to hang out so much with *her*! In these last few months, Pete and Jen had been the only adult friends of Libby's she'd met. And guys? She hadn't been on one date as far as Terry knew, which was weird, since guys checked her out and flirted with her all the time, everywhere they went. When Terry had felt bold enough to ask why she didn't go out with anyone, Libby shrugged and said it wasn't a priority right now, explaining that people in recovery were supposed to be concentrating on getting better and relationships were distracting.

"But not my relationship with you, kiddo," Libby had said. "You're the perfect date. Besides, I'm not in the mood. Believe me, if I met a guy tomorrow who made my heart race, I'd be on him in a minute, the rules of recovery be damned."

This is what Terry liked—no, respected—the most about Libby. She wasn't bullshitty. She always told Terry exactly what she thought, which wasn't always a joy to hear. She called her out on every bitchy remark, rude noise, judgment error, unfair criticism, lack of manners, fashion mistake—you name it. Funny thing was,

Terry didn't feel she was being nagged, like when Papi or Bria did it. She knew Libby was only trying to help her be better. On what Libby called her "wet blanket" days, which fortunately didn't happen often, she warned Terry right up front, so Terry knew to keep the chitchat to a minimum and basically lay low and leave her alone. On these days Libby was sad, crabby and preoccupied, totally droopy as if she actually WAS weighted down by a heavy, sopping blanket. Terry hated wet blanket days and couldn't wait for them to end so Normal Happy Libby, the Libby she didn't worry about, could come back.

Terry glanced at her watch as Pretty Boy gnawed gently on her elbow. Damn, almost 3:15 and here she was playing with the dog and spacing out instead of doing some time on the automatic ball machine before Pete got here. She wanted to take advantage of the half day at school to get a jump on her Practice Countdown to next weekend.

The Palm Club Championships. Her first tennis tournament. And her first victory, if she did say so herself. Only it wouldn't happen this way, fooling around when there were balls to be hit, serves to be served, drills to be run. Terry finished lacing up her shoes and leapt to her feet, driven by a jolt of the adrenaline which had been building ever since she wrote her name on the sign-up sheet. The Palm Club Posers were years of lessons and playing ahead of her, but none of them could work as hard as she could. And not one of them wanted to win as much as she did. She flew out the door, Pretty Boy at her heels.

"Whoa, take it easy, leave some felt on the ball," Pete yelled over at Terry, who had just smashed an overhead inches past his ear. "And get back. We're working groundies now, remember?"

He hit a high topspin lob, forcing Terry to scurry back behind the baseline to get it, which she did, lofting her return deep to his forehand. As they settled into a rally, trading forehands and backhands crosscourt and down the line, Pete couldn't help grinning, pleased with the number of times the ball was crossing the net and staying in. Terry was getting steadier, her groundstrokes becoming more consistent, her patience improving. Her progress in these past three months had been nothing short of astounding. While she still had a tendency to hit out wildly, almost punishing the ball, and go for winners when she should wait for a better opening, she was striking the ball with much more precision and could place the ball with more accuracy than he thought possible at this stage.

After watching hours of tennis matches on video, Terry had developed her own serve using parts of other serves from past tennis greats like Margaret Court and Billie Jean King and Martina Navratilova. Pete was only helping her fine-tune it. When she'd told him she wanted to serve and volley, he had reluctantly devoted time to volley practice while stressing that it shouldn't be her focus at this point. Strong groundstrokes and consistency were the keys to success in junior tennis. Terry thought it was "a drag" to just hit at the baseline and loved nothing better than pouncing on a short ball landing near the service line and smacking it for a winner.

The kid was stubborn, but she worked her butt off. Pete had never seen someone her age with so much drive. Sometimes she seemed a little *too* intense, and he knew Libby worried about this aspect, but as far as he was concerned that intensity was the reason Terry would be playing her first tournament match in a week after having held a racket for the first time an astonishing fourteen weeks ago.

She'd lose in the First Round, of course. But she'd win a few games, maybe even play a close set, and gain her first experience at real match play. Libby didn't think she was ready. Pete and Terry had to badger her until she gave in. Now, the question was, which lucky girl would be her first opponent? It was practically a free ride into the Second Round. He hadn't made up the draw yet, but he'd been thinking of possibilities. There were a number of players in the 16-and-Under age group who were weak enough to give Terry a chance at a respectable showing. Chances were even better in her own 14-and-Under age group, but Pete and Libby had agreed that Terry should play in the older group, given her height and strength. Plus, she was going to be losing a lot in the beginning, and it would be less humiliating being beaten by girls closer to her own size than the often tiny kids in 14-and-Under.

As if reading his mind, Terry leaned on the net after hitting a ball long to end another rally and asked, "Did you make the draw yet."

"Not yet," Pete replied, walking up to meet her. "Why? You have someone in mind?"

"I want to play Slaton," Terry said.

Pete laughed. "Yeah, right. Let's start at the top, why don't we? That's an excellent way for you to have a very short tournament experience." The kid cracked him up. Cubbie Slaton was not only his best junior at the club, but she also held the #15 ranking in the Girls' 16-and-Under in Florida. "Good one, T."

"I'm serious," Terry said, and meant it. She'd watched the Queen of the little Palm Club Princesses play and wasn't as impressed as everyone else was. Sure, she was a super pusher, could keep the ball going all day, but she didn't move well. Terry figured if she could mix it up and make her run, she'd be able to beat her. Boy, would she love to put it to her, show them all, all the bitches who were always fluttering around Slaton and kissing her ass, that their star wasn't so hot after all. Terry knew they dissed her, looked down on her as Libby's Charity Project, but never dared say anything to her face (to be honest, Slaton was the only one who always said hi to her).

"In fact, I'll bet you I can take her," Terry challenged a still laughing Pete. "You just give me the chance, OK? Please, please, puhleeeze…"

"Please what?" Libby asked, appearing out of thin air and walking out on the court to meet them dressed in a white linen pantsuit accessorized by dirty paw prints. The culprit whirled around his mistress, barking ecstatically.

"Hi!" Terry said, giggling and pointing. "Look at your pants."

Libby had obviously just come home from her fund-raising luncheon, the reason Papi had picked her up instead today.

Libby bent over, saw the mess and punished Pretty Boy severely by hugging and kissing him, making herself even dirtier. "Well, it's only fitting," she said, picking up a tennis ball and throwing it for him. "The thing today was for the Big Dog Ranch Rescue. So tell me, Miss Terry, what is it you're begging for?"

"She wants Cubbie as her First Round opponent next week," Pete answered, still snickering, much to Terry's annoyance.

Unlike Pete, Libby didn't laugh out loud, but she did smile in a way that somehow irritated Terry even more.

"And she's willing to bet she can beat her." Pete grinned at Terry. "Sorry, I don't take sucker bets, even when someone *else* is the sucker."

"Are you saying I'm a sucker if I think I can beat her?" Terry fumed, delighted, as always, by any opportunity to argue.

"All right, all right, I hate to break up this love fest," Libby interrupted, glancing at her watch, "But I really want to catch the 7:00 movie, remember, which means we have ninety minutes to get ready and grab an early dinner. So…go!" She grabbed Terry by her shoulders, spun her toward the gate and whacked her on the butt.

"OK, but what about it?" Terry asked Pete as she walked backwards toward the gate.

"Enough!" Libby said, shooing Terry away with both hands. "You know how I hate walking in late to a movie. Now, scram, and I mean it!"

When Terry disappeared around the cabana Pete said, "She can't really believe she can beat Cubbie, can she?"

"Oh Petey," Libby sighed. "Don't you know our girl by now? She can, does, and *needs* to believe it."

10

One week later...Friday afternoon

The only reason Libby put up with the noisy drumming on the dashboard was the mercifully short drive to the club. Plugged into iPod earbuds cranked to a volume guaranteed to destroy hearing, the pulsating bundle of nervous energy rocking next to her was listening to her "psych" music in preparation for her first match.

As if she needed to get jacked up any higher, Libby thought. The car was practically vibrating. As usual, she had mixed feelings about Terry's, uhh, enthusiasm, for lack of a better word to describe the frenzied approach to her tennis. All through this winter and spring, Libby had been so proud of her hard work and progress, and delighted by her genuine interest in the history and technicalities of the game—the legendary players, the stories, the classic matches, the strategies. She was even prouder of her about-face in school from D's and F's to A's, her commitment to staying smoke and drug free, her positive adjustments at home with her grandparents and her acceptance (after a rough couple of weeks) of Libby as mentor and friend instead of probation officer and enemy. She appeared to be happier.

Still...there was an obsessiveness about Terry—in behavior and attitude—which was disturbing. It was dark and angry and seemed to feed off negativity and thoughts of revenge. Jen thought Terry was way too tightly wrapped and should be alternating her tennis lessons with hours on a shrink's couch. Poor Charlie was downright scared of her. Pete encouraged her "intensity" and "focus" and told Libby she worried too much. But Libby spent more time with Terry than they did—a lot more—noticing and hearing things they didn't. They had no idea what a complicated young woman she was.

Terry was smart. She had a clever, wicked sense of humor mature beyond her years. Pretty Boy adored her because he sensed the basic kindness she was so successful at hiding from almost everyone else. There was a soft, playful, giggly Terry who rolled around with him on the floor, who loved to tease Lupe and Diego, who would laugh until Sprite—or Coke—or Starbucks Iced Mochaccino—came out of her nose at something Libby said.

But…there was another Terry who was present far more often. One who was sarcastic and rude and just plain mean, quick to judge and merciless in sentencing. The fact that her tough act was a smokescreen for insecurity and incredibly easy-to-bruise feelings didn't make it any easier to swallow—especially for those who'd never met the other Terry. Like the kids at the Palm Club. Terry had never given them a chance. Right off the bat she'd set herself apart, refused any attempt at conversation, glared at them with disdain, then reveled in how they "dissed" her and looked down on her. Bullshit, Libby had told her. Terry was the snob, not them. She was discriminating against them because of their social class. She'd gotten a snort, an eye-roll *and* a sarcastic "Yeah, right!" in response to that proclamation.

Quick to take offense at any real or imagined slight or criticism, Terry not only held a grudge, she hugged it fiercely. When Libby had suggested she invite a few friends over to go to the beach or hang out at the pool, Terry coldly announced that her "ex-friends" didn't deserve to spend any time with her. Ever again. Once you'd blown it with her, you'd blown it for good.

She hadn't mentioned her mother once in three months.

Libby knew, of course, all about Terry's issues with Isabel, not only from Alberto and Maria, but also straight from the proverbial horse's mouth—Isabel herself. During these past several months of regular phone calls to let her know what was happening with Terry, Libby had found herself liking and totally sympathizing with Isabel, who wanted more than anything to make things right with her daughter. Libby also knew that the sooner Terry started talking about and dealing with these issues, the better. But she didn't want to push too hard. Not yet. Let Terry open that can of worms all by herself.

As they turned into the club entrance and headed to the courts, Libby pulled the earbud from Terry's left ear.

"Hey!" Terry protested, "It's right at the best part…"

"In case you didn't notice, we're here. So, one more time, what's the plan?"

"Get the first serve in. Aim groundstrokes for the baseline. No going for winners unless I'm near the service line. No rushing to the net unless I'm already up there," Terry recited, having already fought and lost the battle over the last two parts of the plan.

"And the buzzwords for the match?" Libby asked, pulling into the parking lot and sliding into a space.

"Steady and patient." Terry leapt from the car and slammed the door, looking as if she was anything but.

"You forgot the most important one."

"Oh yeah!" Terry smacked her forehead with the heel of her hand. "FUN. Gotta remember to have some fun. Believe me, the worse I beat her, the more fun it'll be."

Libby smiled at Terry's back as she rushed ahead of her into the pro shop. While Terry's opponent, Morgan Cunningham, was one of the weaker players in the age group, she'd been a fixture at the club since she could hold a racket and should be able to beat Terry without too much trouble. Libby's hope was simply for Terry to serve well, play some long points and win at least a few games each set.

Her hope was quickly dashed. Libby looked at her watch, then saw Morgan Cunningham do the same out on the court as she stood waiting for Terry's serve to begin the second set. The first set had taken exactly twenty minutes, with Morgan winning 6-0. She'd played better than Libby had expected, hitting deep to Terry on just about every shot, waiting for Terry to make a mistake.

And Terry obliged, whacking the ball too hard instead of merely returning it, going for winners from behind the baseline, serving terribly and rushing to the net behind shots so weak it made it easy for Morgan to pass her.

So much for the plan.

In a way, Libby was glad it worked out this way. She wanted to see how Terry would react. Would she be completely discouraged and just go through the motions in the second set—in effect—quit? Would she continue the kamikaze strategy of the first set and go down spectacularly in flames? Or would she learn from her mistakes and stick to the plan? Libby looked over at Terry, who stood ready to serve, muttering to herself and scowling at the balls she held in her left hand. She'd love to hear what she was saying.

You are so lame, so stupid, such an idiot, Terry had been raging (quietly) at herself. Whatever possessed her to do the opposite of the plan? It was like she had temporary insanity the minute she stepped on the court. She avoided catching Libby's eye, afraid of what she'd see there. Libby had probably written her off already, disgusted by her in general, ready to throw her out of her house and send her off to Detention. OK, probably not. But she had to be disappointed, and Terry didn't blame her. She was disappointed (to say the least) in herself. She could do better, serve a lot better, follow the plan and start thinking. This Morgan (how come all these rich kids had either last names for first names or cutesy names like Muffy, or Lili, or *Cubbie!*) wasn't good enough to be beating her, especially 6-0, damn it!

Then she saw Morgan look at her watch, glance over at her parents sitting up on the terrace and flash ten fingers twice. Twenty more minutes and she'd be off the court.

Terry's face flushed. A surge of hatred roared through her at the smug cockiness of this little bitch. If she thought this set was going to be a replay of the last one, she was sadly mistaken. Holding up the balls to let Morgan know she was about to serve, Terry was determined to play this Libby's way, and even more determined to wipe the smirk off her opponent's blandly pretty face.

This time she quickly reviewed each element of her serve before she did it, then tossed the ball higher than she had the first set, drew her racket back as she bent her knees more deeply, and struck the ball with a sharp snap of her wrist. Sensing it was a good one as soon as she felt the ball leave her racket, she finished the follow-through and got ready for the return.

She needn't have bothered. The ball flew up the "T" in the middle of the court, landed in the far corner of the forehand service box before Morgan could even get her racket back and smacked against the back fence. Terry had served her first ace in a tournament!

Morgan regarded it as a fluke. After all, Terry had gotten so few first serves in, and double-faulted so often during the first set, that the laws of probability told her not to be concerned. She nonchalantly strolled to the backhand service side for the next serve. This time she managed to get her racket back, but the ball whistled by faster than the previous one. Two aces in a row. Morgan shook her head and giggled as she changed sides again.

Terry dumped her first serve into the bottom of the net. Morgan grinned and moved a few feet in, almost to the service line, in anticipation of a weak second serve or, more likely, a double-fault. Viewing Morgan's change of position and the smug look on her face as both an insult and a challenge, Terry tossed the second ball and hit it as hard as she could, knowing it was a dumb, First-Set Terry thing to do. She got lucky. The ball landed directly in the middle of the service box and rocketed into Morgan, who had been standing so close she didn't have time to lift her racket.

A collective gasp came from the small group of spectators on the terrace as Morgan cried out, dropped her racket and grabbed her head. Rather than apologize and see if she could help, Terry opted to stand at the back of the court bouncing a ball off her racket while Morgan's parents, Pete and a few other people cooed and fussed around her. What was the big deal? A little bump on the head. Anyway, she had it coming, moving up that way, taunting her, practically begging for it. Libby would get on her later about not saying sorry, but she didn't care. She *wasn't* sorry.

A few minutes later, Morgan had sufficiently recovered, a wide red blotch decorating the center of her forehead. Terry's turn to smile. 40-0. One more point and she was on the scoreboard. Her first serve went wide. This time she hit her second serve softer, making sure it was in. Morgan returned it deep to Terry's backhand, beginning a baseline rally, the ball sailing high over the net, back and forth with monotonous regularity. Terry hated "pushing" the ball like this and had to keep from going for a winner to end the point. But she'd promised herself to follow the plan, play steady and wait for an opening. Finally, one of Morgan's returns landed short, inside the service line where it was all right to go for a winner, and Terry pounced on it, driving a forehand crosscourt and out of Morgan's reach. Game!

Now, Terry thought, is when this match *really* begins. Feeling much better, she risked glancing in Libby's direction. Libby raised her sunglasses and winked, giving her a thumbs-up.

The second game lasted forever. Morgan's serve was consistent, not a weapon, but strong enough to usually land deep in the service court, setting up long rallies. With Terry playing so much steadier, Morgan realized she was suddenly in a real match now and picked up the level of her own game, outlasting Terry on the final rally to take the game.

The third game was over in five minutes. Terry served two more aces and two serves which Morgan was unable to return. It became the pattern for the second set. Terry won her service games quickly. Morgan won hers after a long struggle and many points.

With the score 5-4 in Terry's favor, they began another of Morgan's marathon service games. It would prove to be the longest yet, rally after rally, five deuce points with neither Terry nor Morgan able to close out their advantage points. At last, the score Terry's ad, Morgan double-faulted for only the second time, handing Terry the game and the second set. She looked over at Libby and saw her standing with Pete by the pro shop door. They both waved. Libby was beaming. Pete, of course, had to pretend to be neutral, but she could tell he was pleased.

Her first set win in tournament play! Terry didn't have time to savor it now, focused as she was on two things. Morgan was tired. The rest of her face was now so red you couldn't see the blotch on her forehead anymore. Her fatigue was affecting her concentration, forcing her into mistakes like the double-fault to end the set. During the changeover at the net, while Terry switched her racket to the one with a dry grip, she could hear Morgan's labored breathing as she drank from a bottle of Gatorade. Terry didn't feel thirsty, or tired. She could *smell* the weakness of her enemy and was ready to move in for the kill.

Terry served to begin the third set. Another ace. This time Morgan hung her head and plodded to the other side of the court, a different player from the one who'd started the second set. Completely ineffective at returning Terry's serve even when she could get her racket on it, she lost the game at love.

Terry had to admit the plan had worked during the second set. But now, with Morgan quickly running out of gas, she decided on a change of strategy, at least for the next game. If it didn't work, she could always go back to the way she played the last set, though Morgan's body language told her there wouldn't be nearly as many rallies.

With this in mind, she waited for the serve. The first one was out, setting up a perfect opportunity to put her revised plan into action. The second serve came in high and soft to her forehand. Instead of returning it deep, Terry hit it hard, placing it at a sharp angle to Morgan's backhand. Caught off guard, Morgan lurched to the side, making it to the ball with just enough time to lob it back, which would have set up another baseline battle. But Terry wasn't at the baseline. After angling her approach shot she'd rushed to the net, so when Morgan's ball floated back she easily volleyed the ball crosscourt.

Morgan had no chance of getting anywhere near it. She frowned and shot a desperate look at her parents, as if to plead, "Get me outta here!"

That volley winner was all Terry needed. For the remainder of the set, she rushed to the net after every one of her serves, most of Morgan's, and in fact, most other shots—whether she belonged there or not. Sometimes Morgan was able to pass her, usually not.

To Terry, *this* was tennis, running and leaping and twisting for balls, not standing at the back of the court trading the same forehands and backhands, over and over until someone happened to miss. She was loving it. This high was way better than any pot she'd ever smoked. Too bad it had to end, at least for this match. Leading 5-1, 40-5, Terry served wide to Morgan's forehand, followed it to the net and was there in plenty of time to smack Morgan's return for a winner with a backhand volley.

Game. Set. Match!!! Terry waited for Morgan to shuffle up to the net and accepted her handshake, which felt like a wet rag, without a word. She walked off the court, gathered her rackets and gear and headed up the stairs to the terrace and Libby's table.

"Congratulations, sweetheart!" Libby stood and gave her a tremendous hug. "I am so proud of you."

"Watch out," Terry said, squirming to free herself. "I'm soaked. You'll get all wet."

"Who cares. You deserve it. You did great out there, especially after that first set."

"I know, sorry about bagging the plan. I guess I was just too nervous or something."

"It's OK, you bounced back. That second set could have easily played out another way."

"Like how?"

"Like you could have gotten discouraged and given up or…"

"That could never happen," Terry interrupted. She stared directly into Libby's eyes and stuck her jaw forward. "You may see me lose, but you'll never see me quit. Never!"

Struck by the force of Terry's reply and the ferocious look on her face, Libby realized two things simultaneously. The first, that Terry was fueled by the fire you needed to be a champion, thrilled her. The second, that the source of the fire was a burning ball of rage, worried her, and made her want to do everything possible to extinguish it. But now was certainly not the time to dwell on it.

"Hey," she forced a laugh. "Lighten up, I believe you. Listen, it's almost 6. Let's get out of here. We can postmortem the match at home. Want me to tell you who you play tomorrow morning, or you want to go see for yourself?"

Terry grinned. "See!" She grabbed Libby's arm and pulled her into the pro shop, where all the draws for the different age groups were posted on a bulletin board. Locating the 16-and-Under sheet she ran her finger past names until she came to *Terry Gomez* with her 0-6, 6-4, 6-1 victory already posted beneath. The excitement she felt at seeing her name was a mild buzz compared to the adrenaline rush she got from discovering the name of her next opponent.

Of all the revelations she'd had during her first tournament match, the one which she believed was the key to winning was, ironically, the only one she didn't plan to share with Libby. The turning point had come when Morgan looked at her watch, flashed her fingers and made Terry hate her. From then on, the more Terry hated her, the better she played. It was simple. It worked, and it would work again because Terry wouldn't have any trouble building up a nice hot hate against the person whose name was opposite hers.

No trouble at all.

⟍ 11

The next morning...

"Terry, this is my husband, Tripp," said Chris Adams, introducing a tall, hunky guy straight out of GQ. "Honey, this is Terry Gomez. I think I told you she's one of my students, right?"

"Oh, of course, hello, Terry, it's a pleasure to meet you."

"Hi," Terry said, thinking, yeah right! Abominable had undoubtedly clued him in on their "very special" student-teacher relationship. Leave it to her to be married to a guy who was prettier than she was. And Tripp? Gimme a break. His parents must have been on some kind of weird trip when they named him. And speaking of weirdness...how weird was it to be having this little chat with her English teacher here at the Palm Club?

"Well, I'd like to wish you luck," Tripp chuckled, "But I think my kid sister would object."

Terry smiled faintly. Weirder still was that her opponent this morning was this guy's sister. Well, half-sister, as Libby had explained the first time she pointed out Penny Adams to Terry (when Libby had taken over Terry's life, she'd set up conferences with all of Terry's teachers. Turns out Libby *knew* Abominable because she'd been childhood friends with Tripp, so she also knew Penny belonged to Tripp's father's second family blahblahblah).

"Chris tells me you've haven't been playing very long," Tripp continued, obviously determined to have an actual conversation. "You know, Penny's been playing since she was six, which is a big head start, so you should count every game you get as a victory and feel good about winning your match yesterday."

"I'll try not to get too discouraged," Terry replied with a totally fake grin as she glanced at Abominable.

Tripp didn't react to Terry's mock polite sarcasm, but Chris had heard it more often than she cared to think about. "Look, hon, there's Page and Will. Let's go sit with them." She turned and walked away without another word to Terry.

"Well, good luck, anyway," Tripp said, following Chris to a table in the middle of the terrace.

"Bullshit," Terry muttered under her breath as she made her way across the terrace and walked down the steps to the first court, where Penny Adams was already spreading out her gear and fastening her limp orange hair into a pitiful ponytail. She didn't acknowledge Terry at all, simply walked out onto the court. If that's the way you wanna play it, fine by me, Terry thought, wondering how this doughy, freckle-covered troll could possibly share *any* DNA with Abominable's husband. Actually, better than fine. Perfect. It fit right into Terry's mental game plan. She wasn't about to make the same mistakes she had in her first set against Morgan.

Choosing her racket and tying a bright red bandanna around her forehead, she walked to the other end of the court, searching for Libby on the terrace directly above them. There she was, sitting at a table near the pro shop with Jen and talking on her cell, waving when she saw Terry looking for her. It was much more crowded today, with a lot more people watching, so Terry was glad to see at least two familiar friendly faces.

As they went through their warm-up, a group of kids scrambled for seats at the far end of the terrace, on Penny's side of the court, dragging chairs and pushing tables together. Penny waved and grinned at her cheering section. Terry recognized most of the usual suspects she saw hanging around Cubbie Slaton, including the Queen Bee herself, of course.

"Hey, Pen," one of the boys called, loudly enough for Terry to hear on the other end, "We want to catch a few waves before lunch, so make this a fast hour, OK?"

Terry didn't bother looking up as she heard the entire entourage laughing like a bunch of rabid hyenas, but her head snapped up at Penny's reply.

"I can do it in 45," Penny boasted, touching off another round of raucous guffawing.

Terry stood at the net, delighted by the bad feelings swirling around the court. "45 minutes sounds about right to me," she chirped, imitating Penny's squeaky voice, "So what are we waiting for? Warm-up's over. You can even serve." Terry tossed the ball she had in her hand at Penny and walked over to her bag for a towel.

Penny missed the ball and scowled at Terry. She was exactly the way her sister-in-law had described. Rude. Mean. Bitch. Totally shocking that she'd beaten Morgan, but then, Morgan pretty much sucked most of the time. Penny couldn't wait to beat her and send her back to whatever hole Libby Shaver had dug her up from.

"Take her apart, Penny!"

"Thrash her!"

"Kill her!"

"Send her back to Mexico!"

Terry laughed out loud at that last one as she made her way over to the forehand service court. Try Cuba, you ignorant moron (not that there was anything wrong with being Mexican. It was just plain wrong in her case). More catcalls rained down on her until Pete told them to shut up. Too bad. She was feeding off it.

This was going to be a blast.

"Just wait," Chris Adams whispered in response to her husband's remark that Terry "seemed like a nice kid" despite everything Chris had told him about her most troublesome student. She had him fooled, as well as most of the faculty at Quigley. Just last week she'd had a heated argument with Jo Meeks in the faculty lounge about Terry's supposed "transformation". She had listened with growing irritation as Jo, Enid Connors and Fred Pontifex took turns heaping praise on Terry's improvement in her grades and her attitude until she couldn't take it anymore. She had retorted that Terry may have improved her grades, but she was still the same angry, hateful, deeply disturbed brat she'd been since the beginning of the school year. Jo, always Terry's defender, had disagreed vehemently, sparking verbal fisticuffs finally broken up by Enid's joke that Chris was envious of Terry's new wardrobe.

Well, Chris thought, noting Terry's fire-engine red Nike outfit clinging perfectly to her tall, slim body, Libby Shaver can dress her up all she wants, but she can't change the basic flaws in her character. On the outside, Terry Gomez was inarguably a beautiful girl, much as Chris disliked admitting it. The ugliness was inside. You could see it easily if you were unlucky enough to have those huge black eyes turn on you, and hear it when that pretty mouth with those perfect white teeth opened and spewed sarcasm and disrespect.

She was slightly ashamed by how much she wanted Penny to humiliate her.

It was humiliating, all right.

Terry didn't beat Penny Adams. She destroyed her. It was Penny's bad luck to catch Terry on a day when her serve was on. She rarely missed a first serve, most of which Penny couldn't return. Her groundstrokes were steady and accurate, her winners devastating. The first set ended 6-0 in 17 minutes, with Penny winning a grand total of thirteen points!

Terry was enjoying herself immensely. Penny looked ready to burst into tears. The entourage had fallen silent at 3-0. She'd been in "The Zone"—the term athletes used for ecstatic, effortless perfection—for the entire set and wanted to stay there for this one. The fact that Abominable was witnessing the massacre of her sister-in-law was icing on the cake.

She wasn't about to let up.

After rapidly losing the first three games of the second set, Penny made a change in strategy that was not only futile, but dangerous. She started coming to the net. The first two times she tried it, Terry lobbed the ball over her head for easy points. The third time she rushed in behind a ball which landed short to Terry's forehand. Terry was on it in a second. Rather than aiming it down the line, completely out of Penny's reach, she put all her strength into the shot and smashed it directly at Penny, who ducked so quickly she lost her balance and landed unceremoniously on her butt. Terry twirled her racket into a machine gun position and pretended to take a shot at Penny. "Next time I won't miss," she said, noting with satisfaction that Dough Girl had begun to cry. She turned and strolled back to serve the next point.

Ten minutes later, Terry served the last in a long string of aces to end the match 6-0, 6-0, 35 minutes after it had started. Totally ignoring Penny, who was approaching the net to shake hands, she quickly gathered up her gear and climbed the steps to the terrace before her opponent had even left the court. She saw Libby standing with Pete at the entrance to the pro shop and was almost there when someone tapped her on the shoulder.

"Terry, wait a sec," Cubbie Slaton said as Terry turned to face her. "I feel terrible about the stuff all those guys were saying, and the way they were acting. I just want you to know I was so mad I went and sat somewhere else, and so did some of the other kids."

"Whatever," Terry shrugged, feigning an indifference she certainly didn't feel. How dare this little princess pity her! "It didn't bother me."

"Well, it bothered me, and I wanted to apologize for…"

"Look," Terry snapped, "Don't worry about me. If I were you, I'd start worrying about this afternoon."

Cubbie flinched as if she'd been slapped. She opened her mouth to say something, but stepped around Terry instead and hurried off without looking back. For one instant Terry had the urge to run after her and say she was sorry, but it passed in a nanosecond and she found herself staring directly into the reflective amber lenses of Libby's sunglasses. While Terry couldn't see her expression, it was clear she sure wasn't smiling, as she should have been after Terry's impressive victory.

"In the car. Now," Libby ordered in the quiet controlled voice Terry had come to fear.

Libby didn't say a word to Terry until she drove through the front gate of the club, then she let her have it.

"That was quite a display you put on back there, and I'm sure as hell not talking about your tennis," she said calmly, careful to control the anger threatening to boil over into her tone.

"But I was just…" Terry started to protest.

"Not another word." Libby wanted Terry's undivided attention, and she wasn't about to be interrupted. "What really gets me is that you were great in the beginning. Penny was being a bitch, and the other kids were terrible, but you went about your business even though you had every right to get rattled. You were getting even by crushing her, which was awesome. Then you did the bit with turning your racket into a gun and dragged yourself right down to their level. And *then*, you refused to shake hands, probably the single most flagrant example of poor sportsmanship in this game, or any other. The absolute worst, though, was your behavior towards Cubbie, who was trying to apologize for something she had no part in."

"I was only trying to…"

"I heard the whole thing, Terry, so don't bullshit me."

"I don't need her feeling sorry for me. That's all I was trying to say," Terry retorted, furious at how unfair Libby was being instead of telling her what a great match she played. "And what was I supposed to do, shake hands with someone who's totally dissing me?"

"Yes," Libby replied, "It's called having class, which has nothing to do with money or social position, and everything to do with character and upbringing. Penny's family is rolling in money, but she has no class. Cubbie has class, though it was thoroughly wasted on you. What I can't figure out is how two classy people like your grandparents managed to have a granddaughter without any."

Terry didn't have a comeback. She was beginning to feel embarrassed, especially about blowing Cubbie off. And maybe she *did* go a little over the top with Penny. "Sorry you're so mad," she said, hoping an apology, half-hearted thought it was, would bring the lecture to an end.

"I'm not as mad as I am disappointed, " Libby said. "And I'm not the one who deserves an apology."

"OK, I'll do it before the match. But please, puhleeeze tell me I don't have to apologize to Penny," Terry pleaded, clasping her hands in mock prayer.

Libby laughed in spite of herself. "You don't have to apologize to Penny."

"Whew," Terry sighed theatrically and swept the edge of her hand across her forehead in exaggerated relief. "Thanks, Lib. And I'm really sorry I let you down. I promise I'll never show poor sportsmanship again, you'll see."

"Oh, I know you won't," Libby said, "Because if you do, it'll be the last time you do it in a tournament, got it?"

"Got it," Terry repeated, happy that Libby seemed willing to let it go for the moment. "Now could we please talk about the plan for this afternoon."

"You mean the plan after your sincere apology delivered without an ounce of sarcasm, right?" Libby asked, taking her eyes off the road to look at Terry and make sure she wasn't just giving lip service.

"Absolutely," Terry said, thinking what a good actress she could be when she really tried.

Terry wiped her sweaty face with a towel and took a long drink of Gatorade, wracking her brain for a strategy to win the next two games to even the match. She'd lost the first set 6-2 and couldn't honestly say she'd played poorly. Yeah, her serve could've been better, and she'd made more than a few stupid shot choices, but overall the problem hadn't been her play. It had been Cubbie.

Cubbie Slaton was a super pusher, all right—emphasis on *super*. Her balls came in hard and deep, keeping Terry way behind the baseline with few opportunities of moving up to hit a short ball. There were no short balls. Quick movement wasn't Cubbie's strength because she rarely had to make the effort. While her serve wasn't as hard as Terry's, it was delivered with a lot of spin and accuracy. It was as if she was playing a whole different game than Penny Adams and Morgan Cunningham. Terry had severely underestimated her. It was one thing watching her play, and quite another actually playing her.

Now it was 4-4 in the second set. Terry not only had to fight for every point, but she also had to deal with the constant noisy cheering of Cubbie's entourage. This morning, against Penny, she had used it to her advantage, but this afternoon it felt different, more supportive of Cubbie instead of against Terry. The negative vibe simply wasn't there, damn it, even though she was sure Cubbie must have given them an earful. At any rate, she couldn't feed off it so she had to concentrate on hating Cubbie (since they'd been ignoring each other so far, even that was proving difficult. The big apology exchange at the net right before the match had consisted of five words—Sorry about earlier. Fine, whatever.

Come on serve, she hissed under her breath, walking to the baseline. She needed four great first serves, preferably aces. Instead she double-faulted twice, hit an easy volley into the net and sent a rare short return so far out it hit the fence, losing the game at love. 5-4 Cubbie. Terry had just experienced her first case of "the yips", a term tennis players used along with "choking" to describe letting their nerves put a stranglehold on their play. Every athlete in every sport dreaded choking, and now Terry knew why. She was disgusted, so furious with herself and so busy raking herself over the coals that she rapidly lost the first three points of the next game. 40-love. Cubbie had three match points. All she had to do was hold her serve and wait for Terry to make another mistake.

"I guess it's too late for the Heimlich maneuver," Pete said to Libby as they stood together on the terrace.

"Don't count her out yet, Funny Boy," Libby replied. Watching

Terry unravel as Cubbie's fans amped up their cheering with every point, Libby was struck by how *alone* Terry was out there. Sure, she brought a lot of it on herself, and there was no denying she was tough enough to take it. But she was also a 13-year-old girl who was much more sensitive and insecure than she'd ever want anyone to know. It had to hurt. Libby felt a surge of affection and protectiveness towards this complicated kid and found herself blinking back tears.

On the court, Cubbie tossed the ball for what she hoped would be her last serve of the match. The ball sliced wide to Terry's backhand, but Terry had anticipated it and sent her return so deep that Cubbie returned short, making it easy for Terry to rush in and hit a winner. 40-15, one match point saved. Cubbie's next serve was out. Her second serve sat up perfectly for Terry to return it crosscourt at a sharp angle and follow it to the net. Cubbie saw her coming and hit the ball too hard in trying to pass her, sending it flying out beyond the baseline. 40-30, two match points saved. Cubbie's next serve was a beautiful torpedo down the T, which would have been an ace against most players. But most players didn't have Terry's quick reflexes and agility. Terry not only returned it, but sent it deep, beginning a long baseline rally which ended with Terry rushing in on a backhand Cubbie had launched high over the net and smashing an overhead winner so hard it bounced in and catapulted over the fence. The crowd gasped, then applauded wildly.

Deuce. Three match points saved.

"I'll be damned," Pete said.

Libby clapped so hard her hands stung.

The battle for the tenth game of the second set of Slaton versus Gomez would go down in the Juniors' record book of the Palm Club. Before it was all over, there would be thirteen deuce points, with Terry having her advantage six times, and Cubbie having seven. The game, which lasted longer than the nine games before it, became a mini drama full of fantastic rallies, awesome winners and great "gets" by both players. The crowd was pulling for both of them. Even Cubbie's friends. It was a shame that someone had to lose.

After winning the thirteenth deuce point when Terry overhit a forehand, Cubbie served for the match for the tenth time, sending a hard first serve to Terry's backhand. Terry's return landed at the service line, giving Cubbie a chance to place a perfect topspin forehand deep to Terry's forehand. It bounced then spun even further back, forcing Terry almost to the fence, where she just managed to flick at the ball, sending it over the net, high and weak. A sitting duck. Instead of volleying it, Cubbie let it bounce first, slicing a drop shot that barely cleared the net on Terry's backhand side, then watched in amazement as Terry sped to the net from the opposite end of the court and dove for the ball, like a baseball player sliding into a base. The tip of her racket caught the ball at the last second, popping it over the net. Cubbie recovered from her shock that Terry even got near the ball just in time to volley it crosscourt for a winner. The match was over.

The crowd was on its feet, clapping and cheering for both girls.

Terry rose instantly to her feet, green clay covering the entire front of her body, both knees speckled with blood and shook Cubbie's outstretched hand.

"Great match," Cubbie said. "I can't believe you got that ball. Are you OK?"

"Yeah, no big deal," Terry replied, brushing off Cubbie's concern right along with the clay from her clothes. "Congratulations." Looking up at the terrace as she walked to the side of the court to gather her gear, she saw Libby and Pete, grinning and waving. What in the hell were they so happy about. She had lost. That was nothing to smile about.

"You've got to be kidding!" Libby said. They were standing by the car in the club parking lot, arguing about what to do next. Libby had suggested heading home for a shower then going to Cafe TuTuTango, Terry's favorite restaurant, to celebrate the great match she'd just played. Terry wanted to go home and practice her serve.

"I'm not," Terry said, scowling. "You don't celebrate losing."

"But you *do* celebrate getting to the Third Round in your first tournament, and sucking it up when people are rooting against you, and gutting it out at the end of that second set, and saving ten match points, and playing the kind of tennis you have no business playing as a beginner."

"So what? If I hadn't choked at 4-4 and lost seven points in a row, I could still be out there playing, and maybe I could be winning instead of being such a loser. A choker *and* a loser."

"That's right, you choked. We've *all* choked, Terry. It's human nature, and it's part of the game. It's nothing to be ashamed of. Just learn from it. The more experience you get, the better you'll be able to deal with the yips. It happens. Move on and cut yourself some slack. How many times do I have to repeat—it's your first tournament. I'm so proud of you, and you should be proud of yourself. Do you realize how close you came to beating the #15 ranked player in Florida?"

"Close isn't good enough. Nobody remembers the score, they just remember who won."

Libby sighed, completely exasperated, and opened the car door. "Look, obviously you're determined to wallow in self-pity, so far be it for me to deprive you. So let's go home and you can serve all night if you want. Knock yourself out, kiddo."

"I'm not feeling sorry for myself. I'm mad at myself. I know I can beat her."

"Then you will the next time."

You can bet on it, Terry promised silently, sliding into the front seat and staring straight ahead, eyes narrowed, jaw set. There were a lot of people and things in the world she hated, and she'd just discovered that losing was right at the top of the list. She had to work harder, run more, drill more.

Starting right now.

⚲ 12

Summer...

For the next three months Terry made good on her promise. There may have been other kids somewhere working as hard as she did, but nobody could possibly work harder. Or longer. Or with more passion. Or with greater desire.

The two weeks between the Palm Club tournament and the end of school had been pure torture for her. She couldn't wait to be finished with the seventh grade and all the silly activities like banquets and dances and class trips that always happened in May (and which Papi and Bria had insisted she attend down to the last miserable one). At the Awards Assembly, she'd been psyched about winning the English and History prizes only because it had made her grandparents so proud, and because it must have *killed* Abominable to have to give it to her. Otherwise, she couldn't have cared less. She'd regarded it all—well, basically, everything—as a distraction from her tennis, an interference with her private agenda. She'd wasted so many years when she could have been playing that she didn't want to blow off one minute more, which is why she'd had her stuff packed and ready to move to Libby's right after dismissal on the last day of school.

The next morning Terry, Libby and Pete had sat down with the United States Tennis Association of Florida's junior tennis schedule for summer and decided Terry would enter three tournaments in July and three in August, leaving the first month completely free for practice, drills, conditioning—and more practice. Terry had been dying to play some tournaments immediately, but Libby and Pete finally convinced her she'd have better results if she used June for training only.

The following four weeks turned out to be one long intense extravaganza of activity.

Terry felt *drenched* in tennis, which was exactly what she'd been craving. She took her former weekend tennis marathon, stretched it to the limit and stuck to it every day with almost religious devotion. When she showed Libby and Pete her schedule, meticulously outlined and printed out, they had quite the chuckle.

6:00	5 Mile Beach Run
7:00	Breakfast
7:30-8:30	Serve Practice
8:30-9:30	Movement Drills
9:45-11:30	Groundstroke Practice on Ball Machine or with Partner
12:00	Lunch Break
1:30-3:45	Match Play
4:00-5:30	Volley Practice on Ball Machine or with Partner
6:00	Dinner Break
7:00-8:00	Serve Practice

Not only weren't they laughing anymore when Terry kept to the schedule for ten straight days, they were begging her to cut back. Pete was concerned that she was running herself down and losing too much weight. Though she ate constantly, even scarfing Power Bars between meals, she still couldn't compensate for the enormous amount of calories she burned. He convinced her to substitute strength training several times a week in place of the movement drills so she could make up for in muscle what she was losing in body fat.

Libby, of course, had additional worries. Terry's maniacal assault on the game could no longer be called anything—focus, determination, intensity, drive, motivation—other than what it clearly was. Obsession. It's all she wanted to do and all she thought about. When she wasn't on the court, or running, or lifting weights, or doing crunches, she was reading tennis magazines, or watching tennis videos or scrutinizing every televised moment of the French Open and Wimbledon, which she would DVR and watch again.

She refused to go out for dinner and a movie the way they used to, claiming she couldn't miss serve practice and that there would be plenty of time for "fooling around" after she won her first tournament. While she knew it was unrealistic, Libby found herself hoping Terry would win one soon, if only to make her slack off a little and maybe reward herself for the progress she'd made.

It was a good thing Libby couldn't read Terry's mind. Terry had no intention of letting up even after she won her first tournament. If anything, she would train harder. It was easy for Libby to be all la-di-dah, let's go see such and such, and eat at this place, and go to that place. Libby had already been there, done that—though in all honesty she'd never been The Best. And Terry wanted to be The Best. She wanted to walk out on the court, preferably Centre Court at Wimbledon, and wipe Jemma York off the face of the earth! Even though Jemma had lost in the semi-finals of the Australian and the finals of the French so far this season, she still held the #1 ranking. She was currently The Best. Besides, she seemed so snotty and above-it-all, the way she never showed emotion, and glided around between points like she had a crown on her swelled head. And of course, the stupid accent that sounded fake even though she *was* from England (no offense to Libby's mom, but she sounded the same way).

Jemma York had become Terry's Holy Grail. But since she knew her fantasy would sound ridiculous, not to mention delusional, coming from someone who'd never played in one Junior tournament (she didn't count the rinky-dink Palm Club tournament since it wasn't a USTA event), she kept it to herself and focused for the immediate future on the junior players in Florida instead. At least out loud.

Logging on to the USTA website, she found the current rankings list for Girls' 16's, printed it and taped it to her bathroom mirror as part of her mental training. Every time she brushed her teeth she lasered in on the list, scrutinizing each name with its jagged red slash through it, signifying annihilation. #1 Kendra Weiss, North

Miami. #2 Jacquie Darden, Tampa. #3 Page Carter, Jacksonville. #4 Gabriela Fonseca, Coral Gables. #5 Erin O'Donnell, Orlando. And so on to #20 Marissa Flick, Sarasota. The #15 slot was so thick with red slashes it was impossible to see Caroline "Cubbie" Slaton's name, but Terry didn't need to see it to know it was there. Though the list went to #50, Terry was interested only in the Top Twenty. She didn't want to imagine losing to anyone lower.

Warning to Kendra Weiss…watch your back, girl.

With Jen gone up north for the summer, Terry's regular practice partners were down to Libby, Pete and Charlie, who were all so good they could play any type of game with any style, making it seem like Terry was playing matches against a wide variety of opponents instead of just three. While she racked up more games with every day, she still hadn't been able to take a set from any of them. The closest she came was 7-5 against Libby one searingly hot afternoon. Afterwards, melting into the chairs under the cabana, Libby said Terry could have won the set, but she got psyched out by thinking Libby should beat her.

"Never underestimate the power of the mind in this game," Libby told her for the millionth time. "It's as—maybe more— important than anything physical you can do on the court. And I'm not talking just about strategizing. It's more about mental toughness, about bearing down when it's easy to let up. About digging deep when things aren't going your way. It's about seeing any gamesmanship your opponent throws at you, like questioning line calls or calling for a bogus medical time-out, as a sign of her own weakness and turning it to your advantage. Mostly, it's about believing in yourself, even when it seems impossible."

Of all the adjectives you could use to describe Libby—gorgeous, kind, funny, moody, generous, rich, tall, thin, and so on—the one Terry thought of first, now that she knew Libby so well, was *smart*. Or wise. OK, smart and wise. Terry listened carefully to Libby's advice, filing it away for someday when she needed it. Libby was her Head Guru, like Pete was her Body Guru. Together they were trying to shape the perfect tennis player, and Terry was thrilled to absorb their efforts.

The more Terry worked on her game, the more convinced she became that serve and volley was the way to go. Not that her groundstrokes hadn't improved. She could now hit all day, steadily, from both sides, with power and precision. From the beginning Pete and Libby had agreed that Terry was strong enough to have a one-handed backhand, which turned out to be a great decision. Her backhand was not only more consistent than her forehand, but it gave her better mobility in getting to the ball and allowed her to chip the ball and charge in to the net behind it. The chip-charge was crucial for a volleyer, which was what Terry considered herself to be. A serve and volleyer.

Terry had now watched enough tennis to realize what an immense weapon a wicked serve could be. For the men, it more often than not determined the outcome of the match. Not so for the women. Terry was shocked that not one of the top women had the kind of serve she could rely on to get her out of trouble or rack up easy service games with aces. For many of them, their serve was actually a disadvantage, which was unfathomable to Terry. Shawn Chillingsworth had the fastest serve, clocked at 122 mph at the Australian Open in January, but she also regularly threw in as many double faults as aces. Terry wanted to be able to count on her serve as a sure thing. So she served thousands of balls, practicing placement, experimenting with different types of spin and speed, grooving her toss until it automatically sent the ball to the 2:00 position every single time.

Whenever she felt bored by the repetition (often) she remembered the day Pete had clocked her serve with one of those radar guns the police used to catch speeders. Her fastest one was 119 mph!!! This would place her at #2 on the tour right behind Chillingsworth, the #3 player *in the world*, who was nine years older, three inches taller, probably 20 pounds heavier and made of muscles on top of other muscles.

Terry was hungrily looking forward to the day when she served Ms. Shawn Chillingsworth off the court and right back into the locker room.

First things first, though. Much as she hated to admit it, and as much as she was chomping at the bit to get a crack at The Real Tour, she knew she had to make her mark on the Juniors in her own state first.

Terry spent the rest of the summer making a mark that looked like a giant sunburst, exploding through the tournaments she entered, leaving a trail of white hot light which left spectators wondering if they needed to buy a darker pair of shades.

Her "debut", as Pete jokingly called it, was close to home at the Gold Coast Junior Tennis Championships in Boca Raton. The buzz started after Terry's first match against an unlucky girl named Sylvie Traina (though in Terry's mind she was simply #28 and therefore must be defeated) who was so rattled by Terry's serve-and-volley blitz that she floundered early and never recovered. 6-1, 6-2, Terry.

Having heard about the big new kid with the giant serve, a lot of people who wouldn't normally have shown interest in anything earlier than a quarterfinal match came by to check Terry out. What they saw caused more than a few mouths to drop open and began a groundswell of whispering—Who is she? Where did she come from? Have you seen her before?—that grew to tsunami size by the time Tricia Bindelglass (#23, to Terry) trudged to the sidelines, wondering how she came to be on the losing end of 6-3, 6-3 to a nobody.

The next morning, during her quarterfinal match, Dulcie Busta-mante's reaction to the bombs being launched from Terry's side of the court was more rage than bewilderment. Dulcie (#18, but seeded #4 in this tournament) quickly began throwing her racket, screaming melodramatically, cursing first in English, then in Spanish directly at Terry. Terry followed Libby's advice, didn't rise to the bait and used Dulcie's meltdown to her own advantage for a 7-5, 6-0 victory.

After the match Libby called Pete at the club to see if he could cancel his afternoon lessons and come down for Terry's semifinal.

"Who's she playing?" he asked.

"Lynn Bloxsom, third seed, ranking #13, tough baseliner."

"I'll go down with you for the final tomorrow," Pete replied, confident that the afternoon would end in victory for Terry.

Three sets and many great shots, unbelievable gets, tense moments and crowd gasps later, Pete proved to be right. Taking the third set in a 7-6 tie-breaker with a vicious crosscourt forehand volley winner, Terry found herself in her first final, which didn't seem to surprise her any more than it did Pete. She expected it of herself, which is why she arrived the next day for her match against the top seed, Jennifer Zilinsky (#6) fully prepared to be cradling the trophy in her arms when it was over.

An hour and a half later she held the trophy, all right. The second place trophy. On the way home Libby interrupted Terry's complaining about how she could have won if her serve had been on, and if she hadn't gone for so many winners, and if she had played smarter on this point and that point, to tell her a few things she needed to hear.

"You're right about all those things, Terry, but in the end she outplayed you, pure and simple. That match wasn't all about you. Jennifer forced a lot of your decisions, made you scramble so you couldn't get set for shots, passed you at the net how many times? She was the better player today. You didn't lose the match. She won it. She deserves the credit, and you should give it to her."

Terry grudgingly saw Libby's point, but it didn't make the loss sting any less, and she still believed deep down that she was a better player than Jennifer Zilinsky.

On an overcast Sunday of the first weekend in August, Terry held

up the winner's trophy to the cheers of an appreciative crowd who
had watched her defeat Page Carter (#3) to take the SeaCrest Junior
Championships of Tampa. Both Terry and Libby breathed a sigh of
relief, but for slightly different reasons. SeaCrest was the third and
last tournament Terry would play since she and Libby had flown
out to the west coast of Florida. Her first two results had been disappointing. Semifinals in Naples. Quarterfinals in Sarasota. Though
she'd lost both to high-ranking players, Erin O'Donnell (#5) and
Lindsay Cross (#8), Terry had been punishing herself (secretly)
with the horrible thought that if she wasn't ripping the Juniors
apart as she'd hoped, how in the hell was she thinking she could
play on The Real Tour? When she finally won in Tampa, beating
the highest ranking player yet, she felt happier about being back on
her timetable than about actually winning the tournament.

Libby, who knew much more about Terry's aspirations and
fantasies than Terry thought she did, hoped the victory would help
Terry take some of the pressure off herself. While she had immediately seen Terry's enormous potential, she never would have
guessed that six months later she'd be beating the girls she had
this summer. Of course, she also could never have imagined how
insanely hard Terry would work. Or the power of the demons that
drove her.

Terry's last two tournament results in August were icing on the
cake of what Libby and Pete considered to be an extraordinary
summer. Terry won her second straight tournament, The Holiday
Park Summer Classic in Ft. Lauderdale (home court of the legendary
Chris Evert), with a win over yet another of her bathroom mirror
enemies, Gabriela Fonseca (#4). The next weekend, at the North
Miami Junior Tennis Championships, Terry shocked everyone
(except Pete and Libby), by handing a three set defeat to Jacquie
Darden (#2), a protege of Shawn Chillingsworth, and considered
by tennis insiders to be The Next Big Thing. When Terry lost 7-6,
7-5 in a close and exciting final to Kendra Weiss, the top-ranked

16-and-Under in the state and the hometown girl, she naturally chose to dwell on that rather than her semifinal triumph.

When the new rankings came out at the end of August Terry couldn't understand how Libby could be so jazzed about Terry's #4 ranking. For one thing, she'd beaten two of the top three. Though she realized the rankings were determined by statistics in the computer, it still burned her to see those other names on top of hers. She also didn't get why Libby thought Terry's being featured as an awesome newcomer and *"one to watch"* in the Junior Roundup in *TENNIS* magazine was such a big freaking deal. Who cared about the Juniors?

She had bigger fish to fry. She imagined it constantly and had it all planned.

The stunning conclusion of Terry's recurring Wimbledon fantasy was something she turned over and over in her mind, using it as fuel when she was tired and incentive when she doubted herself: after beating Jemma 6-0, 6-0 for the worst defeat in a final in Wimbledon history, Terry stands at Centre Court with the Tournament Director, microphone in hand, and thanks all the people who helped her get where she was today. Her grandparents, Pete and Charlie and Jen. And Libby most of all. When the Tournament Director asks if her parents are there to watch her greatest moment, Terry replies, "No, both my parents are dead." Then she looks over at the box where Isabel sits, having flown uninvited from Los Angeles to share Terry's success.

Isabel is crying. Terry is happy at last.

⚲ 13

Two months later...Halloween

"Give me a sec, T," Libby gasped, bending over and leaning on her racket as she struggled to catch her breath after a super long rally which had both of them racing all over the court.

"Aww, come on," Terry chided, bouncing the ball at hyper speed, itching to serve. "I'm not falling for one of your little head games this time." Finally, *finally* she had Libby at 6-4, 5-3, 30-30, two points from beating her for the first time. Whenever Terry had come close to victory in their previous matches, Libby had psyched her out, or made it so Terry psyched herself out. Well, not today. She was in The Zone. Her serve was on. This baby was hers.

Libby's gasping trailed off into a weak, sputtering cough. "No, I'm serious," she croaked, walking over to the cabana. "Hang on a minute. Let me get some water."

What an actress, Terry thought. She wasn't about to get lured over there and start acting all sympathetic so Libby could break her rhythm and snatch the match away. Again. "I'll be waiting right here, if you don't mind," she said, lightly jogging in place in the shade by the fence. She was still kicking herself for blowing off her usual long Saturday morning run. She had spent last night at Papi and Bria's, and instead of hauling her butt out of bed and hitting the road, she'd slept in and gorged on Bria's chocolate chip pancakes instead.

Normally, she wouldn't have been there on a Friday night since they'd all decided to continue the summer schedule of Terry living at Libby's and visiting with her grandparents on most Sundays when she didn't have a tournament. But last night Papi and Bria had made her go to the lame Halloween Dance at school. Even worse, Bria had forced her into wearing a costume, if you wanted to call a black leotard and tights, a hairband with pointy ears and whiskers painted on her face (how embarrassing) a costume. Terry had spent the entire two painful hours alternately standing by the door talking to Mrs. Meeks and sitting in the darkest, most obscure corner she could find. Even though eighth grade hadn't been too bad so far, and definitely an improvement on last year, she still wasn't thrilled to participate in any activities other than her classes. And she still didn't have—or want—any friends. She just wanted to do her work, earn her A's and beat it out of Agnes Quigley the instant the final bell rang so she could get back out on the court.

She knew that Bria, mostly, and Papi, too, wanted her to have a "normal kid's" life, so she tried hard (but usually failed) not to get too pissed when they insisted on her attendance at Geek Events like the one last night (which hadn't been as humiliating—whiskers and all—as the Fall Family Festival the school held in Hillcrest Park where her grandparents had dragged her to every booth and introduced themselves to every teacher who had the slightest connection to Terry). This morning though, when she'd stumbled sleepily into the kitchen to see them both rushing over to her with big white vampire fangs glistening in their mouths, she had laughed so hard she couldn't possibly stay mad. Even now she giggled, thinking of the two of them with those fangs, the least scary people she knew.

She looked over at Libby, who was holding up her finger asking for one more second as she drained her water bottle. Nope, time to end the charade. "Ready?" she yelled, walking to the service line where she stood, hands on hips, tapping her foot to say, yeah, ready to give up the act? Give the girl an Oscar!

"You bet." Libby set the bottle on the table and returned to the court. "Thanks for the breather. I know it was bad timing."

"No problem," Terry replied sweetly. She held up the balls in her hand to let Libby know she was about to serve. She felt an ace coming on and ripped the ball straight down the T. Out. Damn! She sliced her second serve far out to Libby's forehand, forcing Libby to make a lunge for it, which she promptly dumped in the net.

"Good one," Libby said, moving over to the ad service side. "I believe that gives you match point, Miss Gomez, but it's not over till it's over."

Oh, it's over, all right, Terry thought, visualizing how she wanted to play this next point. Over in three strokes, if it went her way. Tossing the ball slightly higher than usual she hit a hard topspin serve wide to Libby's backhand then followed it to the net in perfect position to put away the weak return for a forehand volley winner.

"I won!!!!" Terry screamed, tossing her racket in the air and dancing around, arms waving wildly.

"You won!!!!" Libby screamed even louder, running around the net post and hugging Terry, the two of them gleefully jumping up and down while holding hands like a pair of little kids, their words leapfrogging over one another's.

"I can't freaking believe it!"

"You played that last game beautifully"

"Yeah, even after your psych."

"Psych? Oh, uhhh, that—well, you hung tough. Can't fool you anymore."

"You didn't let me win, did you?"

"Absolutely not."

"Then you're not mad at all I beat you, right?"

"Kiddo, I am *thrilled* you beat me. I've been expecting it for the last month now, so it's about time you creamed the old lady."

"Hey, let's call Pete."

"Go ahead, rub it in, bragging rights are yours. In fact, I'll help. My cell is right over..." Libby broke off her sentence, the broad smile fading from her face at what she saw over Terry's shoulder. Alberto Gomez and another man approaching the cabana.

Terry turned around to see Papi and his friend Mr. Costa walking onto the court. She looked into her grandfather's red, swollen eyes and knew even before he hugged her and whispered hoarsely through his tears that something terrible had happened to the person they both loved most.

Terry stood in the doorway of the kitchen in her grandparents' house hours later. In front of her, the small living room overflowed with people she had known her whole life, close friends and neighbors of Papi and Bria's, who took turns sitting on the couch with Papi, hugging him, holding his hand, patting him on the back. Behind her a squad of ladies headed by Mrs. Costa bumped into one another as they searched the cupboards and drawers of Bria's kitchen for what they needed to keep the tons of stuff to eat and drink everyone brought moving onto the dining room table.

It all seemed totally unreal to Terry, like she was watching a movie she didn't want to see. A movie where a man kisses his perfectly fine wife good-bye , takes a twenty minute ride because his granddaughter needs to be somewhere else, runs a bunch of errands and returns to find his wife lying on the floor in the hallway, not moving, not breathing. He calls 911 and tries to breathe for her until the paramedics come and take her to the hospital, where he watches through the glass as the doctors and nurses try to get her back. He sees them fail. She is gone. Sudden massive cerebral hemorrhage, the doctor tells him. A stroke. She likely didn't know what hit her and surely didn't suffer...Ugh! What a horrible, sad movie. Terry wanted to bolt from her seat and leave the theater. But she couldn't.

Bria was dead. On some level she knew this was true. But her heart couldn't accept it. She kept expecting to see her grandmother appear at any moment, asking why everyone was here and what the party was for. Maybe that's why she had felt so calm during the ride back here from Libby's, with Papi and Mr. Costa both crying while she kept saying, it's OK, it's OK, over and over to make them feel better. The calmness had stayed with her during the rest of the afternoon and evening, taking care of Papi and answering the phone and helping serve food and pour drinks. Maybe she was keeping it together and being strong for Papi because it *was* just a horror movie. Or a nightmare. The movie would end. Or she would wake up. Bria would be alive and everything would go back to the way it was when she had woken up this morning.

People thought she was in shock. "Pobrecita!" she heard them say, "Look at her, it hasn't hit her yet."

Maybe they were right.

"Hey, sweetheart?" Terry heard Libby's voice behind her. "Let's move out here so we're not blocking the doorway, huh?"

As they slid into the crowded living room and found an unoccupied space to stand by the bookcase, Terry noticed Libby holding a fresh cup of coffee, steam rising from the top. It must be her tenth cup since she'd gotten here, where she really didn't need to be.

Terry had told her as much, back at the Shaver's house when Libby said she'd be over later, and again on the phone when Libby called asking what she should bring. And even though Terry kept insisting she was fine, here Libby was anyway, looking at Terry like she felt so sorry for her, which is one of the things Terry really hated. In fact, everyone was looking at her the same way, as if they expected her to burst into tears or faint or something.

"You doing OK?" Libby asked, sipping coffee and studying Terry's face over the rim of her cup.

"Yeah, it's just weird, you know?" Terry said, hoping Libby wouldn't ask her to describe the weirdness. It would be too hard explaining about the movie and how they were all characters reading lines from a script.

"Actually, I don't. I haven't had anyone die who was nearly as close to me as you were to your grandmother. I can only imagine how you must be feeling right now, especially with it being so sudden."

"I'm all right, but I'm worried about Papi." Terry looked over at Alberto. He hadn't moved from the couch and was staring down at the picture he'd been holding all afternoon and evening of him and Bria on their wedding day. His body seemed shrunken, his handsome, dearly familiar features twisted by grief into a face she'd never seen before. It scared her. "No matter what I do, I can't make him feel better."

"Oh, sweetie," Libby put her arm around Terry and squeezed. "There's nothing you need to do. It's what you are for him, his granddaughter who loves him. And tomorrow, when your mom gets here, he'll have the two of you together to lean on."

Terry stiffened at the mention of *her* and pulled away from Libby's embrace. "I still don't get why you told Papi you'd pick her up. They *do* have cabs at the airport."

"And after taking that red-eye flight from L.A., believe me, it's much nicer to have your own ride. Besides, Alberto is in no condition and Mr. and Mrs. Costa are making the arrangements for the funeral and reception. It's the least I can do," Libby replied.

"Well, it's more than she deserves," Terry snapped. It's a wonder she was even bothering to come.

"Look, Terry, I know you've got some pretty major issues with your mother, but…"

"You don't understand," Terry cut her off, "And I know what you're going to say, that for Papi's sake I should give it a rest and try to get along with her. Well, don't worry. I agree. I'll act the part in front of Papi, even if it makes me sick."

"Good decision, but what I was going to say was maybe you should have a little more sympathy for your mom, who just lost *her* mother, and that maybe if you cut her a break and talked to her as a person rather than the enemy, you might feel differently."

"Uhh, maybe," Terry said, as the voice in her head yelled, "When hell freezes over!"

Libby meant well. She had no way of knowing just how much Terry hated *her*, so she didn't realize what a preposterous suggestion she was making. The only person, other than Papi, who would understand, who knew how deeply Isabel had hurt her, wasn't here to sympathize, and would never be again. For the first time on this long and awful day Terry felt the loss of Bria like a sharp blow to her chest. She wanted to slump to the floor and cry and cry like the night of her twelfth birthday.

But of course, she didn't.

Libby lay on a chaise by the pool, scratching Pretty Boy under his chin and watching Terry swim laps. It had been six days since Maria Gomez' death and Libby was still waiting for something she hoped like hell would happen soon. Thinking back over the events of the past week, it was difficult to believe how many times it could have, should have happened, and hadn't.

Terry's mother had told her not to hold her breath.

"I think she's still in shock," Libby had remarked to Isabel over coffee at the airport Starbucks. What a pleasure it had been to finally meet the woman she'd been e-mailing and talking with on the phone for ten months. Though she'd seen many pictures of Isabel, nothing had prepared her for the dazzling woman sweeping down the concourse to meet her. It was as if Terry had stepped into a time machine and emerged at age 30.

Terry had known, right from the beginning, that Libby kept Isabel informed about every aspect of her daughter's progress—in school, with tennis, in her behavior. What Terry didn't know was how the e-mails and phone calls had quickly increased and lengthened to the point where Libby and Isabel had become friends. They shared a great deal of information and had a lot more in common than Terry could imagine. Because of their friendship and the confidences it nurtured, Libby understood Terry far better than Terry thought she did.

What she couldn't understand, she had explained to Isabel, was Terry's refusal so far to break down and cry for Maria, whom she so clearly had adored.

Isabel had shaken her head sadly and said, "Thanks to me, she's built a wall around her heart so high and strong that *nothing* can reach her—even losing Mami. I know. I've tried."

Libby had felt a shiver snaking down her spine.

The shivers had returned full force when Libby and Isabel walked into the Gomez' house, and Alberto met them at the door, crushing his daughter to him and holding her for dear life, both of them crying, rocking each other, trying to soothe. Libby had looked past them through her own tears at Terry, who stood frozen and dry-eyed, staring at Isabel with a hateful look that Libby wanted to slap right off her face. When Isabel had finally let go of Alberto and moved towards Terry, Libby couldn't bear to see what would happen and left the fractured family to grieve (at least two of them, that is) in private.

Still, she had kept expecting it to happen. It was only natural. Opportunities for it to happen, instances when *surely* it would, had come and gone. She had waited at the funeral home the next day as she watched Terry bend over Maria's open coffin and kiss her on the cheek. She had waited at St. Juliana's Catholic Church as Terry sat next to her grandfather and listened to Father Trezza saying what a wonderful, kind and loving person Maria Gomez had been.

She had waited at the cemetery as Terry placed a lily on her grandmother's coffin before it was lowered into her grave. She had waited later back at the Gomez house during the reception as Terry played the perfect hostess, making sure everyone had enough to eat and drink and handing out Kleenex to those who needed it. She had waited for the last two days as Terry, who had insisted on "getting back to normal", ran and practiced her serve and did her drills and played with Pretty Boy just as she usually did.

Libby was still waiting for Terry to shed a tear.

And now, watching Terry churning through the water with the same savage intensity she applied to everything she did, Libby realized with a terrible certainty that she'd be waiting forever.

Terry can't cry.

Terry can't cry.

The thought chilled and frightened her. For Terry. And it made her sadder than she'd been in a long time.

⚲ 14

*One month and three weeks later...
the week after Christmas*

Of all the reasons why Terry was so happy to be playing in the Orange Bowl Junior Championships, the most obvious ones weren't the biggest. Sure, this tournament was one of the "majors" on the junior circuit, right up there with the junior versions of the Grand Slams. And yeah, it was an international event with players from South America and Europe and all over, just like The Real Tour, only for kids. And of course, you had to be pretty hot to get right into the main draw (like she had) instead of having to qualify. AND it was held at the Key Biscayne Tennis Center in Miami, home of the Sony Ericsson Open, considered to be the unofficial Fifth Grand Slam of The Real Tour. These were all superb reasons, but they came in a distant second, third, fourth and fifth to number one.

Because she'd had to train for and play in this tournament she had the perfect excuse for not flying to Los Angeles with Papi to spend Christmas with *her*. Now, as she sat in the locker room at the Tennis Center (maybe in the very same spot as Jemma, or Shawn, or one of the other stars on The Real Tour had sat!), getting ready for her quarterfinal match, she was thinking how this reason alone would have made up for even a First Round loss here (which, thankfully, didn't happen).

The whole holiday season had been a total downer, as anyone would have expected. Thanksgiving had fallen only three weeks after Bria died. Papi and Bria used to have a huge dinner at their house, but this year everyone had gone to the Costas' house instead. She and Papi had gone, too, though Terry knew it was going to be weird and sad and just plain miserable, which, of course, was exactly the way it had turned out. Everyone had been afraid to talk about Bria, but by not talking about her, they'd accidentally made it worse, especially for poor Papi, who'd been doing a pretty bad imitation of living since October 31. Terry was certain she'd hate Halloween for the rest of her life. It was like she'd lost *both* her grandparents that terrible day.

Since Thanksgiving had been such a catastrophe, Papi decided that trying to get through another holiday pretending things were the way they used to be, would be unbearable, so he'd planned the trip to visit his daughter for the two weeks around Christmas and New Year's without even asking Terry what she thought! He had just assumed she'd go.

The last thing she'd wanted to do was make Papi feel worse, so she hadn't gone ballistic and said that if anything was unbearable it was being around her and Gack (which was the truth). Instead she'd gently explained how the Orange Bowl tournament was a major big deal and how she had to train especially hard the whole month of December (also the truth) so she couldn't go to L.A., much as she wanted to (huge lie).

Spending Christmas with Libby and her family had at least distracted her somewhat from missing Bria and Papi. Because the Shaver Christmas traditions were so different from her family's (or what used to be her family), it had been easier for Terry to get wrapped up in them rather than dwell on all she'd lost. Instead of having the big celebration on Christmas Eve—Medianoche—the way Cuban families did, Mr. and Mrs. S had gone out to dinner with Libby's aunt and uncle while Libby and Terry stayed home and watched *It's A Wonderful Life* on TV. Very low-key and perfect for Terry's mood. The next day a bunch of the Shavers' friends came over for a fancy brunch which seemed more like a cocktail party than a Christmas Dinner, with everyone all dressed up and drinking champagne. Except for the great presents she'd gotten from Libby, Mr. and Mrs. S, Lupe and Diego, and Pete and Jen,

Terry could have easily convinced herself that Christmas hadn't happened this year.

Practicing and working out in overdrive these past three weeks had also been a great distraction. She had played more with Pete, Charlie and Jen because Libby hadn't been feeling well lately. In fact, longer than just lately. All through November, Terry had noticed how tired Libby seemed a lot of the time, even if she hadn't really done anything strenuous. When they played, she had to stop and catch her breath after every long rally, and she had this dry little cough that never seemed to go away. She was slowly but steadily losing the weight she'd gained and was starting to look sort of scary skinny. Every time anyone—Terry, Pete, her parents—had suggested she see a doctor, she'd just blown it off. It wasn't until she'd become so dizzy hitting with Terry, actually plopping right down on the court (!!), that she made an appointment.

The doctor, Libby had told her afterwards, ran a bunch of tests, gave her an antibiotic and some other kind of medicine for the iron in her blood, and said if she followed his instructions and took it easy—no tennis, no exercise, period—she should start feeling much better. And it had worked! Libby wasn't her old self yet, but she wasn't nearly as tired, or coughing as much. Still, she had to watch from the cabana and restrict herself to verbal coaching as Terry prepared for her first really big tournament. On the way down here to Miami, she had praised Terry for working so hard and said she should be proud of herself, regardless of the outcome.

So far, the extra effort was paying off. Her First Round match against Samantha Something-Or-Other from Atlanta had been a breeze 6-1, 6-2, no sweat. She'd had to scramble more against Martine LeBeque from Grenada, but still won 6-4, 6-4. Yesterday, she'd gotten to avenge her loss back in the summer to her Third Round opponent, Kendra Weiss, beating her this time in three sets, 6-4, 5-7, 6-3 (proving, once and for all, in Terry's mind, exactly who was #1 in the Florida 16's, no matter what the computer said).

In fifteen minutes she was due on the court to play her quarterfinal match against Helena Sanchez-Rojas, the tiny dynamo (nicknamed The Flea) from Caracas, Venezuela, who had wiped the court with Jacqui Darden in the Third Round. Taping the final bandage over the blister on her left heel, Terry replaced her double socks and tennis shoe, stood and pivoted around a few times to make sure she couldn't feel raw flesh grinding against leather. Satisfied, she grabbed her gear and jogged from the locker room, primed for battle. She couldn't wait to crush the midget.

Two hours later Terry sat slumped in the very same spot, peeling the bloody socks from her left foot and wondering if she could possibly feel any more humiliated. Now she knew that everyone called Sanchez-Rojas "The Flea" for reasons other than her size. Like the infuriating insect, the girl had moved with uncanny intuition and quickness, darting around the court, getting to balls which should have been winners, forcing Terry to hit so many more shots that she'd gotten frustrated, went for too much and missed. Instead of hitting primarily flat, hard groundstrokes, The Flea had used a variety of spins and slices, drop-shotting and lobbing, mixing up the pace to drive Terry crazy, making her go for impossible winners just to end the damn point. To make matters worse, Terry hadn't had a good serving day, getting few first serves in, and The Flea took full advantage, jumping on each slower second serve and sending back a return with so much "work" (tennisspeak for spin) on it that Terry found herself lunging awkwardly at balls which weren't bouncing as she expected. After Terry netted these returns or sent them flying out, The Flea would give a brief nod then scuttle back to wait for the next second serve to slice and dice. During the entire miserable three sets she had jerked Terry around the court like a sadistic puppeteer punishing a rag doll.

Irritating, Relentless. Impossible to pin down. Utterly flea-like.

Final score, 4-6, 6-3, 6-4, Helena Sanchez-Rojas.

"Well, kiddo, congratulations are in order," Libby said, appearing from between two rows of lockers and sitting on the bench next to Terry.

"For *what*??? For getting my butt handed to me by a dwarf?"

"No," Libby laughed. "For surviving your first encounter with a genuine, hard-core South American clay-court specialist. Almost as dangerous on the hard stuff, as you just found out."

"But I didn't survive. I *lost*, Lib, in case you didn't notice."

"Yes, but you took a set and you didn't give up out of sheer frustration. Believe me, the girl you just played is a perfect example of the breed. When I was on tour, I hated facing the girls from Spain and France, and South America. It was always physically and mentally exhausting and left me feeling wrung out and pissed off. Sound familiar?"

"Yeah, exactly," Terry agreed and grinned in spite of herself. Libby always knew how to make her feel better, even when she felt lower than bottom-dwelling pond scum.

"Chalk this one up to experience and learn from it," Libby said. "Then just keep moving forward. And right now, forward means into the shower. Then we'll go have a big, greasy fattening early dinner and I'll let you in on the secrets of beating Ms. Helena Sanchez-Rojas and all of her diabolical kind."

On January 5th, the day before her fourteenth birthday, Terry received a letter:

Dear Terry,

This is a hard letter to write. I wanted to say this in person, but since you won't really speak to me, this is how it has to be. We've been apart for almost two years now, which is far too long for a daughter to be separated from her mother. I miss you. I miss being your mother.

I know you haven't forgotten how happy we once were. I'm also sure you remember why I had to go to L.A. without you, so I won't bore you by repeating the reasons. What I DON'T think you remember is the promise I made, that our separation would be

TEMPORARY. I meant it. I wanted you to come out by the end of that first summer so you could start 7th grade here. But you wouldn't even look at me when I visited, and you wouldn't speak to me on the phone, so I waited. I was hoping as time passed you'd come to understand and forgive me and believe how much I have always loved you.

Terry, Jack and I are getting married, and we BOTH want you to move out here and live with us.

I wanted to tell you when Bria died, but everything was so awful, and you were so hostile, I decided to wait— again. When you didn't come out for Christmas with Papi, I thought the best way would be to write this letter and let you think about it. Please, please think about it. Have a wonderful birthday, my precious girl.

Love,

Isabel

As Terry read the letter, her hands began to shake with anger and blood rushed to the surface of her skin, flushing her face with outrage. How dare she! Was this her idea of a swell birthday present? Sending this piece of trash that made it sound like it was mostly *Terry's* fault they were apart? That because Terry had the nerve to still be hurt and angry, they couldn't be one big happy family??? Precious girl, my ass.

She held the letter—and the enclosed check for $200—over the toilet bowl as she burned them, watching the ashes drift slowly down and disappear into the water. Then she flushed with grim satisfaction.

Happy freaking birthday.

Libby couldn't believe it had been a year since they'd last gathered in this office, but it was somehow the end of January again, and here they were, hanging on Judge Walpole's every word. Well, at least Terry was. Libby and Alberto already knew what the judge was going to say and had spent the past few days discussing and making arrangements for the near future. Regarding Terry and her grandfather as they sat side by side, Libby marveled at the huge difference one year had made in all their lives. Mostly positives, and one enormous tragic negative.

Glancing at the empty chair off to the side, then once more at Alberto, she wondered what it would be like to love someone so deeply that their death made you want to follow them. Last year Alberto had been a boisterous, laughing, supremely happy person who loved life and looked ten years younger than a man in his mid-fifties. Within three months of Maria's death, he'd caught up to his real age and in the past year had aged ten years beyond. Deeply in mourning, it was all he could do to simply get up and go to work, put one foot in front of the other.

While Libby could see how his deterioration upset Terry, it didn't surprise her that Terry took it in stride, the same way she'd absorbed the blow of losing her grandmother and carried on as usual. And the fact that Libby wasn't surprised made her all the more worried about Terry.

In so many ways, the Terry of today was a much improved version of last year's Terry. There were all the reasons to be proud of her accomplishments—her about-face in school, the cold turkey on pot and cigarettes, and, of course, her tennis, which was nothing short of remarkable.

But.

Libby knew the old Terry, the bitter, angry, hate-driven Terry, was still lurking just beneath the surface. And still calling the shots. This is what ate away at Libby's hope that she was making a difference. For while she didn't doubt Terry loved and trusted her, she couldn't help feeling Terry wasn't any further along in dealing with the central issue of her unhappiness. This had to be dealt with soon, and Libby looked forward to bringing it up as much as she'd welcome a root canal with no anesthetic.

As for herself, if anyone had told her she'd go for more than a year alcohol and drug- free, she'd have rolled her eyes and given them one of Terry's *"Yeah, right's"*. But she had. No booze, no coke, no smoke, no pills—except for the ones she was forced into taking now. No more individual or group therapy. No more AA or NA meetings. She was clean, sober, emotionally healthy again.

And apparently sick as hell. In the words of Alanis Morrisette, "Isn't it ironic, dontcha think?" Yessiree, ironic and #2 on the list of things she dreaded having to discuss with Terry. Well, let's get *this* over with, she thought, focusing her attention back on Judge Walpole, then she'd take Terry to lunch and try to scratch at least one item off the list.

"...And so, Miss Gomez," the judge was saying, obviously wrapping up his review, "...taking into consideration all of the elements we've discussed today—your remarkable improvement and achievement in school, the cessation of your drug use and behavior problems, and the twelve glowing progress reports submitted by Ms. Shaver, not to mention your dedication to mastering the game of tennis—I have no qualms about ending your probation and ordering your juvenile record expunged. Congratulations, Ms. Gomez. I wish all of my cases had as excellent an outcome."

Judge Walpole rose from his seat and extended his hand to Terry, who even as she shook it was glancing over at Libby, worry already flattening her smile of a moment ago. After congratulating Alberto and Libby as well, the judge ushered them to the door, wishing them all the best and declaring that he was sure he'd be reading about Terry in the newspaper someday.

As they walked to the elevator, Terry turned to Libby and asked, "So now what?"

Talk about a loaded question! "Well," Libby replied in a deliberately casual tone she certainly didn't feel, "For right now, how about lunch? It's our anniversary, after all."

Terry couldn't stand the suspense much longer. Stirring the straw in her Coke so hard it created a whirlpool in the glass she frowned at Libby, who was chattering away about So-and-So's such-and-such, blahblahblah, the same as she had on the way over here in the car, when all Terry wanted was a REAL answer to her question.

When the judge had said her probation was over and her record expunged, she'd thought , excellent, way to go Gomez! But almost immediately after the initial elation, she had rushed out in a bad way, wondering what this actually meant. Probation over. Did this mean Libby's part was over, too? Would Libby expect her to move back with Papi now?? Could she still work out with Pete and Charlie and Jen??? Was she on her own with tennis now???? What did it mean?????

Libby had driven straight here to Bradley's without asking Terry where she wanted to go. The same restaurant where they'd had their first lunch ever. What was Libby trying to tell her? Was this supposed to be their last lunch? Was this Libby's way of saying Buh-bye, see ya later, kiddo. Have a nice life and don't let the door hit you in the butt on the way out? Arghhh, she had to know.

"Just hit me with it straight up," she interrupted Libby, who looked startled by the anger in her voice. "Is this it? Probation's over, so I guess your obligation's over, too, right? Why don't you just come out and say it? I can take it."

Libby threw her head back and laughed so hard she started coughing and didn't stop until she drank half her glass of Evian. It certainly wasn't the reaction Terry expected. Now she really didn't know what to think.

"Oh, Miss Terry, you are so predictable!" Libby said, reaching across the table and putting her hand on Terry's arm. But Terry snatched both arms back and folded them across her chest, waiting for an explanation. "You still think the best defense is a good offense."

"What are you talking about?" Terry asked, though she knew very well what Libby meant. She was always lecturing Terry about lashing out when she felt insecure or threatened, especially when there was no reason to be insecure and no real threat at all.

Ignoring the question, Libby took another sip of water and sat back in her chair, looking at Terry with an expression Terry recognized as pity. "Sweetheart, do you really believe I would just step out of the picture at this point?"

Terry shrugged. "I don't know. I guess maybe not. But the judge said…"

"Terry, please listen to me, and no butting in, OK? The end of your probation has nothing to do with our relationship, except that I don't have to do those pesky monthly progress reports anymore. Your grandfather and I knew about the judge's decision a week ago and have already made arrangements for us to continue the same as before. Nothing is going to change, unless, of course, there's something you want to do differently. I love having you live with me. I love helping you with your tennis, and I love being a part of your life. I never want you to feel I'm doing something because I have to. I want to. You've done more to help me get through this year than all the therapy sessions and meetings and volunteering combined. Remember our old deal? Quid pro quo? Something exchanged for something? Kiddo, you have more than held up your end of the bargain. I am so proud of you on so many levels. I only wish you'd give yourself the credit you deserve."

Libby paused as the waiter arrived and set their food on the table. Terry was glad for the slight interruption. She felt so ashamed of herself for thinking Libby would bail on her, and so relieved that nothing was going to change.

When Libby continued, it was as if she'd been reading Terry's mind. "Now, there is one thing that has to change, unfortunately. It seems I've got a bit of a problem with my heart, and…"

"Whaaat??" Terry was instantly alarmed.

Libby held up her hand. "Wait a minute! No need to panic. I have an irregular heartbeat, and one of the ventricles in my heart is enlarged and not working as well as it should be. At first I though

I might have done it to myself with all the abuse I put my body through, but my doctor says it's congenital, and there's no way of knowing how or if the alcohol and drugs were a factor."

"Do you need an operation? They can fix it, can't they?" Terry was feeling panicked.

"No, no, nothing so dramatic. Chill out, it's not as bad as it sounds."

"But you've been feeling better!"

"I know, and if I continue with the meds and taking it easy, I'm sure I'll feel even better. But, the point is, T, I can't play tennis—or any sport—for quite awhile, so you're going to have to rely on Pete and Charlie and Jen, and anyone else you can find who can give you a workout. Actually, it's not such a big change, after all, since you started thrashing me on a regular basis anyway."

"Yeah, but you've been sick. When you're allowed to play again, it'll be like it was."

Libby shook her head. "Sick or not, it was only a matter of time before I couldn't challenge you anymore. You've gotten too good!"

"Not true," Terry said, poking at the turkey sandwich she hadn't felt like ordering in the first place. "I could never be too good for you."

They looked at each other and smiled.

🎾 15

Two and a half months later...

At the end of March the best professional tennis players in the world come together at the Key Biscayne Tennis Center on Miami Beach to battle it out for the big bucks and the championship of the Sony Ericsson Open, the richest and most prestigious tournament aside from the four Slams. Throughout this first weekend, all of the stars of both the mens' and womens' tours were playing their early round matches, so it was possible, if you timed it right, to watch Shawn Chillingsworth easily handling her much lower ranked opponent, then scurry over to another court in time to see the adorable Aussie Bad Boy, Chris Renshaw, win his match, then rush across the complex to see Japan's Keiko Tanaka. Or Germany's Rolf Dresbach. Or Pieter De Broon from the Netherlands.

Or Tatiana Kraskova, #2 in the world, crouched to receive serve not thirty feet from where Terry sat in the front-row stadium seats reserved by Libby for the entire tournament.

Terry couldn't believe how much bigger the Russian star was in person. In fact, all of the players she was so familiar with from watching on television seemed bigger, stronger, more imposing. Even Analise Rouselle, the 5'6" Frenchwoman who was always described as "tiny" and "petite", was actually buffed and powerful when you saw her up close. For the first time in her life, Terry thought being 5'11" might not be so bad after all and maybe she could grow another inch or two before she made it to The Real Tour.

She was having an awesome time. How cool was it to be a part of this—the players, the other sports, movie and TV celebrities (she'd seen nine so far!), the huge media presence, the cheering crowds of rabid tennis fans—the whole, crazy carnival atmosphere! She wanted to do and see everything and felt frustrated because there was too much to see and do. Libby said she was like a little kid with a free pass to the Magic Kingdom at Disney World. It was true. Terry was enchanted with *Real Tour World*. It was more exciting than she'd ever imagined in her countless hours of day (and night) dreaming and she was wanted more than anything to live in it 24-7.

The down side was that the players didn't just seem bigger in person. They were *better*. Watching televised matches, you didn't realize how hard they hit the ball, and how fast they moved. Even the players who never made it past the Round of 16, whose names were unfamiliar to anyone who didn't follow tennis, were totally impressive. Like Eva Kessler, whom Terry had just watched lose a close first set tie-breaker to Kraskova. She was a perfect example. Kessler, from Switzerland, was ranked somewhere in the 30's, yet she was smacking the ball with such force and accuracy and covering the court so well that she'd almost taken the set. Though it killed her to admit it, Terry realized that if she was out there playing Kessler (a nobody compared to Kraskova) she'd be having her butt handed to her, no question.

Arrgghhh! How depressing. True, she'd come a long way in a short time, but she had a long way to go, which became more apparent with each match she saw. OK, fine, she thought. She knew what she had to work on. It only made her *more* determined. Her best improvement strategy was to set a goal then do everything in her power to achieve it. She was still steamed over coming up short of her last goal, to be #1 in the Florida 16's. When the new rankings had come out at the end of January she was #2 behind Kendra Weiss. While Libby was congratulating her on her jump from the previous rank of #4, Terry had been inconsolable, especially after beating Kendra at the Orange Bowl. It wasn't fair, was it? What did the stupid computer know anyway?

Well, at least her new ranking guaranteed her a high seeding and a good draw for her Next Big Goal. Junior Nationals in Kalamazoo, Michigan in May. She had about a month and a half to prepare and now, jacked up by the adrenaline jolt (not to mention a cold, hard reality check) provided by being here and seeing the best players in the world, she couldn't wait to get back to work.

The crowd erupted after Kraskova ended a long rally with a spectacular overhead smash, pulling Terry's attention back to the match. After the hotly contested first set, Kraskova had already raced ahead 3-0 and appeared to be halfway to a second set blowout. Terry scanned the entrance nearest their stadium box seats for Libby. On their way in for the match they'd bumped into one of Libby's friends (again), and Libby had sent Terry ahead, saying she and her friend were going for iced coffee to catch up, so she'd meet Terry in their box.

Here was another thing which was cool, but kind of annoying at the same time. Since they'd gotten here, all day yesterday and today, Libby had been bumping into and catching up with "old friends". Like, a million of them! The cool part was that a lot of them were famous, either players or other people Terry recognized from the tabloids. The annoying part was that so much of Libby's attention was being hogged by all these people that Terry was feeling a little pushed to the sidelines when this was supposed to be her special time with Libby. She was trying to be mature and understanding about it. After all, Libby *had* been away from this world for a long time. And who *didn't* love her? Uhh, nobody in their right mind. But still...

There was a third, weird part of Libby seeing all her old buddies which bothered Terry. She could see the shock of Libby's appearance reflected in everyone's eyes, though they always struggled to hide it. Libby had grown even thinner than she'd been right after Christmas. Her cheekbones, naturally chiseled, were now so sharply edged it looked like you'd slice a finger open if you touched them. Being so blond and fair, Libby had never been very tanned, even when she was playing tennis all the time. But now, she was so white she blended right in with the white jeans and T-shirt she was wearing today. Terry thought she looked beautiful, regardless.

But now, instead of looking like a Viking Queen, she was more the pale, fragile, lovely Beth in one of Terry's favorite books, *Little Women* (although Terry immediately discarded this comparison, because everyone knew what happened to Beth, and Libby simply needed time to recover, so it was ridiculous to even think it up in the first place). Libby insisted that she felt a little better and that all the medication she was taking was upsetting her stomach, which was totally understandable. If Terry had to swallow the handful of pills Libby did several times a day, she wouldn't be interested in food either.

Speaking of Libby...Terry took her cell phone from the pocket of her shorts and thumbed the first number on speed dial. Predictably, Kraskova was killing Kessler 5-0, and Terry was anxious to move on to another match. She had an hour before the next stadium court match, the match she wouldn't miss for anything. Jemma York vs Mia Lindstrom. Terry planned to study Jemma's every move and file it away for future reference.

"Hiya," Libby answered over noisy laughter in the background.

"Well, you missed a great first set, but..."

"But Kessler's already mentally in the locker room, I know, we've been watching it on the screen."

"Where are you?"

"The cafe with all the tropical stuff, you know, next to the gift shop near Court Three. Come meet me and we'll head over to Six. E.J.'s down a set and 0-1 to some qualifier from Morocco."

"Whoa, poor E.J.! Be right there." Terry pressed "end" and hurried toward the exit. E.J. Wyatt, #2 and America's Favorite Tennis Hottie, drew huge crowds wherever he went and Terry doubted she and Libby would be able to get close to the court. Unlike in the stadium, seating at all the other show courts wasn't reserved, so it was dog eat dog if you got there late. So be it. She could be a mean dog. Terry streaked to meet Libby, white teeth gleaming in her best snarling pit bull grin.

Outside the Caribbean Cafe, Libby kissed her friend Pam good-bye and watched her lope away down the crowded walk with the same giant, giraffe-like strides she'd had when they played on the Stanford tennis team together. It had been ages since she and Pam had gotten together, and while it was great seeing her, Libby felt exhausted from their little reunion.

So what else was new? Spying a nearby bench she plopped down to wait for Terry. Being sick sucked big time, as her young charge would so eloquently put it. There were a lot of days when she felt fine, better than she had since October—not doing cartwheels, but almost like what she remembered as "normal". On not-so-good days, like today, it was as if she moved sluggishly through a thick fluid, never managing to gulp enough air to completely fill her lungs. Everything took extra effort, from the simple act of getting dressed, to the much more complicated activity of popping up at the Sony after a lengthy absence looking like death warmed over. To the friends she'd last seen at the height (or depth) of her Bad Old Days, she probably didn't look much different, but to those who knew her only from her days on the tour before she quit, she was surely a candidate for Intensive Care. While she hated lying to all these folks, explaining her appearance by saying she was getting over a particularly nasty and stubborn viral infection, she wasn't about to launch into the explanation about her heart problem. It was too complicated. Besides, there were only a few people who knew about her illness, and she wanted to keep it that way.

Drawing a shallow breath, Libby glanced around, drinking in the atmosphere. As a player, the Sony had always been her favorite tournament. Everyone showed up unless they were injured, and the competition was fierce. But there wasn't as much pressure as at the Slams. The vibe was more casual and fun, though the amount of money at stake could hardly be called casual. She had always played well here, reaching two quarters and one semifinal. Sitting here on this bench, quietly gasping for air, she thought how distant she was from the hard-charging girl who played that semifinal.

What saved her from free-falling into a well of depression, particularly when she was so sick of being sick she could scream, was Terry. Focusing on Terry had helped save her once, in the difficult months immediately following her rehab. Now it was helping her again. Listening to and commenting on Terry's never-ending strategizing and goal-making. Guiding her through school work and life lessons and her budding tennis career. Being a mentor, a disciplinarian, a friend—basically...a mother.

Yessiree, it was saving her, but she couldn't let it continue in this way.

Terry had a mother, and it wasn't Libby.

Libby had known about Isabel and Jack's engagement the day after it happened back in September. She knew how much Isabel had wanted to tell Terry when she'd flown in for Maria's funeral, and how disappointed she'd been that Terry wouldn't come out with Alberto at Christmas. Isabel had read Terry's birthday letter to Libby over the phone before she sent it. Libby's heart ached for the woman who had become such a close friend. Isabel wanted her daughter back. And Terry needed to be back with her mother whether she realized it yet or not.

Libby had waited several weeks for Terry to mention Isabel's letter then finally asked her about it, prompting the biggest blow-up of their relationship, with Terry accusing Libby of conspiring with Isabel behind her back and wanting to ship Terry back to Isabel so she could be rid of her, and Libby patiently trying to explain Isabel's position and assuring Terry that, no matter what, she'd always be part of Libby's life. When it was all over, Terry had apologized to Libby, but stubbornly refused to say another word concerning her mother.

Well, you're not the only one who's stubborn, Ms. Gomez. Libby was determined to bring about this reconciliation and had been quietly laying the groundwork. Bumping into her old friend Pam Hutchinson had been by design, not accident. Pam coached the UCLA women's tennis team as well as private students and a few of the younger professional players. She was here with her UCLA #1, who'd made it into the main draw as a qualifier. Libby and Pam had grabbed the only time they could both meet to follow-up on the phone conversations they'd had over the last two months. By now, Pam knew all about Terry, who would need a tennis coach when she moved to L.A.

Terry appeared suddenly beside her and grabbed her arm, pulling her off the bench.

"C'mon, we're missing all the action, we'll never get seats!"

"So, what's the hurry?" Libby laughed, letting herself be dragged along and thinking Terry could just as easily pick her up and carry her. "Like you said. We'll never get seats."

Terry was wedged between two burly guys in the seventh row near the service line, cheering for E.J. Wyatt to continue his second set comeback after being down 4-1 against a player from Morocco whose name no one could pronounce. When she and Libby had arrived at the entrance to the jammed Court Six they agreed to split up and find any seat they could. Scanning the crowd to see where Libby ended up, she weirdly heard someone say Libby's name directly behind her.

"...I told you, to the right and down three rows...it's her, Libby Shaver, you remember, the rich girl, the one they called The Heiress..."

"That's not her. Too scrawny..."

"Scrawny, yeah, but it's her. Remember how she partied her way right off the tour. I read where she was in rehab not long ago."

"Looks like it didn't work. Classic coke-head, she must weigh, what ninety pounds?"

Pure rage shot through Terry, igniting her entire body. Heart hammering with fury, she leaped to her feet and whirled around on the two women behind her, who instantly cowered at the look on her face.

"Shut up, you disgusting pigs," Terry spit at the women, who were, indeed, both seriously overweight and squeezed unsuccessfully into neon-colored Lycra outfits. "What gives you the right to judge someone you don't even know?? Someone you don't even deserve to be on the same planet with. Someone who's worth more than your fat asses multiplied a million times over? Huh, answer me?" Terry reached out and slapped away the cups each was holding. "What's the matter, tongues too full of flab to move? Speak up!"

The women were whimpering and looking around wildly for help. The people around them stared. The burly guys laughed.

Fists clenched and ready to sail into the puffy, clownish faces of her victims, an enormous irony suddenly occurred to Terry. In defending Libby, she was reacting in *exactly* the way Libby wouldn't want her to. Libby's voice echoed in her head. Be cool. Be classy. Walk away.

Though it was too late for the cool, classy part, Terry obeyed the final command, turning and hurrying to the aisle to get as far away from those morons as possible before she did something else that Libby wouldn't approve of.

She hated disappointing Libby more than most of all the other things she hated.

⚲ 16

Six weeks later...

"Don't let up, don't let up, don't let up," Terry chanted to herself as she crouched menacingly at the service line, poised to launch yet another vicious attack the instant the ball left her victim's racket. Across the net, Katie O'Halloran bit her lip and prayed she could hit her second serve with enough pace to keep Terry from doing what she'd done for the entire set—hammer the return for a winner. Tossing the ball, she hit it solidly with decent speed, but directly into Terry's lethal forehand.

No chance. Terry reacted so quickly she had her racket back and waiting to take a full swing, blazing a yellow blur straight down the line. The umpire leaned into her microphone and announced, "Game and set, Miss Gomez. She leads 6-1 in this Girls' 16-and-Under Final match."

As the players walked to the side of the court for the changeover, Katie approached the umpire's chair, said she needed to use the restroom and hurried off, clutching a towel and a bottle of water.

"You might as well go too, if you'd like," the umpire told Terry.

"Nope, I'm good," Terry replied, perching on her chair and scrabbling in her bag for a fresh wristband. Bathroom break, my butt, she thought. O'Halloran was just trying to break her momentum. As if! Not that Terry could blame her. She'd been on fire the first set, getting most of her first serves in—six of them aces—volleying well, scoring winners from the baseline, exploiting O'Halloran's erratic backhand. Exactly according to plan.

In fact, this whole week had gone precisely the way she'd planned, starting from the moment she arrived here at Kalamazoo College in Michigan and checked out the draw. She was seeded #8 (it should have been higher, considering Kendra Weiss, who she'd beaten, was the third seed, but never mind), which put her in a bracket to eventually meet #1 Jill Koricke (she could hardly wait to get a crack at *her!*) from San Diego in the quarterfinals. Analyzing her potential path through the tournament, she had pictured "T. Gomez" in boldface, with straight set victories noted in parenthesis, multiplied five times to form a big black arrow pointed at the final.

Actually, The Plan had started way back when she returned home from the Sony, fresh from the thrill of watching major league tennis. Studying the best pros in the world up close and personal had made her see that if she wanted to make the jump from the minors (worse, really, the Little League!!) as soon as possible, she had to start playing like she belonged on The Real Tour. She needed to be dominating in the Juniors to make it clear—to herself and everyone else—that she was beyond tournaments for kids.

So she'd trained harder than she ever had, to the point where even Pete was ordering her to throttle back. Since Libby, of course, couldn't play and Jen had broken her ankle skiing in Colorado, her practice partners for match play had dwindled to Pete and Charlie, who near the end had both begged her to stop bugging them for "just one more set, puhleeeze". By the time she was ready to leave for Michigan, she'd been confident that if she played smart, kept her head straight and stuck with her usual strategy of turning everyone across the net into an enemy, *nobody* could come close to beating her.

And nobody had. In her first three matches, against opponents from Georgia, Texas and Pennsylvania, she'd lost a total of *eight* games. After upsetting Jill Koricke (easy to hate given her status as the Golden Girl of the 16-and-Unders) 6-4, 6-2 in the quarters, she had demolished the fourth seed, another Californian, Cricket Carruthers from Beverly Hills (totally easy to hate, if only for her stupid name) 6-1, 6-1 to land in the final.

Now if O'Halloran would get back out here, already, Terry could continue the massacre. One more set and the title was hers. She had to admit that winning Nationals would be pretty cool, even if it was the Juniors. The tournament organizers tried to make the finals as much like The Real Tour as possible, with changeover chairs and linesmen (but no ball girls and boys) and a much bigger crowd here in the stadium at Kalamazoo College than she'd ever played in front of before. Libby and Pete were sitting in the third row of the center section, right across the court from Terry's chair. Libby saw her looking over and gave her a thumbs up then leaned across Pete to say something to her friend Pam. The same Pam Libby had run into at the Sony. Even before they'd all had dinner together last night Terry had decided she wasn't going to like Pam because she lived in L.A. and Terry didn't like anything having to do with L.A. But Pam was so, so nice and laid back and funny that Terry couldn't *not* like her. Plus, since she was such a great old friend of Libby's, she had to be cool, right?

The sound of scattered clapping made Terry look over to see her opponent jogging from the stadium entrance. As O'Halloran reached her chair and bent to grab her racket, the applause grew into a roar of encouragement for the #2 seed who was clearly now the underdog. Well, they could clap until their hands bled, for all Terry cared. She stood and walked out to the service line eager to seal the deal she made with herself. Move in for the kill. Show no mercy. The loudest cheering in the world wasn't going to save O'Halloran from going down in flames.

"How much is this going to rattle her?" Pam asked, nearly shouting to be heard over the crowd's roar of approval when Katie O'Halloran won the first game of the second set.

"You mean losing the first game?" Pete made a brush-off gesture with his hand to indicate no big deal.

"No, I mean having the crowd rooting so hard for Katie."

Pete and Libby looked at each other and howled with laughter.

"And that's hilarious because…" Pam said, obviously puzzled by their reaction.

"Because if you knew Terry the way we do, you'd be rolling in that aisle over there yourself," Pete said, still chuckling over the notion of Terry getting upset over any circumstance she could interpret as negative, challenging or confrontational.

"C'mon, Pamela Jean," Libby teased, "You're not getting so old your memory's failing, are you? Don't you remember me saying how Terry revels in a situation like this? Given the slightest opportunity to be pissed off, she'll grab it and run."

"Yeah, she feeds off it," Pete agreed. "The kid gets a buzz off bad vibes."

"She wants to see the crowd as being *against* her instead of what they really are, which is for Katie to get back in the match and make it a competitive final," Libby added.

"Doesn't sound like a very mentally healthy—or happy—way to play," Pam said.

"No kidding," Libby said, turning her attention back to the court, where Terry had just dropped the second game at love. This was getting interesting. The switch in momentum from Terry to Katie had nothing to do with the crowd and everything to do with the Katie's change in strategy. The player who had taken a well-timed "bathroom break"(Libby had to admit she would have been tempted to do the same in Katie's woeful Reeboks) was not the same player who returned. Poor Terry was probably having a nightmarish flashback to her torture at the Orange Bowl by The Flea.

Clearly, Katie had finally realized she wasn't going to outhit Terry (though that should have been obvious after the first few games of the first set), so she was now taking pace *off* the ball and putting more work *on* it, making it harder for Terry to get in a groove and take full swings. While this type of game was ideal on clay courts, it could also be effective on hard courts like this one if played cleverly. And right now, it was as if Katie O'Halloran was channeling Helena Sanchez-Rojas. This girl didn't get to be #2 in the country for nothing.

What Libby couldn't wait to see is how Terry handled it. After the Sanchez-Rojas debacle, both Pete—on the court—and Libby—through verbal instruction—had taught Terry everything they could about slices and spins, drop-shots and lobs, pace-mixing and strategizing. They'd made her play set after set "throwing junk" as Terry put it, even though she hated playing that way.

"This isn't tennis," she'd whine.

"Oh, yes, it is," they'd reply. "It's simply a different part of a complex game and it's just as important—and can be as deadly—as power and speed. You need it to be a complete player, so you can fight fire with fire if you have to."

Okay, T, time to slice and dice, Libby willed a silent command down to the court. And sooner rather than later.

As if reading Libby's mind Pete whispered in her ear, "Let the junk throwing begin."

They needn't have worried.

After cursing herself for the two double-faults in the first game and for being in denial about O'Halloran's new junk throwing strategy during the second game, Terry decided she better screw her head back on straight unless she wanted to find herself in a third set. Though it killed her to have to do it, she'd chill out on the pace, slice her serves, give the net a rest, bag going for winners on every stroke and wait patiently (haha) for O'Halloran to make the error.

She won the next six games.

After shaking hands at the net, Terry beamed and waved to the cheering crowd. She shot a thumbs up at Libby and Pete then walked to her chair to gather her gear with only one thought foremost in her head. It wasn't that she had just thrashed the #2 player in the United States, 6-1, 6-2. It wasn't that she'd beaten the #1 player on the way to the final. It wasn't that she not only hadn't lost a set, but lost only 19 games *total* (which had to be some kind of record). And it wasn't that she was the new, undisputed Girls' 16-and-Under National Champion.

It was that she was one step closer to The Real Tour.

Libby peered at the screen of her laptop computer, trying to concentrate on the task at hand. In the two weeks since coming home from Nationals, Terry had been nagging her incessantly about setting her summer tournament schedule. When she'd left with Diego this morning for the last day of school, she was pleading all the way out the door for Libby to pleasepleasepuuuhleeze go on line and start figuring things out because tomorrow was the first day of summer and there was no *plan!!!!!*

Libby chuckled, thinking how frantic Terry got when she didn't have a plan, a schedule, a routine, a goal. While she teased her all the time about the obsessive-compulsiveness (usually in a failed effort to get her to let up a little), Libby had to admit it was a major factor in the phenomenal progress Terry had made with her tennis in *15 months*. Ever since last summer's success in her first tournaments, Terry's name had been mentioned more and more frequently as a player to watch in the world of junior tennis. Now, after her incredible performance at Nationals, tennis insiders were buzzing about *her* instead of Jacquie Darden as The Next Big Thing, a player with the potential to one day make a mark on the professional tour (and it certainly didn't hurt that she was tall and beautiful and admirably articulate when she wanted to be).

Both Libby and Terry were deliberately vague when asked—by the press or anyone else for that matter—how long Terry had been playing and why hadn't they seen her before? The truth would only raise suspicion, if not outright disbelief. Really, who could watch Terry and imagine she'd first picked up a racket a little over a year ago? People were already skeptical about her being only 14. Her slashing serve-and-volley game set her apart from the other American juniors as much as her height and strength. She had much more in common with the legions of tall, powerful Russian teenagers currently crowding the ranks of the pro tour.

This summer would be another step forward in Terry's tennis

development. After her victory in Kalamazoo, she had insisted on entering the Girls' 18-and-Under division and wanted, unlike last summer, to play as many tournaments in as many different places as possible. Neither Libby nor Pete had any reason to object, so Libby was presently searching the USTA website for events and dates to allow the maximum amount of entries.

If only she wasn't so tired! Simply looking at these schedules and all the effort and arrangements they represented made her want to curl up here on the couch and take a nap.

Again. She was the Nap Champ. At least she wasn't constantly nauseated anymore, though she still couldn't care less about eating. The dizzy spells weren't as bad, but the constant need to gasp for air was an ongoing pain in the ass. Her doctor told her it was to be expected and she needed to take it easy.

Ha! How was that supposed to happen? How was she going to get Terry to all of these tournaments all over the country when walking from the house to the tennis court in her own backyard left her exhausted? For obvious reasons, Libby particularly wanted her to enter a number of tournaments in Southern California, which right now seemed as far away as Sydney, Australia. Where was she going to find the physical and emotional energy she needed to set the stage for the much-needed Terry-Isabel reconciliation?

The answer was, she couldn't do it all. She needed help. It was time to pitch an idea simmering on one of her brain's back burners ever since she got sick. This morning's activity of scrolling through lists of tournament possibilities just made it boil over. She'd been honest about her illness with Pete right from the beginning, so it wouldn't come out of left field when she made her proposal. If he could take a leave of absence from the club for the summer (the slowest season for him), Libby would pay him to be Terry's personal coach, to travel with them, or with Terry alone when Libby couldn't make it, to basically be a second Libby for Terry.

It was the perfect solution. In fact, she'd call Pete right now and ask him to lunch tomorrow. Locating the phone under a bunch of pillows next to her, she was scrolling through her contacts when it rang, making her jump. Wouldn't it be spooky if it was Pete?

It wasn't Pete.

Instead, it was Charlotte Taylor, Libby's old friend and sometimes doubles partner from the tour. Charlotte was now an administrator with the British Tennis Association, and the reason for her call made Libby shriek so loudly that Pretty Boy jumped on the couch to lick her face and Lupe came running to see if she was hurt or under attack.

Every year the directors of each of the four Grand Slam tournaments gave several "wild card" entries into the draw, sort of like a free pass. Usually wild cards went to highly ranked players who'd been injured and missed part of the season, or former champions trying to make a comeback. Or promising junior players from the country hosting that particular Slam (for instance, the US Open always gave wild cards to the Girls' and Boys' 18-and-Under National Champions). Charlotte told Libby that this year the BTA had decided to give one of the Wimbledon wild cards to the winner of a special raffle. The names of the 18's and 16's National Champions from all of the participating countries were put into a blind drawing, and just twenty minutes ago, at 4:00 pm London time, the President of the BTA had read the name of the winner.

Miss Teresa Gomez, USA, Girls' 16-and-Under National Champion.

"I couldn't believe it when I saw your name as her coach and contact person," Charlotte exclaimed. "I practically fell on my face rushing back to my office to call you! This couldn't *possibly* be the same girl your mum was telling me about when she was over last year???"

"She's the one, Char," Libby laughed giddily, still reeling from the news. "Believe me, I'll tell you all about it when I see you. It's a long story."

"Listen, I've got to pop off. I'm in a rush and late as usual, right? But I wanted to give you a quick ring to let you know I just sent an e-mail to Terry to give her the good word and tell her to expect an official invitation by registered letter."

"Thanks for calling, sweetie. I don't want to keep you, so a million kisses and we'll talk soon."

"Okay, luv, a million kisses back. Toodles."

Libby pressed "end" and looked at her watch. 11:30. Terry wouldn't be home for *four* hours! How in the world could she wait that long? Her fingers trembled with excitement as she called Pete.

"I'm free, free, free at last," Terry sang, sailing onto the terrace where Libby and Pete sat on the couch drinking iced tea. "Hear that, Pretty Boy," she said, dropping onto the floor next to the dog and burying her face in his fur. "F-R-E-E spells free!!! No more teachers, no more books, no more Adams' dirty looks. And no more Agnes Quigley Middle School!"

"Hiya, sweetheart. How was your last day?"

"We didn't do squat of course," Terry replied, sitting up and scratching Pretty Boy's belly. "The best part of the day was that it's over. So, what's up Petester, how come you're here?"

"What? I can't just come over and hang with my girls—ooops, and Boy, sorry buddy," Pete said, watching Pretty Boy writhing and whining in ecstasy.

"Sure, but you've usually got lessons now."

"Yeah, usually, but I thought it was more important to come over and help set your summer schedule. Lib said you're driving her crazy and won't stop until we do it."

"Great!" Terry leapt from the floor and plopped down next to Libby, eagerly eying the laptop on the table. "Let's see what you've got so far."

"Okay, just cool your jets," Libby said, sneaking a sideways glance at Pete and fighting to keep from grinning like a lunatic. "We've got a lot of options, especially for June. But before we get to that, you might want to check your e-mail first."

"How come?"

"Because it may factor into our plans."

"But…"

"Just do it, T, before Libby blows a gasket," Pete pleaded.

"Wellll, okay," Terry said, eying them suspiciously as she pulled up her e-mail. It was the second one, and it read:

> *Dear Terry,*
>
> *My name is Charlotte Taylor. I'm a friend of Libby Shaver's and a member of the British Tennis Association. I'm so very pleased to say you've won a special raffle which included National Junior Champions from all over the world. As the winner, you will be given a wild card into the Main Draw of the Wimbledon Tennis Championship to be held June 22-July 4 at the All England Club. You'll be receiving a registered letter shortly from the BTA and the Club to officially invite you to the Championship.*
>
> *Many congratulations. I'm looking forward to meeting you.*
>
> *Sincerely, CT*

"This has to be a joke!" Terry's eyes were huge as she read the e-mail over and over.

"No joke, sweetheart. You're going to play at Wimbledon," Libby said, blinking back tears at the pure joy lighting Terry's face.

"I'm going to *Wimbledonnnnnnnn*," Terry screamed, bringing Pretty Boy bounding onto the couch and Lupe running to the rescue for the second time that day.

17

Three weeks later...

Terry's serve hit the court and skidded past Pete so fast he found himself swinging at nothing but air. Again! This was her sixth ace and only her third service game this set.

"Good one," he yelled as he walked over to the backhand side in preparation for the next rocket launch. If she kept blowing them by him at this rate it could get embarrassing. At least it was just the two of them out here right now, no witnesses to his impending humiliation at the hands of a 14-year-old girl. The fact that Terry served like no other 14-year-old girl, or boy, or most adult players, for that matter, couldn't sugarcoat the dismal truth that she was acing him right and left and making him struggle to hold his own service games. Him! A grown man! A professional, for Pete's sake (no pun intended).

Well, for THIS Pete's sake, he wished she'd take a little smoke off the ball, or miss a few, but for Terry's sake, he was thrilled. They'd been in England for the past two weeks so Terry could get used to playing on the grass, but it could just as easily have been two days. Terry had taken to the slippery surface like a figure skater to ice. While most other players, himself included, approached the grass with caution and not a small amount of reluctance, Terry had glided around gracefully from her first running steps. Her game was custom-made for this slick, fast surface, and boy, did she know it. Look at her over there, chomping at the bit to fire off another cannonball and follow it to the net to easily put away the few pitiful returns he'd been able to manage. Serve-and-volley specialists waited all year for Wimbledon and the few warm-up tournaments leading up to it. It was their best chance for great results. Tennis history was full of serve-and-volleyers, predominately men, whose only Grand Slam victory had been Wimbledon.

Pete hadn't a doubt in his mind that Terry could be unbeatable on grass someday, and no slouch on clay and Har-Tru as well. She was developing an aggressive, all-around game which would make her a tough opponent at any professional tournament on any surface, anywhere in the world in a few years from now. Lucking into this Wimbledon wild card was a great way for her to get her first taste of The Bigs (or, The Real Tour, as she called it) by competing for what every player regarded as the most prestigious, most coveted title in tennis.

Pete didn't know who was more stoked—Terry, or he and Libby, who were both ecstatic about Terry simply being here and were hoping her luck would hold and she'd draw a First Round opponent who wouldn't blow her off the court. One thing was certain. If she served the way she was now, no one, *no one*, could blow her off the court.

"Serve 'em up, T. Make my head spin," he called across the court, crouching to get ready for what he truly wanted, despite his ego, to be another ace. Terry obliged, bringing the score to 3-3. The battle of serves and volleys lasted only another fifteen minutes, passing quickly as grass court matches usually do, with Pete finally breaking Terry's serve and taking the set 6-4.

"Way to let me off the hook that last game," Pete said, approaching the net as Terry headed toward him, stamping her feet like a little kid.

"Arrgghhh! 30-0 I had you, and I go and throw in *two* doubles, then that easy volley, then that skyball forehand..."

"Waaaiiit a minute, that forehand wasn't your error, merely a feeble response to my blistering backhand down the line, but those others, yeah, I agree." Pete dropped his racket and squeezed his throat with both hands, sticking out his tongue and crossing his eyes for good measure.

"I did *not* choke," Terry protested, "It was more like..."

"Gagging?"

"No!" Terry punched him playfully in the shoulder, but it was still hard enough to knock him back a few inches.

"Seriously, T, " Pete said, rubbing his shoulder. He sometimes forgot how strong she was. "Those were your only doubles the entire set, and you can make winners all day off that high backhand volley you blew, not to mention the dropshot you tried at deuce, which was the worst possible choice in that situation. What's the rewind shot?"

The rewind shot, in Pete's training lingo, was the one you hit if you could rewind to that point in the match and do it over. Terry didn't have to think hard because the moment she'd gone for the stupid dropshot she knew it was wrong, but she'd done it anyway. "Sharp angle crosscourt, follow to the net," she replied.

"Absolutely, and why do you think you chose the dropshot?"

Terry shrugged. "I don't know," she answered, though she did, and Pete knew it, but he'd make her listen anyway.

"I do. You started thinking how all you had to do was win two more points and you could even the set at 5-5, rack up the most games you ever have against me, then win the next two games and beat me for the first time. Gag! Two doubles. You think some more about how the game should be over, but now it's 30-30. Gag! You miss that easy volley, my ad. You get a reprieve when I miss the winner I went for on your shaky second serve. Deuce, huge point, which is when I force you to hit long with my brilliant backhand. My ad and you've already mentally lost the game so you try the epically misguided dropshot to prove it—the final, death-gurgling *gag!*"

"You're right," was all Terry could say since it was totally true. It used to freak her out when Pete did this, told her exactly what she was thinking, like he was inside her head, spying on her, or something.

"Remember, nobody is immune to pressure, self-inflicted or otherwise. I've seen classic meltdowns by Wyatt and Kraskova and Chillingsworth and…"

"Jemma York doesn't choke," Terry declared, much as it killed her to say it.

"Oh no? See, this is a perfect example of the point I was about to make. There's a big difference between feeling like choking and actually doing it. At this level, the mental part of the game is as big—if not a bigger—than the physical part. It's only human to get tight, everyone does, but the most successful players learn how to fight through the nerves, and that's maybe the biggest factor between being Top Twenty and All The Rest. I agree, Jemma is one cool customer, but don't believe for one minute that she doesn't start swallowing hard during a second set tie-breaker of a Slam when she's dropped the first set and needs the breaker to stay in the match."

"Yeah, and I melted down just practicing. Great."

"Are you kidding? You've got major mental toughness. You just haven't learned yet how to harness it and shape it into the weapon it'll be someday. All I'm saying is there's no shame in getting nervous, but if you can't admit it to yourself at the time, *in* time, you can't beat it."

"So if I had just admitted—to you—that I choked the last game I could have saved myself this whole lecture?"

"Exactly," Pete laughed. "Now, let's take a water break and we'll do the next hour all tie-breakers, simulated match play, Centre Court conditions. And if you don't mind, old girl," he chirped, switching to a comically exaggerated British accent, "I raaaather fancy you calling me Miss York, Your Highness, if you please."

"Watch out, Jemma, you freakin' ice cube," Terry warned, raising her fists and assuming a boxer's stance." I'm gonna burn your British butt into a one pathetic pile of ashes."

Workout finished, Terry and Pete left the tennis and pool area for the long walk back through the "grounds" to the main house, though "house" was hardly the word to describe the home of Libby's Aunt Astrid. Located in the London suburb (here they called it a borough) of Richmond upon Thames, it was by far the grandest place Terry had ever seen, easily twice the size of the Shaver's home in Palm Beach. The first time they'd driven through the massive front gates, she could have sworn they were visiting a castle, or a college, that's how huge it was. There wasn't just A garden, but multiple gardens covering the entire property (Papi would go wild here) and a maze made of hedges and topiary lifted straight from the movie *The Shining*. Terry could see boats and barges and rowers gliding past on the Thames River right from the tennis court. Didn't it figure that Libby would have an aunt who lived in a crib like this?

They'd been coming out here every day from the Shaver's townhouse in another London borough called Kensington and Chelsea so Terry could get the feel of the grass court, which she'd loved instantly. It wasn't at all like regular grass, soft and squishy and tickling your ankles. Instead it was cut extremely short and had the feel of a carpet, hard but with some give, too. It was hard to describe, way different than any other court she'd played on. Sure, it was a little slippery, but she couldn't understand why so many players didn't like it. Why, there were even some who refused to play Wimbledon because of it! Grass court tennis was, above all, *fast*, and fast was Terry's middle name.

She still couldn't believe she was here in England, an ocean away from home and Papi and everything familiar. Over the last couple of weeks, when she wasn't practicing, Terry had seen what there was to be seen in London, courtesy of her tour guides Libby and Pete. Whether she'd wanted to or not. She didn't have much interest in what she referred to as the C & C's—castles and churches. Trips to Westminster Abbey, St. Paul's Cathedral, the Tower of London, Buckingham Palace, Windsor Castle, this Castle,that Castle… had been pretty ho-hum. The old English guys who built these mammoth piles of stone thousands of years ago hadn't had much imagination. The National Gallery in Trafalgar Square, was cool, but really, how much time could you spend looking at stuff behind glass and ropes?

She preferred hanging out where the Shavers lived, cruising the shops on The King's Road and High Street and Knightsbridge, home of the famous Harrods department store. She loved visiting the Portobello Market in Notting Hill and being able to choose a meal from any country in the world from the trillions of cafes sprinkled throughout Kensington-Chelsea. Leave it to Mr. and Mrs. S to live in a ritzy (here they called it posh) part of the city. Their townhouse had three floors full of gorgeous furniture and paintings and sculpture, just like the Palm Beach house, and they hardly ever spent any time here, according to Libby.

What Terry enjoyed the most was simply soaking up the atmosphere of being in a foreign country, though England was probably the least foreign country you could visit. Still, there were differences. Sure, people here spoke English, but their accents made it sound like they were trying to talk through a mouthful of hot soup. She had a hard time understanding some of the more extreme cases (Aunt Astrid, for example) and simply nodded her head and smiled, too embarrassed to admit she didn't have a clue what they were saying. They were, after all, speaking the same language.

They used different words, too, for the same thing. Loo for bathroom. Knickers for underwear. Mo-BILE for cellphone. Football for soccer. Chips for french fries. And it seemed as if everyone smoked here, which was maybe one reason why so many people had such brown gnarly Halloween teeth, as opposed to home, where people were addicted to cosmetic dentistry and teeth-whitening products instead of cigarettes.

But the major difference between Brits and Americans, according to Terry's current mindset, was Wimbledon Fever. In the US, Wimbledon was a big deal only to tennis fans, which were far outnumbered by football, basketball and baseball fans. The sports section of local papers would give it a page each day. Besides the Tennis Channel, it was on ESPN during the week and on one of the big networks on both weekends. That was it.

Here in jolly old England it was all Wimbledon, *all the time*.

It was insane.

For the past week you couldn't switch on the "telly" without seeing Wimbledon warm-up coverage. Clips from Wimbledon's past. Interviews with players. Experts making predictions. Bookies making odds. Gossip galore and on and on and on. Giant pictures of players (especially Jemma York and Kip Sutherland, Britain's best male player) loomed on billboards and covered the sides of buses. It was all people talked about.

And then there were the tabloids. For one thing, there were tons more here, and they made *In Touch* and *US Weekly* at home seem boring in comparison. Terry was embarrassed to admit she was becoming addicted to the taste of trash. During Wimbledon Fever stories about tennis players and tournament buzz way outnumbered stories about movie, TV and rock stars, footballers and people who were famous for being rich or committing some horrible crime or weighing 500 pounds.

Pictures of Jemma and some of the other so called *"Tennis Hotties Ready to Sizzle on the Court"* were plastered on page after page, every day, with over-the-top commentary about their supposed romances and family problems and eating disorders. It was pretty gross, but Terry lapped it up anyway. Nobody got more space in the tabloids than Juliana Belluci—*"Everybody's Drooly Over Juli"*— an Italian player who hadn't won a single tournament but made millions in endorsements because she looked great in a bikini, which Terry thought was really unfair. When Terry had said this to Libby, Libby laughed and said Juliana helped promote interest in tennis and Terry shouldn't take all the tabloid garbage seriously. No one else did.

Libby should know. A few days ago there'd been a picture of Libby and her friend Trevor Stewart, the British soccer (oops, football) star, in the *Tatler*, one of the most outrageous of the tabs. A photographer had snapped them walking on the street after a lunch date. Terry noticed Libby was a bigger celebrity here than at home. Strangers recognized her on the street all the time, said hi, wanted to stop and chat like they were buddies. Libby said they considered her all Brit, instead of only half, and didn't seem to mind.

The problem was that Libby was so thin and pale in the picture, and the story running with it had rehashed her drug and alcohol problems and implied she was using again. The "proof", they wrote, was "in the picture". Terry had been furious. She thought Libby should defend herself, demand an apology, threaten a lawsuit. Libby just blew it off, saying there were about a zillion more important things to think about. Let it go.

One thing Terry wasn't letting go of was her growing obsession with beating Jemma York. In her own country. In front of her devoted fans. Every time Terry saw Jemma's smug face (which was ALL the time now, here in Jemmaville), or heard her on TV, prattling on with her snotty accent, she felt the familiar and welcome surge of hatred she considered as much a weapon in her game as her serve. Despite her ongoing fantasy of facing Jemma on Centre Court for the Final, Terry wanted so desperately to have a shot at her imagined enemy she wouldn't even mind a First Round meeting, a distinct possibility since as the #1 seed, Jemma would be given the luxury of an easy first match against the lowest of the low-ranked, or a complete nobody—like Terry. And Jemma would, of course, play every one of her matches on Centre Court, so at least two out of the three parts of the fantasy could come true.

Deep down, in the secret part of Terry's brain where her most embarrassing, ridiculous, pathetic and evil thoughts crouched in the dark, was the gut feeling she could actually beat Jemma. She'd watched her play on TV plenty of times, studied videos of her matches played over the last two years, and better yet, analyzed her every move from a first row seat as she'd won the Sony back in March. Jemma didn't have the best forehand, or backhand, or serve. She wasn't the quickest, or fastest, or strongest, though she *was* better at all these things than 90% of the other players. What put her ahead of the 10% who were better at all those things than she, and what kept her there, at #1, were two weapons stemming from the same place—her brain.

Jemma was a brilliant strategist, a tennis genius. She worked a match like a chess game, ruling over the court as Queen of the Board. Her game was all about consistency, precision and mental toughness. *She never lost her cool.* Terry admired her more than any other player for these reasons. And hated her for them too. But…they didn't make her invincible. After hours of observation and thought, Terry believed she had a way to challenge Jemma on her own terms—and come out the winner.

Too bad she couldn't share her thoughts with Libby and Pete, who would no doubt howl with laughter and tell her she was maybe a few sandwiches short of a picnic. Since the day they'd found out about the wild card, all those two could talk about was what a great experience this would be for Terry. How lucky she would be to take *a* set off her First Round opponent, whomever she turned out to be. Just soak up the atmosphere and have fun, they repeated, over and over, until Terry wanted to scream. Clearly, their confidence in her ability to make it to the Second Round was zip.

So she was only 14, with no ranking and no experience beyond junior level. So what? So this was the world's greatest tournament with all the best players. Was that any reason to lower her expectations? She was totally disappointed in their attitude.

She'd show them. She's show everyone…

"Yo, Earth to T, come in, do you read me?"

"Sorry, what?" she asked, realizing as she pulled herself out of her head that they'd almost reached the house and she hadn't heard a word Pete said.

Pete knocked softly on her right temple with his fist. "What's going on in there?"

"Uhh, nothing, just spacing," she lied, unwilling to divulge her "delusions of grandeur", as Pete would surely call them.

"I said, what are you up for doing this afternoon?"

"How about another workout after lunch?"

"No way. You know what they say, all workout and no play makes Terry an obsessive fruitcake and Petey a tired boy."

"Who's they?"

"You know, them, the 'they' people…"

"Hey you guys, perfect timing," Libby called out,

jogging—*jogging*!—down the stone walkway from the back terrace to meet them and waving something high over her head. It was the fastest Terry had seen her move in a long time. Libby may be dangerously skinny and kind of grayish white these days, but she was still beautiful, especially this very moment, all tooth commercial perfect smile stretched wide and icy blue eyes glittering with excitement.

"I just talked to Charlotte," she gasped, reaching them and instantly bending over, hands on knees, to catch her breath. "The… draw…is…finished…and…"

"Hey, take it easy, Lib, catch your breath," Terry said, noticing the cellphone in her hand and thinking, hurry up, Lib, spill it! The Wimbledon draw was made in great secrecy and wasn't supposed to be released to the press until tomorrow. Obviously Libby's friend Charlotte had gotten a sneak peak.

"Way to go, Char!" Pete exclaimed. "This calls for a drum roll—and the answer is…Miss Terry Gomez, USA versus…"

Libby straightened up and announced gleefully, "Miss Shannon Hatfield, Australia!"

The three of them looked at one another and burst into a collective *Whooohooo!!!*

Why the hooraying? First and foremost, Terry had beaten the odds by not drawing a highly seeded player. Second, Shannon Hatfield was ranked somewhere in the 60's, like 66, or 67, and was a "name" only to tennis fans who regarded her as just one of a group of young, talented but indistinguishable players who rarely made it past the Second Round of a major tournament. Terry remembered watching on TV as Keiko Tanaka shredded her in the First Round at the Australian Open six months ago. More significantly, she remembered exactly how Tanaka had performed the execution.

Heart racing, adrenaline pumping, Terry turned to Pete and declared, "The 'they' people are wrong. All workout and no play puts Terry through to the Second Round."

The window of opportunity had just cracked open and she was going to leap through it feet first and hit the ground running.

⚲ 18

Opening Day of the Wimbledon Championship, All England Lawn Tennis Club...

Terry fidgeted next to her in the back seat of the Bentley, gazing out the car window, lost in the pre-match psych ritual with her iPod and incapable of being reached unless forcibly unplugged. Pete was up front, driving and bantering with his long-time, not-so-secret crush, Libby's mom, Glynn. Libby was grateful they were all otherwise occupied because it left her alone for a little jaunt down memory lane. How many times had she made this trip out to The Club, in how many different emotional and physical states? Her mind spooled backwards, images of herself at various ages and stages flickering before her eyes.

Seven-year-old Libby, running and slipping, giggling and tumbling on the grass, trying to return balls fed by her mother, whose parents had been members of the club since Glynn was Libby's age. Twelve-year-old Libby watching the Ladies' Final from her family's box and earnestly swearing to her parents that they'd be watching *her* down there one day. Sixteen-year-old Libby, all long arms and legs and swishy blond ponytail, narrowly losing the Junior Wimbledon title, drawing the biggest crowd ever for that event and being hailed as England's best hope for future Wimbledons. Twenty-one-year-old Libby, newly graduated from Stanford and the reigning NCAA Champion, making her first appearance in the Main Draw and making it to the Third Round as the British press dubbed her "The Heiress" and agents scrambled to represent her.

Twenty-four-year-old Libby, nerves frayed from weeks of being an entire country's main focus of attention, crumbling under pressure during the third set of the Semifinal, then reading in the

papers the next day how "Our Lib" had been transformed over-
night into "America's Heiress Disinherited!!!!".

Her favorite memory was of the following year, the year she had
made it to the Final. It had been the same old craziness, of course.
The deeper she'd advanced into the draw, the more frenzied the
press had become, especially the tabloids, which had her romanti-
cally linked to every famous British man over eighteen and under
eighty (all enormously entertaining to Terry, who was hooked on
the tabs and salivated over the scrapbooks of old clips saved by
Libby's mom). At that point, Jemma York and Kip Sutherland had
still been merely promising juniors, neither generating much in the
way of buzz, so Libby, despite her unfortunate American half, was
all England had to hope for and cheer on to the brink of madness.

But she'd learned her lesson. She had ignored the hype and
didn't pressure herself to please the fickle Brits who had been so
quick to disown her the previous year. She'd played the match of
her life, defeated by the #1 seed Paulina Polichenko of Belarus after
an electrifying, heart-wrenching 12-10 third set which had the
normally reserved Wimbledon crowd screaming and doing "The
Wave". Both players received a standing ovation after the match.
The Duchess of Kent had said, "We're so proud of you my dear,"
as she handed her the gold runner-up plate rather than the Venus
Rosewater Dish, on which Libby had dreamed so many times her
name would be etched one day.

It was the closest she had ever come to winning a Grand Slam.
And it would be the high point of her tennis career, the peak from
which she'd begin the long slow slide into the Madison-Kaplan
Institute. But she didn't know that then.

"Lib, tell your mother to stop picking on me!"

Pete's voice jerked Libby abruptly back to the present, where
she could see they were approaching the outskirts of the village
of Wimbledon.

"I'm hardly picking on you, dear," Glynn retorted (in the throaty,
theatrical voice that struck fear into people who didn't know she

was a cream-puff). "Simply pointing out that you still haven't learned how to drive properly."

"It's not my fault everything here's on the wrong side," Pete whined, catching Libby's eye in the rear-view mirror and winking.

"As I recall, your road skills are no better at home. Need I remind you of a certain incident involving my precious daughter, a rainy night and one disreputable hunk of junk…"

"All right, you two, time out," Libby laughed, thinking how many of these mock squabbles she'd heard over the years. Glynn and Pete were one of each other's favorite people (Their constant teasing and sparring used to make Libby jealous back when she was around Terry's age and madly in love with Pete, who'd treated her like a little sister while flirting shamelessly with her beautiful mother.) She was glad they were both here, for the amusement value as well as the fact that it made things easier for her.

Glynn, a devoted tennis fan and accomplished player, tried to make every Opening Day at Wimbledon and was usually a regular throughout the two-week tournament. This year, however, Libby suspected her presence had more to do with concern over her daughter's health than tradition. Since arriving two days ago, Glynn had attached herself to Libby's side, clucking and fussing until Libby had to beg her to stop hovering. They'd had a nice chat earlier this morning about the difference between helping and smothering, and Glynn had promised to at least pretend to chill out.

Pete got it right. After arguing about accepting a salary (which he hadn't wanted, but Libby insisted on, otherwise no deal), he'd agreed to travel with them as Terry's coach and Libby's partner in management. He knew exactly when to step in and when to back off. He didn't freak out whenever she had a coughing fit or examine her with a fearful eye to determine whether she was any thinner or paler than the day before. And he never, *ever*, treated her like she was a fragile glass sculpture ready to shatter at any moment. Unlike her mother. And Terry.

Libby glanced over at Terry, still plugged in but now sitting up straight and checking out the traffic snarl they were stuck in as they inched closer to the Club. She'd had similar talks with Terry to the one she'd had with Glynn, about letting up on the fretting. It hadn't made a difference. Terry constantly asked her how she was feeling, could she get her some tea, did she take her pills, how about something to eat? It drove Libby crazy and made her upset, especially now since they'd been in London, that Terry was worrying about *her* instead of thoroughly enjoying herself.

So…she had done her best to be the "old", meaning the healthy, Libby for Terry, doing the tourist thing, shopping, eating out. It exhausted her, but it was worth it. Terry was having a blast. And she was so excited about today! All she could talk about the last 48 hours was the Shannon Hatfield strategy. Libby, and even Pete, had to admit the idea of Terry beating Hatfield wasn't preposterous. Highly unlikely but possible. Shannon Hatfield was one of those many players who had excelled in the Juniors only to struggle once they hit the pro tour. Leave it to Terry to remember the Tanaka match, though Libby had to remind her that there was a big difference between watching the #4 player in the world dismantle an opponent, and being able to do it.

"There it is!" Terry exclaimed, yanking the earbuds from her ears and pointing ahead.

The All England Lawn Tennis Club had a stuffy old-fashioned name that made you imagine ladies in hats, knee-length skirts and white stockings, trotting daintily on the grass, delicately tapping the ball with small wooden racquets, and gentlemen in long trousers with ascots around their necks, leaping over the net to shake hands—everybody promenading about with umbrellas and cups of tea, and perhaps a foxhound or two on a leash. It probably had been like that once, but today's Club was a sprawling modern tennis center built to accommodate and pay homage to tennis' premiere event and the throngs of tennis fans who flocked here each year.

The grounds—gardens, walkways, fountains, public spaces—were lovely and immaculate, providing visitors with plenty of room to walk from match to match, or find a pleasant place to take a break and people-watch. Food, drink and souvenir vendors popped up every few feet, making it easy to get your fill of fish-and-chips and strawberries and cream, or buy a huge felt tennis ball for autographs. Strategically placed giant screens allowed video access to the main show courts, so if you couldn't get a seat or claim a spot to stand, you could still enjoy the action. The Clubhouse was , of course, for members only, a luxurious retreat from the teeming masses, where high tea was served promptly at 4:00 no matter what type of battle was raging on the adjacent Court Two.

The mood was quite different, supercharged rather than leisurely, over at the Competitor's Complex in the Millennium Building. It was here that the players could take advantage of the dining facilities, mini-gym and interview rooms designed specifically for their comfort and convenience. The other Grand Slam venues were similar to all this, but what set Wimbledon apart was the one thing no other Slam had, the hallmark of the tournament, the tradition beloved by the British, the nemesis of many and the delight of others.

Grass. Yards and yards of painstakingly cultivated and manicured green living carpet stretching over 19 courts.

Centre Court, the location of every tennis player's most elaborate fantasy, seated 13,810, while Court One next door could fit 11,249. The courts closest to these two had room for large numbers of spectators as well, but the viewing accommodations got smaller the farther away the court was situated from Centre Court.

It was on one of these courts in the hinterlands, Court 19—the farthest you could get from Tennis' Greatest Stage and still be at Wimbledon—where Miss Terry Gomez and Miss Shannon Hatfield began their warm-up at 11:00 am sharp on a chilly, overcast Opening Day in front of a crowd of five.

Shannon Hatfield was approximately ten minutes into the warm-up when she realized a major attitude adjustment was in order. When she'd seen the draw and learned after asking around that her opponent would be the lucky little junior wild card, she'd been ecstatic. It was about time she pulled an easy First Round. Shannon had been the Australian Girls' 18-and-Under Champion once upon a time, and no one had to tell her, four years later, what a cruel world of difference there was between junior and professional tennis. Barely making enough money to stay on the Tour the first three seasons, she'd finally started having some good wins, clawing her way up the rankings to #67. She deserved this break. *A Junior!* And a 16's Junior at that! Thank you, Gods of Tennis, she had thought—until about ten minutes ago, when she walked out on the court with Terry Gomez.

For one thing, there was nothing "little" about this junior. The girl was *huge.* Shannon was 5'8", 140 pounds and—suddenly—small. She was having a hard time believing Terry was only 16. As they started trading groundstrokes, and Shannon felt the power coming off Terry's ball, saw how well she moved on the grass, how quick she was at the net, her concern increased and grew into full-blown anxiety when Terry began her practice serves.

What bothered her the most, though, was this kid's body language and the expression on her face. She acted as if she belonged here, as if she played a match at the professional level—*at Wimbledon*—every day. As if she could actually win this match! The nerve! Shannon wasn't about to let some American brat start messing with her head, or rob her of an easy chance to make it to Second Round. She won the toss, a good omen, and elected to receive, counting on Terry to throw in a few nervous double faults. When the first serve whipped by her for an ace, she realized what a mistake she'd made and how premature, and just plain wrong, her earlier happiness with the draw had been.

The more frequently Shannon Hatfield questioned calls and argued with the umpire, and snapped at the ballboys and gave her dirty looks, the happier Terry was. Those lessons she'd learned from the Tanaka match were coming in handy. Hit almost exclusively to the weak Hatfield forehand because she'll quickly get frustrated with making so many errors. Expect every second serve to land in the same place (how dumb was that? Didn't she have a coach?) and be ready to return it for a winner. Pull her in short and low on her backhand. Above all, encourage her bratty behavior and gamesmanship. Some players fed off it, but Hatfield wasn't one of them. She would self-destruct.

So far, it was working perfectly.

Terry perched restlessly on her chair during changeover. In the lead 5-3, about to serve for the first set, she marveled again that she wasn't more nervous. Excited, sure, especially when she arrived here this morning and had to push through the crowd of photographers and reporters at the Player's Entrance (where E.J. Wyatt and his entourage, including supermodel Bijou, were right in front of them!). And when she'd been in the locker room getting dressed (unfortunately in one of her new boring white outfits, instead of her usual neon colors because of the stupid, out-dated, all-white rule here) right next to Mia Lindstom, just about the biggest name she'd see in this locker room (the stars used a different one). And when she'd seen her name , right up there in black and white, in the Main Draw along with the great names of the game.

And, absolutely, when she had stepped onto Court 19 to warm up, she'd been incredibly excited. But not nervous. From the moment her feet hit the grass and she stroked the first ball, she had felt—right. She also felt she had the advantage because she'd watched Hatfield play, knew her weaknesses, while Hatfield knew nothing about her except that she was a junior player and most probably a pushover. As a bonus, Hatfield's nastiness during the Tanaka match had made her easy to hate, always essential for Terry's motivation.

She looked across at the small seating space where Pete, Libby and Mrs. S huddled, along with two guys who Terry assumed belonged with Hatfield. It was really nice of Mrs. S to come all the way out here in the cold and support her when she could be in the Shaver's box at Centre Court watching Kip Sutherland play his first match, or warm and cozy in the glassed-in observation deck of the Club enjoying Tatiana Kraskova's match. She and Mrs. S had nothing in common except the one thing that gave them a special bond—loving and being loved by Libby. Terry suddenly wanted to reward Libby's mom for being here by finishing Hatfield off as quickly as possible.

"Time," called the umpire.

Exactly, Terry thought as she prepared to serve, time to wrap this up. She knew she'd gotten under Hatfield's skin and beating her was only a matter of...well...time.

She won the game at love.

With the final score 6-3, 6-2, Shannon Hatfield barely brushed Terry's outstretched hand at the net and instead of saying Congratulations (even though she didn't mean it), or Good Match (even though it really hadn't been) she said something that made Terry laugh.

"You're not really 16, are you?" she accused, narrowing her eyes at Terry as if she could wring the ugly truth from her with a menacing stare.

"No, I'm really not," Terry replied, flashing her a gigantic white smile and walking over to shake hands with the umpire.

"Well, that's not right! It's illegal," Hatfield sputtered, following Terry. "You're not a legitimate 16's Champion if you're over 16!" Forgetting to shake hands with the umpire in the heat of her temper tantrum, she screamed at him instead, "She just admitted she's older than she's supposed to be! She's in this tournament under false pretenses! Somebody needs to do something about this!"

"Knock yourself out," Terry said. She quickly gathered her gear, leaving Hatfield to continue haranguing the umpire, and joined Libby, Pete and Mrs. S, who were already standing and anxious to leave the unpleasant scene unfolding in front of them.

"Way to go, T. You literally drove her crazy," Pete chuckled.

"Bravo, my dear! Marvelous of you to beat that dreadful young woman," sniffed Mrs. S, giving Terry a peck on the cheek.

"Well done, Sweetheart!" Libby hugged her, glancing back at the still raging Hatfield, "Look, she's still carrying on. I hope she doesn't follow through with this and try to make trouble."

"So what if she does?" Terry said as they hailed a courtesy golf cart for the ride back to the main complex. "Do you *really* think she'll want people to know she got thrashed by a 14-year-old? Nahh, she's going to feel just like what she is...a loser."

"Point well taken," said Mrs. S.

"I guess you're right," Libby said. "It's just too bad your first match here had to end on such a sour note."

"Doesn't bother me," Terry said.

"So tell us, Miss Gomez," Pete asked with his comical, barely understandable British accent, pointing an imaginary microphone in her direction, "How do you feel after winning your first match, crushing young Hatfield with relative ease?"

"One down, six to go," Terry replied.

✎ 19

Four days later...Friday afternoon

Terry listened to the conversation happening several lockers away and could tell that Yelena Grobina and a player she didn't recognize were trading mean and funny 411 despite the fact they were doing it in Russian. Gossip was universal and it sounded pretty much the same in every language. No matter where you were at this tournament—here in the locker room, at the Competitor's Complex, at the matches, on the grounds (but not so much at The Clubhouse)—you heard Spanish, French, German, Russian, English, of course, and a dozen other unidentifiable languages mingling to create a chaotic soundtrack which was fun to listen to even though you couldn't understand most of it.

Whatever Grobina and her friend were saying, Terry was glad for the distraction. Her stomach gurgled and she yawned constantly and unnecessarily, a sure sign that her nerves were stretched and quivering in anticipation of the match she was about to play. She hadn't felt nearly as wired back on Wednesday in the Second Round, which now seemed like two *years* instead of two days ago.

At Wimbledon, everyone played every *other* day with the exception of the women playing their Fourth Round (known as the Round of 16, or just the 16's) and the Quarterfinals back-to-back. So after beating Shannon Hatfield on Monday, Terry had spent Tuesday morning at Aunt Astrid's, practicing and psyching herself for her next opponent, an American veteran who was one of the oldest players on the Tour. Patricia Timmerman was even older than Libby, whom she'd played against many times.

"Trish is the best," Libby had told her. "You'll never meet a sweeter, classier person. She never pulls the kind of bullshit you saw in your first match. Excellent sportsmanship at all times. Everyone loves her. In fact, back in the day, we used to tease her about being too nice for her own good. C'mon, bitch it up, Trish, get mean! But she'd just laugh. She doesn't have it in her."

Since Terry's strategy was obviously not going to be able to include hating Patricia Timmerman, and since she'd never watched her play, she'd had to rely solely on what Libby could tell her, which boiled down to patience. Consistency, apparently, wasn't Timmerman's middle name. Libby had advised that if Terry could keep the ball in play longer than she normally wanted to, she'd have a chance. Timmerman didn't have any big weapons, but she had every shot in the book and knew when to use them, not to mention tons of experience. Ranked #84, she had surprisingly upset the #11 seed, Arianna Sandoval, in the First Round, so she was obviously playing well.

After several hours of practicing looooonnnggg (and boring!) rallies with Pete, Terry had been overjoyed to head back out to the Club to watch some mens' matches and meet Libby and Mrs. S for "High Tea" at the Clubhouse (where Jemma York, who'd automatically become a member when she won two years ago, had been holding court at a table by the window, everyone fawning over her like she was the actual freaking Queen of England). Later, she'd wanted to stay and see the end of Chris Renshaw's match (it didn't get dark in England until almost 9:00), but Mrs. S insisted they get home so Terry could get a good night's sleep before her match the next day, though Terry was certain it was really Libby she'd been worried about. And rightly so. Libby had fallen asleep the moment they got in the car and didn't wake up until they pulled into the underground garage at the townhouse.

The next afternoon, on Court 11, this time with a "crowd" of maybe 20, down 0-5 in the first set, Terry had welcomed the first surge of hate (well, honestly, more annoyed dislike) for her opponent. Not because Timmerman wasn't everything Libby had said she was. In fact, Timmerman had introduced herself to Terry in the locker room, remarked on how much she adored Libby, said she envied Terry the fun and excitement of just beginning her tennis career and that she was really looking forward to their match.

No, ironically it was because Timmerman was so nice that she'd given Terry an encouraging and sympathetic smile and patted her on the back during the last changeover, feeling sorry that she was thrashing on Terry. If there was another thing Terry hated—along with the gazillions of things she hated—it was being the object of pity. Not that her play hadn't been pitiful. Though she'd followed Libby and Pete's advice, trying to keep the ball in play until Timmerman made an error, nothing had worked. Timmerman hadn't been making unforced errors while Terry had sprayed balls all over, double-faulting, missing easy volleys.

She'd been furious with herself, but Timmerman's well-intentioned show of sympathy had infuriated her more, so much that she'd promptly won her first game, serving three aces in the process, and had finally woken up from her coma. Timmerman won her serve to take the set 6-1, but Terry had regained her confidence and came out with guns blazing in the next set, which was a reversal of the first. Timmerman's level of play had dropped dramatically while Terry's soared. 6-2, Terry. She still felt she had the momentum, leading 3-1 in the third, when at 30-30 in the fourth game, Timmerman had run for a wide ball to her forehand, slipped and gone down hard on the grass, twisting her left knee and having to retire (which just meant quit in tennisspeak) from the match, leaving Terry the winner.

Talk about a bummer! Terry knew in her heart she'd have won that third set and felt cheated by having it "awarded" to her. Libby and Pete had both told her to let it go, it happened all the time, it was part of the game, just accept it as a lucky break and look toward the next match.

The next match, as in ten minutes from now. Stifling another nervous yawn, Terry straddled the bench in front of her locker and checked the contents of her tennis bag for the fifth time, continuing to obsess, as she had for the past 48 hours, about what—well, really who—lurked dangerously in the her immediate future. After the premature end to the Timmerman match, she had rushed over to Centre Court to watch the duel which would determine her next opponent, but hadn't been at all surprised to see the winner already standing in the middle of the court, blowing kisses to the cheering crowd.

Shawn Chillingsworth.

As if there had been any doubt, considering her opponent had been a low-ranked Spanish clay-courter. Shawn's name had jumped out at Terry the moment she'd looked at the draw as the first major hurdle she would hit, so she'd been thinking about this possibility from the start. But somehow, seeing Shawn out there grinning and waving and lapping up the adulation had made Terry suddenly wonder what made her imagine she belonged on the same court as the dazzling superstar. Shawn "Chills" Chillingsworth, #3 in the world, was the undisputed glamour girl of the Tour (except for Juliana Belluci, but she was more of a model than a player) and one of the most famous and beloved athletes, male or female, in America. Before Terry had ever picked up a tennis racket, she'd heard of Shawn. Shawn had her own clothing, shoe and racket lines with Nike (Terry had a lot of "Chilli" outfits). Her endorsement was plastered on ads for expensive watches, digital cameras, sports drinks, cars and on and on. She gave to and raised a great deal of money for her favorite charities and sponsored a summer camp for disadvantaged kids near her home base of Philadelphia.

Brash and outspoken, entertaining and flashy, Shawn was a fan favorite and sportswriter's dream. More striking than pretty, she accentuated her exotic looks with elaborate hair extensions and weaves. Both of her sculpted upper arms sported large tattoos, one a trailing garland of flowers, the other an African tribal mask. She was the opposite of Jemma York on court, her emotions easy to see on her face and in her voice as she talked (and sometimes screamed) to herself—the umpire, the line judges, the ball girls and boys—even the fans.

Shawn's game, unlike Jemma's crafty strategizing, was pure power and slashing attack, *all the time.* She was either on or off. On her off days she still managed to win 90% of the time. When she was on, even Jemma and Kraskova couldn't beat her.

Terry loved watching Shawn play as much as everyone else did and admired her fearlessness in going for the kill shot on every point, which was why she had spent yesterday at Aunt Astrid's alternately practicing and freaking out. While pounding serves and volleys (Terry, Libby and Pete had all agreed this was the key to playing Shawn) Terry had resolved to think of Shawn as just another opponent, not as Chills. No sooner had she convinced herself that her own serve was better, that she moved as well and was probably faster, than her confidence pendulum had swung wildly in the opposite direction and she'd swear that Chills would blow her right off the court. It had been that way all yesterday, and all last night as she'd pretended she could fall asleep, back and forth between believing she could win and fearing she would be annihilated.

Then, earlier this afternoon as she and her entourage (ha) had arrived at the Club, something happened which made the pendulum swing once more, then freeze in place, and not in the position you'd guess. As Terry, Libby, Pete and Mrs. S were walking down the main concourse toward the Competitor's Complex, two little English girls had approached Terry, who wasn't dressed for the match yet, but whose bulging tennis bag identified her as a player. Each girl had one of the big felt autograph balls, and one of them had held her ball out to Terry, asking, "You're a player, right? Will you sign, please?"

"Sure," Terry said, delighted, as she held out her hands to take the ball and attached pen.

"Who are you?" the other little girl asked, eying Terry suspiciously.

"Terry Gomez," Terry replied. "I'm new. This is my first tournament."

"She's nobody," the brat announced to her friend, "Look, there's Rolf Dresbach, come on!"

They had run off, leaving Terry with her hands empty and her feelings hurt. Libby said to ignore them, just silly little kids, but by the time Terry had reached the locker room she'd worked up a fine righteous anger. How *dare* those little bitches call her a nobody? She was somebody, somebody who was a National Junior Champion, somebody who had won two rounds at the greatest tournament in the world, somebody who was strong and fast and good enough to compete with any woman on the Tour.

Somebody who could hold her own against Shawn Chillingsworth, and maybe even win.

Anger was Terry's strongest motivator, and as she left the locker room she gave silent thanks to those little girls for helping her screw her head on straight and tap into her best resource.

Libby drank in the atmosphere of Court One, historic stage of so many great Wimbledon dramas, including a few of her own. Conditions were just about perfect on this sunny, windless late afternoon, with the temperature a delightful 73 degrees. She'd always preferred playing here rather than Centre Court. You had the thrill of a show court and a big crowd but less pressure. The stadium was packed right now, which meant that over 11,000 people were getting their first look at Terry.

The moment was almost surreal. Who would have imagined that the same kid who stood across the court from her last January, swatting wildly at balls for the first time in her life, would be warming up for a Third Round match here against Shawn Chillingsworth? Libby knew better than anyone what Terry was capable of, but she'd still been surprised at the Hatfield result and, quite frankly, shocked that she'd taken a 6-2 set from Trish Timmerman, with every indication she'd have taken the third set as well if Trish hadn't gotten hurt. Taking that fall may have been a blessing in disguise for her old friend. Better to retire from the match than be defeated by a 14-year-old when you had nearly 20 years on her.

Yes, thanks to Shannon Hatfield's misguided protest (which, true to Terry's prediction, had backfired on her), Terry had been "outed" for her true age, which had been duly reported in a small item in the Wimbledon section of Tuesday's *London Times*. Not much attention had been paid at the time, but the buzz had grown considerably after the match with Trish, when it became clear Terry was headed to a meeting with Shawn. Terry's picture had appeared in the paper (the *Times*, not one of the tabs, thank God!) for the first time yesterday with an accompanying long paragraph highlighting her age and her connection to Libby, which had placed her officially on the public radar. The fans here this afternoon were no doubt as anxious to see the New Girl, the Novelty, the Youngest Player in the Main Draw, as they were to support the beloved Chills.

Down on the court trading groundstrokes with Shawn, Terry looked as nervous as Libby had ever seen her. When she wasn't focused on the ball, she kept her head down and fussed with her racket strings, avoiding eye contact with Shawn. She wasn't checking out her surroundings either, no sneak peeks into the stands, not even over here at them. Libby didn't blame her. It was the smart thing to do (she remembered the first time she had played in front of a crowd this big. The butterflies already cruising around her stomach had gone into a frenzy the moment she heard the sheer volume of the applause as she and her opponent appeared on the court).

Terry was wired, all right, but she was also something else Libby recognized.

She poked Pete and asked, "Do you see it?"

"What?"

"Terry's face, her body language."

Pete watched Terry smack an overhead that bounced off the court and sailed into the stands. Shawn turned to watch it fly and said something to the people sitting in the box above her that made them all laugh. "Oh, yeah," he said. "What do you think ticked her off? That thing with the autograph?"

"Or maybe something that happened in the locker room. Or Shawn out there doing her Chills thing. Could be anything, right? We know how skilled our girl is at turning a careless gesture into a major insult. Whatever, she's ready to rumble."

"And Shawn's too loose. She doesn't know what she could be dealing with."

It was true. All through the warm up, Shawn had seemed as if she was out there for a casual practice—putting little effort behind her ball, moving lazily, joking with the courtside photographers, the ballboys and girls, the fans. It was one of her trademarks. Everyone else warmed up while Chills "chilled out" (which drove most opponents crazy and was surely Shawn's intention all along). But Pete was right, she was clowning around more than usual. And she was a notoriously slow starter with a tendency to run hot and cold. Libby and Pete had made sure Terry knew to be aggressive from the first point. If Shawn started true to form and was running cold, the match could be competitive.

One of Terry's practice serves went wild, accidentally hitting Shawn in the arm. Shawn touched her index finger to the spot where the ball hit, then jerked it away and shook it as if it had been burned. Then she blew on her arm as if to put out the fire, eliciting howls of laughter from the crowd.

Terry, who for once had been watching Shawn, turned abruptly and walked away, looking over at Libby, Pete and Glynn for the first time.

"There it is, Code Red," said Pete, rubbing his hands together with glee. Code Red was Terry at her highest level of angry determination and intensity.

"Exactly," Libby said. "Poor Chills has no idea what she just did."

Shawn Chillingsworth did a lot more thinking and strategizing on court than she was given credit for, and what she'd been thinking since the first five minutes of the warm-up was that Terry Gomez might be trouble. At the ripe old age of 23, Shawn had already been on the Tour for six years, Top 5 for the last three of them. She was a shrewd and quick judge of her opponents' abilities, which was why, as the warm-up continued, she mentally prepared herself for a struggle while pretending to be more interested in entertaining the crowd than paying attention to Terry.

This kid had major power behind her ball. She moved well, especially for someone Shawn estimated to be about 6 feet tall (at 6'2" herself she appreciated how difficult it was to get low and smoothly coordinate super long arms and legs). Her volley and overhead skills looked solid. And her serve! Though they were serving at the same time to opposite sides of the court, Shawn watched Terry from the corner of her eye, noting the fluid motion, excellent toss and speed as the ball flew over the net. It was alarmingly similar to her own, which was even more cause for concern. By the end of warm up Shawn knew she couldn't afford a slow start today and was happy to win the toss and serve the first game. Two games later, after struggling through three deuce points to hold her serve, then losing the next game in four shockingly quick points, she knew that starting slowly was going to be the *least* of her problems.

Having just broken Shawn's serve for the first time, Terry stood ready to serve for the first set at 5-4. She was waiting for the crowd to stop cheering. They smelled the possibility of an upset, and Terry did too. During the warm-up she'd built up a good hate for Shawn, which had been helping her put every ounce of strength into all her shots, but especially her serve. She'd been coming to net after every first serve and volleying for a winner almost every time (plus, her serve was blessedly on today, so she rarely had to hit a second). Because of the net rushing, she won her service games quickly. Shawn, on the other hand, didn't come to net behind her serve (a big mistake in Terry's opinion) and had to work harder to hold. But even then, Shawn's service games weren't much longer because they were both whacking the ball as hard as they could and going for winners. Terry was playing Shawn's own game (admittedly also her game) against her, and now she had a chance at taking the first set.

"Quiet please," the umpire said.

The applause died down except for one loud voice crying out, "Come on Chills, send her back to her playpen!"

Shawn turned in the direction the voice came from and yelled, "Hey, *you* come out and play her! It's not as easy as it looks!"

The crowd roared.

Terry swallowed the tiny smile threatening to erupt on her face. She couldn't afford to stop hating Shawn right now.

But six points later she did allow herself a grin in the privacy of her towel as the crowd went nuts when she won the first set.

The second set was a twin of the first, fast and furious, with each player holding serve, more like a mens' than a womens' (or ladies' as they stubbornly continued to say here) match. The crowd slowly shifted its support to Terry (who wasn't used to being a favorite and had to admit she kind of liked it) though they certainly didn't abandon Shawn. At 4-5 Shawn, but leading 30-5 in this tenth game, Terry hit a serve which registered 124 mph on the big screen courtside. The crowd erupted. She'd just broken the record Shawn had set at the Australian Open six months ago!

Shawn looked at the screen then turned to Terry and applauded with one hand clapping her racquet face, pushing the crowd into an even louder frenzy.

Terry held up a hand to acknowledge Shawn's gesture while fighting to remain calm. She had to win this game to stay even, or Shawn would have the second set. She had to put everything out of her head—her opponent, her new record, the crowd, the drama— and focus on the two chances she had here at 40-5. Serving wide to Shawn's forehand, she was midway to the net when she realized it wasn't wide or fast enough, giving Shawn time to rip a passing shot down the line. One chance down. 40-30. She missed her first serve and, swallowing hard, made a decision that might not be the smartest but might surprise Shawn. Instead of hitting a slicing, weaker second serve, she went for another ace and followed it to net. Sure enough, Shawn was caught off guard and netted her return. 5-5. The next game proved to be the longest of the match, going to deuce five times before Terry broke Shawn's serve for the second time, taking the lead 6-5. She'd be serving for the match!!!!

Sitting in her chair during the changeover, Terry's arms and legs were shaking, her heart hammering. Sipping constantly at her water bottle because there was no saliva in her mouth, she didn't dare look behind her at Libby and Pete because they were probably freaking out too, which would make her *more* freaked out.

No choking, no choking, no choking, she pleaded to herself. No choking *just because you're on the verge of beating Chills at Wimbledon!!!!* What if she blew this chance and had to play a tiebreaker? What if she lost the tiebreaker? What if she suddenly woke up from this dream in the third set and completely fell apart? What if…Arrgghhh, stop it! Focus on your serve. Four great serves and you've got the match. Four little points. She chanted silently to herself and tried to breathe deeply until the umpire called time.

Terry walked out onto the court, trying to block out the thunderous applause and concentrating on one thing. All the hours and all the thousands and thousands of serves she'd practiced were in preparation for this exact situation. *Get the first serve in.* That was the key.

And that's what she did. Two aces and two rockets that set up volley winners.

Game. Set. Match. Miss Gomez.

Terry was already at the net, and as she waited for Shawn to shake hands, she waved and gave a thumbs up to Libby and Pete, who were standing and clapping wildly. As psyched as she was about winning the match, it pleased her even more to see how happy it made the two people she most wanted to feel proud of her. She wished this moment could go on forever.

Shawn approached the net and Terry was shocked to see she was grinning. If Terry had lost she'd be beyond bummed right now.

"Congratulations, Terry, you played a great match," Shawn said, holding out her hand and grasping Terry's warmly in a thumb-clasping handshake.

"Uhh, thank you, you too," Terry stammered. Though she'd just beaten her, she was overwhelmed by actually talking (and holding hands—in a way) with *Chills*.

"Giiirrrlll, you are The Real Deal," Shawn said, placing her hand against Terry's back as they walked to the umpire's chair. "Enjoy this, cause the first big wins always the best, and you're going to have lots of these, believe me."

"I hope so," Terry said, still shy about being in the presence of such a star.

"Oh, there's hope, all right," Shawn laughed, "Just do me a favor and at least win your next round, okay? It's easy to have a letdown after a match like ours."

"I'll try," Terry replied. She reached up to shake the umpire's hand then waved to the crowd as they gave both her and Shawn a standing ovation.

She had every intention of doing Shawn that favor. And then some.

⚲ 20

Two days later...Sunday

Terry couldn't stop shuffling gleefully through the papers littered on the floor around her. Everywhere she looked she saw her picture and her name, or one of her NEW names, in big bold letters:

TERRY THE TEEN TERROR TOPS CHILLS!

CHILLINGSWORTH OUSTED BY NEW SENSATION TERRY GOMEZ!!

LOOK OUT FOR TERRY THE TEENINATOR!!!

"Hey, I like this one best," Terry held up the page and waved it in front of her face.

"Just call me the Teeninator from now on," she demanded in a terrible imitation of Ahhnuuld's Austrian accent.

Libby and Pete both looked up from their own papers and burst out laughing, like they had all morning since Pete ran to the corner newsstand at the crack of dawn to make sure he snagged every tabloid. The Shavers had the *Times* delivered, but everyone (OK, mostly Terry) knew the tabbies would be the most fun to see.

It was Middle Sunday, which meant no tennis at Wimbledon, a sacred tradition which was broken only if rain had delayed too many matches during the first week. But it was raining today, giving Terry, Libby and Pete a perfect excuse to lounge around the townhouse, devouring the papers and continuing to savor Friday's triumph. Though she'd had 36 hours to digest her victory over Shawn, Terry still felt deliciously full from the experience. And from all the awesome stuff that was happening because of it.

As soon as the match was over she and Shawn had been escorted to the Competitor's Complex for the post-match press conference.

Since she hadn't been invited to one after winning the first two rounds ("nobodies" didn't exactly get mobbed for interviews), it was her first time facing all the cameras and reporters. Naturally, Shawn had gone first, so Terry paced the hallway outside, getting more and more nervous, thinking of Libby's earlier advice to "just be yourself—only nicer. And if someone asks you a question you don't want to answer, flash those gorgeous teeth and say politely that you'd rather not comment. It's better to say nothing than something you may regret later or something that may be misinterpreted. Always give credit to your opponents and *never* sound boastful about yourself or your game. Show them what a class act you are."

She'd heard loud laughter as the door to the conference room swung open and Shawn flew by, punching Terry playfully on the arm. "They're all yours, knock 'em dead Ms. Terry. Catch ya later."

As soon as Terry entered the room, she'd been overwhelmed (but dazzled!) by the bright lights of the television cameras, the continuous flashes of the photographers, the sheer number of people focused on her. After the first few questions she'd relaxed and started to enjoy talking about the match and how it felt playing Shawn and how much fun she was having and what she thought about her Round 16 opponent Analise Rouselle. Then some guy had asked if Libby was still coaching her. Terry had replied that Libby and Pete May were her coaches. The same rude-sounding asshole had followed up with, "Is this a subtle way, then, of Libby Shaver stepping down as your coach due to her personal problems?"

It had taken every ounce of self-control Terry had to reply, *politely*, "Libby is my coach and my friend and I can't imagine her 'stepping down' from being either one. As for the other thing you implied, I have no comment."

But she hadn't smiled when she said it.

Except for that one bad moment, the press conference had been great. Then, as soon as she left the Competitor's Complex, she'd been surrounded by kids clamoring for her autograph! For real this time!

And yesterday, when she, Pete and Mrs. S (Libby had felt a little tired and stayed home) had gone back to watch the men play their Third Round matches, photographers kept taking her picture and she could see people looking over at her, actually pointing at her.

So far, this being kind of famous thing had been pretty cool.

And now, all this, she thought, eying the heaps of newsprint. It *was* cool, but it was also a little bit weird, like it was happening not to her, but to some other Terry Gomez. A Terry Gomez the sportswriters were calling "beautiful" and "graceful" and "charming" and "poised beyond her years". Just who in the hell were they talking about? Sure, she could understand the nice stuff they wrote about the way she played, about her "deadly" serve, her "lightening-quick" reflexes at net, her "slashing" groundstrokes. But "beautiful"? Hardly. It embarrassed her as much to read it as it always did when Papi said it (of course, when she called Papi as soon as she could after the match, he said he'd watched every minute and she never looked more—you guessed it—beautiful).

"Listen to this," Libby said, reading from the *Daily Mail*, "... asked about Gomez' serve and volley game, Chillingsworth replied, 'Well, the next time I see Libby Shaver, I'm giving that girl a piece of my mind. Serve and volley was her game and now she's created a monster in her own image to terrorize us all. Thanks a lot Libby...'" Libby giggled, "So, Teeninator, just call *me* Dr. Frankenstein."

Terry leapt from the floor, stretched her arms out and lurched around the living room, moaning, "Master, Maaassterrrr..."

Pete made a face and held the paper he'd been reading away with two fingers as if it reeked. "Ahh, Doc, you'll be interested to know that according to the *Tatler* here, you've promised your 'adorable ward'—that would be you, Teeninator—that as soon as Wimbledon's over you're popping straight back to rehab so you'll be all straightened out in time for the Open."

Libby and Pete both roared, which made Terry furious.

"How can you guys laugh at this?" Terry said, snatching the

paper from Pete and scanning it herself. "How can they get away with writing stuff that's so not true?"

"Yeah, look, they called you adorable!" Pete hooted.

"I'm serious," Terry said. "I still can't understand why you don't sue them, or make them take it back."

"I keep telling you, T, it's not worth getting upset about," Libby replied. "Believe me, they've written worse things about me, and other people, than that. If you want to be serious about something worthwhile, start thinking about tomorrow."

"Duhh," Terry said and bolted from the room.

"Have any idea what that's about?" Libby asked Pete.

"Not a clue," Pete said and went back to reading the papers.

Libby sipped her coffee and examined a photograph of Terry stretching for a volley, arms and legs appearing a mile long, thick dark braid swinging out straight behind her. The kid was photogenic, all right. Gorgeous in every picture. The press was having a field day with their new obsession and Libby's voice mail was already full of calls from agents, sponsors, and company reps salivating for a chance at getting to Terry first. She had no intention of returning any of those calls while Terry was still in the draw and she'd instructed Terry to turn down all interviews except for the official post-match press conferences. Libby had seen too many young players thrust into the limelight prematurely only to crash and burn. This was *not* going to happen to Terry.

Libby had been so proud of the way Terry handled her press conference. Not that she'd doubted for one minute Terry's ability to express and conduct herself well, but it was a lot to handle all at once for an adult, let alone an adolescent. Libby and Pete had been watching on the big screen right outside the Complex, where all the "big name" conferences were shown live. Terry hadn't been a big name, but she'd beaten one. Libby held her breath when the questions concerning her were asked, knowing how defensive and aggressive Terry could turn in a second. When Terry answered as diplomatically as any seasoned star, Pete had hugged her and chuckled, "The kid's already a pro."

Her point exactly. Libby worried it was too much, too soon. Pete kept telling her to relax, enjoy the ride while it lasted, which probably wouldn't be beyond tomorrow, when Analise Rouselle would restore order to the world of womens' tennis and send Terry back to the Juniors where she belonged. Pete reminded Libby that though Terry had played above their expectations, she'd also been damn lucky, with the weak Hatfield as her first opponent, with Trish upsetting Sandoval, then getting hurt, with Shawn being too loose and getting caught off guard. How much luckier could she get?

Well, Libby thought Terry was also lucky to be playing Analise tomorrow instead of Natalia Volodieva, the fifth seed. Analise was ranked #6 in the world but had been seeded #10 here because she always did poorly at Wimbledon. A fantastic player on clay and an excellent one on hard court as well, Analise hated the grass and had vowed loudly and publicly every year after losing in the first three rounds *never* to return to Wimbledon. But she always did, and she'd never made it to the 16's before.

Until now. Beating Volodieva and facing an unseeded wild card like Terry had presented Analise with the best chance she'd probably ever have at winning Wimbledon. Ironically, this could present a problem for the popular French star. She had always been emotionally fragile, becoming easily frustrated, discouraged and down on herself when a match wasn't going her way. Especially a big match. She had choked away a lot of great opportunities in her career, which was disappointing to her many fans who appreciated her lovely game and her warm and gentle on-court disposition. The harder they rooted for her, the more nervous she became. In some ways, she was a victim of her own popularity. So immense was the pressure on poor Analise to win the French Open in her hometown of Paris that she practically had a nervous breakdown each year while she tried and failed to accomplish it. Now, *everyone* was expecting her to knock over the upstart American teenager.

But Analise had a pretty dismal record meeting great expectations, which could work in Terry's favor.

Much as she looked forward to tomorrow's match, Libby wished she had more energy to enjoy it. She'd felt worse yesterday and this morning than she had in a while, and she knew precisely why. She could practically hear Dr. Bissinger scolding her that she was doing too much. Too much! It was pathetic when "too much" meant simply riding back and forth to the Club and watching tennis matches. The coughing, the shortness of breath, the palpitations and constant sleepiness were supposed to warn her to take it easy. But how much easier could she take it short of lying on the couch all day, which she wasn't about to do when Terry was playing at Wimbledon, for pity's sake!

Glynn, ever the eagle eye for Libby's "symptom surges", had noticed and was shifting into smother mode again, which was another good reason for Libby to be thrilled that her dad was arriving today. He was a master at chilling her mom out. Douglas Shaver wasn't the world's biggest tennis fan, and this London home was his least favorite, but he was as excited about Terry's success as they all were and was eager to see her play.

So this was her plan. She wouldn't lift a finger today, all day, and she'd go to bed really early so she'd be fresh for tomorrow and beyond. Unlike Pete, she had a feeling Terry's luck wasn't quite ready to run out. In fact, she was so convinced of this that she'd spoken to both Alberto and Isabel yesterday while Terry, Pete and Glynn were out at the Club. If Terry could make it to the Quarters, she just might find herself with a bigger entourage!

Terry rushed back into the room. "Here!" With a dramatic flourish, she handed Libby a sheet of paper. "See, I *have* been thinking about tomorrow."

Libby looked at Terry's meticulously itemized game plan, complete with lists of Analise's strengths and weaknesses and different strategies for every situation. She grinned and handed the paper back to Terry. "No kidding. Think this might be overkill?"

"No such thing," Terry said.

Terry needn't have planned so diligently after all. Her opponent was about to do all the work *for* her. As Analise Rouselle walked out on Court One Monday afternoon to begin warming up for her first Round of 16 match, she was amazed she could draw a full breath. It was as if a 50 pound weight sat on her chest. Her mouth was so dry her tongue stuck to her teeth. The relaxation techniques she'd spent the last hour practicing with the sports psychologist who traveled with her hadn't helped at all. Her nerves were shot and the match hadn't even started!

Annalise was already so wrapped up in her own head that the tall American girl on the other side of the net could be anybody. It didn't matter. What mattered was that she *couldn't* lose this chance. Everyone thought she should have won a Grand Slam by now. Sportswriters called her "The Best Player Without A Slam Title". Her coach, her friends, her parents, her sports psychologist, her masseuse, the press—*everyone*—said winning this match was a sure thing, then just three more to the title. Easy for them to say. How was she supposed to win when her arms and legs felt full of sand, so heavy she could barely move? When she won the toss, she had a brief surge of hope. Surely it was a good sign, right?

It was the last positive thought she would have.

Terry knew after the first four games of the first set that her intuition about her opponent had been dead on. She had watched Analise play plenty of times on television, including last year's French Open quarterfinal when she blew a 6-2, 5-1 lead and lost to Mia Lindstrom. Each time she watched her, it seemed to Terry that Analise never played to win. She played not to lose, which is how you played when you choked. And Terry could plainly see she was choking big time. Double-faulting. Spraying balls way out or in the bottom of the net. Making stupid choices, like drop-shotting when Terry was mid-court. Having to repeat her toss two or three times before serving.

Terry won the first set 6-2 in twenty-five minutes. Or rather, she should say Analise lost the set because Terry hadn't had to do much except be a warm body on the other side of the net. She didn't even have to bother hating Analise. In fact, she almost felt sorry for her. Almost. In the middle of the second set, Terry actually got angry with her. She wanted to yell at Analise, "C'mon, shake it off—fight, damn it! This is *Wimbledon!!!*" The crowd obviously felt the same way. They cheered for Annalise, tried to get her going. Terry couldn't blame them. It was a terrible match, probably as painful to watch as it was to play.

In the end, Analise was no match for her greatest opponent—her own fear. She had tears in her eyes when she shook Terry's hand after dumping a final shaky forehand into the net, then showed better hustle getting off the court than she had during the whole match.

The final score was 6-2, 6-2.

Terry took no pleasure in the victory—if you could call it that—and acknowledged the crowd's polite but mild (they'd rarely seen such a poor Second Week match here) applause with an unenthusiastic wave. As she walked off the court she felt frustrated, irritated—and totally baffled. How could Analise just give the match away? It was inconceivable to someone like Terry, who liked to fight, who loved the drama of the battle and actually craved winning.

She was so bewildered that it took her a full minute to realize she was in the Quarterfinals of Wimbledon! Since the match was tomorrow, her psyching process had to power up immediately. She'd play the winner between #9 Regina Shuster from Germany and #12 Dragana Maravic of Serbia, both tall, strong, scrappy players who wouldn't roll over and die the way Analise did. She'd be ready.

Terry's mental preparation for her next match was abruptly suspended two hours later when Dragana Maravic, the famously fun-loving Serb who'd never beaten Shuster in their six previous meetings, was doing a spirited victory dance in the locker room after her match and slipped on the wet floor. One concussion and one broken right wrist later, Terry was assured a place in the Semifinals on Thursday without having to play one point.

It wasn't called a walkover for nothing.

Terry was bitterly disappointed, of course, feeling that she hadn't earned it. Once again, Libby and Pete assured her that walkovers, like retirements due to injury, were part of the game, that every player quickly pushed the misplaced guilt aside and tried to take advantage of their good fortune.

"I think the Tennis Gods might be in your corner, kiddo", Libby joked, though she knew that the person who would probably be waiting for Terry in the Semi's could wipe the smile off anyone's face.

⚲ 21

Ladies' Semifinal Day...Thursday

The hype surrounding the Kraskova-Gomez match had reached a fever pitch by the time the players stood at the entrance to the locker room, ready to walk out onto Centre Court for the first scheduled Semifinal. Kraskova had instigated this latest in a series of media frenzies at the press conference Tuesday following her easy Quarterfinal victory against Eva Kessler. When asked how she felt about her next opponent, Kraskova had given one of her characteristically churlish replies in a heavy Russian accent which made her sound like Ivan, the freakish robotic boxer in one of the *Rocky* movies

"Is ridiculous," she drawled, sounding bored enough to yawn and stretch out for a nap. "American child , I give tennis lesson to. Her luck over now. Is only warming up for Final, no?"

Tatiana Kraskova had been ranked #1 in the world before Jemma bumped her down to #2 eighteen months ago, which had done nothing to improve her already—and always—sour disposition. Perpetually crabby and argumentative on-court and down-right mean off-court, Kraskova was the player everyone loved to hate. She regularly taunted her opponents during matches then insulted them with surly remarks to the press. She was nasty to line judges, umpires—even ballgirls and boys, all of whom who shook in their tennis shoes upon learning they had to work a Kraskova match.

Adding to her fearsomeness—many called it poetic justice—were looks which reflected her inner ogre. At 6′1″ she was built rather like a refrigerator—a big rectangle of solid muscle without defining curves. She wore her hair in a buzz cut, regrettably drawing greater attention to beady rat eyes, a fat lump of a nose, crooked teeth and no chin to speak of.

The contrast between Kraskova and Terry was the cherry on top of the sundae to the salivating press corps. The headlines were merciless. *"Beauty vs the Beast"* was the natural and prevalent theme, of course. *"Crass vs Class"* reflected Terry's refusal to comment on Kraskova's negative remarks about her. Finally, *"Can the Teeninator Crush the Incredible Hulk???"* had to be the prime example of media absurdity. Yesterday's and today's papers had hyped this pairing with such over-the-top glee that the expectations here on Centre Court seemed primed for a heavy-weight boxing bout rather than a tennis match. When the fighters—oops, players—appeared in the ring—uhh, on the court—the normally reserved and tennis savvy crowd roared, eager for battle.

Warm-up over, Terry sat in her chair, feet tapping anxiously, ready to leap back on the court when the umpire announced the start of the match. How many times had she imagined what it would be like to play here, on the most awesome court at the most famous tournament in the world? So far, her imagination had done a pretty decent job predicting the adrenaline rush of walking into a stadium filled with nearly 14,000 clapping, cheering fans. During warm-up, she'd felt as if her nerves would burst through her skin, but in a good way, not a freaking out, choky way. Of course, in her ultimate fantasy, Jemma was her opponent, not the Incredible Hulk (the most fitting nickname for the Russian, in Terry's opinion), who was sitting on the other side of the umpire's chair at the moment, already bitching to the umpire about removing one of the ballboys who'd had the bad luck to throw a ball out of her reach.

Terry couldn't help but glance over at her last obstacle to the Final and Jemma. The good news was that Tatiana Kraskova was ridiculously despicable, so Terry didn't have to waste an ounce of energy coming up with a creative reason to hate her. On their way out of the locker room (as a Semifinalist, Terry now had the privilege of using the same "A" locker room the top seeds used), Kraskova had roughly brushed by her to be first out the door. Then, as they'd waited at the entrance to Centre Court to be introduced,

The Hulk stretched her fish lips back in a grotesque imitation of a smile and announced matter-of-factly through a stained jumble of teeth, "You vill lose." Yup, no problem with the hate factor today. The Hulk was so cartoonishly horrible it made Terry wonder, not for the first time, if it wasn't all a big act on Kraskova's part, like playing the villain in professional wrestling.

The bad news was that Kraskova had a lot of weapons. Her serve was almost as fast as Shawn's (and Terry's) and had a wicked kick to it, hitting the court then veering sharply to the right or left. She was left-handed, which made it harder for right-handers like Terry. She had a wicked topspin forehand which she loved to drive cross-court so it would bounce high on the other player's backhand side, and a deadly back-spinning drop-shot. Her reputation for running her opponents until they dropped was legendary.

But, but, but...Terry was convinced that all these strengths could be challenged. She'd watched (studied) Kraskova plenty of times, twice in person at the Sony and plenty of times on TV and video. When The Hulk served, she positioned her feet differently at the service line according to the direction she would kick her serve, so if you paid close attention you could anticipate where it would go. And yeah, her topspin forehand was dangerous, but it was also predictable. She *always* went to the backhand. Though she had confidence in her own backhand, Terry figured if she reacted quickly she could run around her backhand and make the return with her more powerful forehand. As for the drop shots, no worries. Getting to them required flat-out speed which Terry had to spare.

Finally, if Kraskova thought she could run her into the ground she was sadly mistaken. All the miles of running and hours of conditioning had made Terry an endurance junkie. She thrived on grinding it out if she had to. Unfortunately, her opponent was the same. The Hulk wasn't the fastest on her feet, but she would keep them moving for as long as it took to get the job done. "Winning ugly" in tennisspeak meant winning no matter how off, or tired, or choky you were, winning with whatever rabbits you could pull out of the top-hat on a day you should have lost. Kraskova was the Queen of Winning Ugly (and not because even on the days she played her best she was still *was* ugly).

So bring it on, Hulk, I'm ready. Terry shifted her attention to the Shaver's box, which was directly across from her in the first row of elevated seats. In all of her fantasies about playing here did she ever imagine that Libby *wouldn't* be sitting there. Instead, Pete was all alone, waving when he saw her looking over.

Libby had woken up this morning with a slight fever, and though she'd insisted she felt okay, Mrs. S made her call Dr. Bissinger, who had strongly advised her to stay home and rest. Libby was heartbroken and apologized over and over to Terry for having to miss the match and promising she'd be better for the Final. Terry was too worried about Libby to be mad at her for apologizing, of all the things she didn't need to do. Libby kept saying she was fine, but Terry knew deep down that all the doctor's orders and parents' arguing in the world couldn't have kept her from this match unless she truly felt sick.

"Remember, I'll be glued to the TV, kiddo, so you better not do anything you wouldn't want me to see," Libby had told her as she gave her a good luck hug at the door.

Mr. and Mrs. S decided to stay and watch the match with Libby, so it had been just Terry and Pete driving out to the Club with Pete trying the entire ride to make her stop fretting over Libby and focus on The Hulk. Of all the reasons why she needed to win this match, the biggest was so Libby could be here to watch her win Wimbledon and make almost every part of Terry's dream come true.

"Players, begin play," the umpire announced.

The thousands of fans packed around Centre Court, or watching on the giant screens on the Club grounds or riveted to a television screen somewhere in the world weren't to be disappointed if they'd hoped to witness a blood-thirsty clash. So far the Kraskova-Gomez match had been the tennis equivalent of a pit bull dogfight. After two and a half hours of two tie-breaker-deciding sets with a combined 246 points played, and the last twelve games with another combined 118 points, the combatants were dead even with the match *still* up for grabs. There was no tie-breaker in the third set at Wimbledon. They had to play it out, no matter how long it took.

Kraskova had taken the first set 7-6. Terry had taken the second set 7-6 after saving three match points in the tiebreaker, much to the delight of the crowd. They were now at 6-6 in the final set. Each game of each set had gone to deuce at least twice, and some a lot more. The momentum had swung wildly, often within a single game. Punches were immediately answered by counter-punches. Terry would serve an ace for one point then get passed at the net the next. Kraskova would jerk Terry all over the court then close in for the kill only to have Terry blow a winner by her a moment later.

Terry had to wait before serving to begin the 13th game because the stadium was in the midst of doing "The Wave". The crowd was solidly behind her, as they'd been throughout the match, though not so biased as to rudely applaud Kraskova's errors (though if there was anyone who deserved to be treated rudely it was she). They wanted Terry to win almost as much as she herself did, and at this point she needed all the encouragement she could get.

Incredibly fit as she was, Terry had never been so tired, physically and mentally. She was playing at the highest sustained level of tennis she'd ever experienced—with no end in sight. Kraskova had sunk her rotten teeth into this match and wasn't letting go. Terry couldn't think of any strategy she hadn't already tried. The best she could do was continue holding her serve and pray The Hulk would miraculously cave on her own serve, like double-fault four times in a row. Yeah, in her dreams.

"The Wave" was finished and the umpire called for quiet. Terry served wide to Kraskova's backhand and was rewarded with a rare precious easy point as Kraskova dumped the return in the net. 15-0. When she came in behind her next serve and volleyed the weak return for a winner and 30-0, she dared to hope she could hold her serve at love and save enough energy to win the next game without collapsing. Instead, she double-faulted. 30-5. Oh-oh. Not now. Please, puuuhhhlleeezzze, serve, don't let me down *now*, Terry begged The Tennis Gods. The added spin she put on her next first serve went wild, hitting one of the photographers in their box at courtside. Having to pause for the nervous laughter of the crowd to subside sure wasn't helping her own growing-by-the-second case of the dreaded throat-closing, stomach-churning, brain-sucking yips.

She tossed the ball for her second serve. It was a poor toss and she should have caught it and tossed again, but Rule #1 in The Choking Manual is Never Make The Smart Move. She served into the bottom of the net. Second double-fault in a row. 30-30. Adding insult to injury, Kraskova strolled back to the forehand service court clutching her neck with her right hand while sticking her tongue out, drawing boos and catcalls for what seemed like the millionth time during the match. Normally this would have enraged Terry, but she was already so mad at herself she couldn't waste any of it on The Hulk. "Come on, get a grip," she yelled (in her head, not out loud. Libby wasn't here, but she was watching).

The Tennis Gods must have been listening because she managed to place a decent first serve in which Kraskova returned to begin another long (especially for grass) grueling rally Terry won by drop-shotting Kraskova. 40-30. Terry drew a deep breath, feeling a little less choky now. Make this one count, she ordered, tossing the ball and gathering all the strength she had left into pounding the ball as hard as she could. The serve flew straight up the T. Kraskova lunged, swung and missed it completely. It was clocked at 131 mph! Terry had broken her own record!

When the number flashed on the big screen, the stadium crowd went crazy.

So did Kraskova, who stormed to the umpire's chair, declaring that the serve was out and making a challenge.

The umpire and the line judges (and the Shot Spot camera, for those watching on TV) agreed it was in.

Terry quickly walked to her chair for changeover and sat watching the spectacle of a classic Kraskova Meltdown. Instead of using the changeover to rest and regroup, Kraskova marched back and forth between the umpire's chair, the service line judge and the imaginary spot just past the service line where she insisted Terry's serve had landed. She raged in English and Russian, flapping her arms and stomping her feet like a giant little kid throwing a tantrum. The loud disapproval of the crowd merely incited her to more histrionics. It wasn't until the umpire warned her that she was in danger of being penalized a point that Kraskova piped down long enough to go to her chair, where she threw her racket to the ground and sulked until time was called.

Terry walked back on the court with renewed confidence, though she'd watched her opponent enough not to assume that Kraskova had fallen apart. Unlike most players, The Hulk wasn't distracted by a meltdown and sometimes even got jacked up by one.

But not this time. Kraskova's powerful jaws had unclamped from the match, leaving Terry free to take advantage of a double fault and an error while blasting three winners to take the game, set and match. 6-7, 7-6, 8-6.

Kraskova wouldn't look at her and barely touched her outstretched hand at the net, but Terry couldn't have cared less. She looked over at Pete, her huge smile faltering as she glanced at the empty spot next to him.

She was having an easier time believing she'd won a Wimbledon Semifinal than she was believing that Libby hadn't been here to see her do it.

"*She did it*" Libby screamed, hopping around in front of the big screen television where she'd been pacing for the last two games.

"Careful, luv," Glynn cautioned half-heartedly, since she was nearly as excited as Libby.

"Oh, come on, Mom, lighten up. I'm fine," Libby said, reveling in a close-up of Terry's beautiful face and dazzling smile as she stood at the side of the court waving to the jubilant crowd.

And she *was* fine. Her temperature was back to normal and she was feeling much better than she had earlier this morning, so much better that she wished she had ignored Dr. B and her parents, trusted her body to pull her through (though it hadn't given her much reason to believe in it lately) and gone to the match anyway. And *what* a match! She was so proud of Terry, not only for raising and maintaining her level of play but for out-gutting the infamously gutsy Kraskova. And for keeping her head on straight, especially after those two doubles near the end when she was clearly approaching the gates of Choke City. But mostly she was proud of the way she'd conducted herself. Class all the way, especially in contrast to her opponent, who'd baited her constantly with no success.

How proud Alberto and Isabel would have been, too, if only their flight hadn't been delayed. Damn, what rotten timing! They were supposed to arrive this morning in time for the afternoon Semi-final. As it turned out, the delay had put them in the air during the match, so they'd missed the whole thing, though there was a decent chance that Air Brittania showed it during the flight. She hoped so. She also hoped with all her heart that this surprise for Terry would be the beginning of a reconciliation that needed to happen for the entire Gomez family.

Now they all had the Final to look forward to. Libby was certain that whatever little bug had punked her out this morning had already run its course. In fact, she had more energy right now, felt more *normal* than she had in a long time. Certainly she realized that the thrill of Terry's victory had more than a little to do with it, but she also sensed that the feeling of wellness would continue long enough to see this girl who'd become so precious to her walk out onto Centre Court for the match of her life.

22

Thursday Evening...

Terry fidgeted in the car all the way back to London. She couldn't wait to see Libby and go through their ritual postmortem of the match. Of course, Terry had already spoken to her on the phone right after returning to the locker room to get ready for the press conference, but all they'd done was scream in unison. Libby had been so excited that Terry felt somewhat guilty about wanting to stay and watch the other Semifinal. She must have sounded guilty, too, because Libby had told her to relax, enjoy the match, take notes and she'd see her at home.

By the time she'd finished with the press stuff and rushed to join Pete in the Shaver's box, Jemma had won the first set 6-3. Great... go Jemma! Terry then spent the second set silently but madly rooting for the one of the two main characters in her vivid fantasy life. No offense to Keiko Tanaka, whom Terry would love to play—and beat—one day—just not this particular Saturday. No, it was *Jemma* who needed to be on the other side of the net. When Jemma obliged and put Keiko away 6-3, 6-3, Terry had been elated—and oddly relieved.

"Give it a rest, will you, T?" Pete pointed at the dashboard of the Bentley, currently in use as a drum for Terry's jackhammering index fingers.

"What? Oh, sorry." Terry leaned back and tried unsuccessfully to sit still. She felt like an electrical current was buzzing through her body and shooting through her arms and legs with nowhere else to go.

Pete chuckled. "It's OK. You just need to blow off some extra energy. I should let you out here and let you run the rest of the way. It's only a few more miles."

"Do it! I know the way back." Terry reached for the door handle as if she was going to leap from the car while it was still moving.

"No way. Libby would kill me."

"As if," Terry said. "She would never kill you, Petey. She *loooooves* you. Besides, killing you would take too much effort and she has to conserve her energy for more important things."

"What could be so important? Some little thing like the Wimbledon Final?"

"Seriously, do you think she'll be OK? She said on the phone that she was feeling better, but you know how she is, right?"

"Listen, she rested all day, so chill out," Pete said. "And when we get home, don't fuss over her because it bums her out to see you worrying. The best way you can help Libby feel better is to let yourself enjoy every minute of what's happening, all right?"

"Yeah, all right," Terry reluctantly agreed.

"And don't forget, Miss Teeninator, there's the small matter of psyching yourself to play Number One," Pete said.

"Oh, don't worry about that," Terry said in an odd tone that made Pete glance over at her. "But it can't hurt to do double workouts tomorrow and…"

Pete shook his head. "Too much, especially after the match you just played."

"But it's not a big deal…" Terry protested.

"Yes, it is…" Pete interrupted.

They still hadn't reached a compromise by the time they drove up to the townhouse.

While Pete went to park the car, Terry bounded up the stone steps and burst through the front door, shouting, "We're baaaackkkk!"

"In here," Mrs. S called from the living room.

Dashing through the foyer, she headed in the direction of the voice then came to a dead stop in the doorway when she saw who was sitting on the couch with Mr. and Mrs. S. For a moment she couldn't move because she couldn't believe her eyes.

"Corazon!" Alberto Gomez' face lit up at the sight of his granddaughter as he rose to greet her.

"Papi!" Terry rushed to hug him, reveling in his Papi smell of aftershave and cigars. She hadn't seen him in almost a month, the longest she'd ever gone in her *life*, and it made her so happy to see how great he looked, like the old Papi before Bria died. She stepped back, still holding his hands, stammering in her excitement, "Wh-what are you doing here? How did you get here??"

"I swam across the ocean, naturally," Alberto laughed, delighted at how thrilled Terry was with her surprise.

"No, I mean, when did you decide to come? How come you didn't let me know?"

"I didn't know myself. I just wished I could watch my granddaughter play in her big tournament and magically, here I am!" Alberto teased.

"C'mon Papi, tell me," Terry pleaded. Mr. and Mrs. S were yukking up a storm. So they were in on this, too, obviously. And Libby and Pete, no doubt.

"All right, no more torture," Alberto promised. "Libby called after you beat the French girl and said there was a good chance you could win the next match and play again today, so she was booking a flight for Wednesday in case, but our flight was delayed, and we missed it."

"You know I won, right?" Terry still couldn't get over Papi standing here in the Shaver's living room, all joking and casual, like he flew to London every day to watch his granddaughter play at Wimbledon. It was kind of surreal.

Papi chuckled and hugged her to him. "We watched you do it! They showed it on the plane, every minute of it. It wasn't as good as being there, of course, but I told all the people sitting around us that you were my granddaughter, and before we knew it, the whole plane was watching and rooting for you. When you won, the clapping and cheering was so loud I was afraid the plane might break apart! We are so proud of you, corazon!"

Terry had been so caught up in listening to Papi that it just now occurred to her that he kept saying "we".

She was opening her mouth to ask exactly who "we" was when she heard female giggling drifting toward them from the foyer. As it got closer, she realized she didn't even have to ask before Libby appeared in the doorway with her arm around the shoulders of the one person she most dreaded yet most wanted to see.

It seemed that *both* main characters of her Wimbledon Fantasy would be in place on Saturday after all, as long as she played it cool between now and then. Arranging her features into an imitation of happy surprise, Terry the Actress moved forward to greet her and Libby.

Subtly watching Terry from across the table during dinner, Libby couldn't yet decide whether she should be patting herself on the back for her brilliant idea or smacking herself for throwing Terry and Isabel into an awkward and potentially disastrous situation. This surprise reunion had seemed like a great idea at the time, but now she wasn't so sure. She couldn't get a good read on Terry, which was odd considering how well she knew her.

When she and Isabel had made their appearance earlier, the expression on Terry's face had gone through a series of rapid changes before settling into a pleasant mask punctuated with a smile that didn't quite reach her eyes. While she hadn't hugged Isabel, she hadn't been rude either, a vast improvement from the only other time Libby had seen them together, at Maria's funeral. And so far throughout dinner, as they had all relived Terry's triumph on the court that afternoon, and as Isabel and Alberto described how everyone back in the States (well, everyone who followed tennis), was going Terry Crazy, Terry had been fully engaged in the conversation and as responsive to Isabel as to everyone else, even asking her several questions. At one point, Isabel had looked over at Libby with wide eyes and raised eyebrows, as if to say, well this is new!

Still…Libby couldn't put her finger on it, but there was something about the way Terry was acting…and just like that it hit her. Terry *was acting*. Well, if the act was for her benefit, if Terry was simply trying to please her by at least pretending to get along with Isabel, at least it was a step in the right direction. These next few days presented a perfect opportunity for the Gomez family to begin healing itself, and Libby was determined to help it happen in any way she could. Listening to father, daughter and granddaughter sharing a laugh just now over something Alberto said, Libby allowed herself the first genuine glimmer of hope that it would all work out.

Terry lay across the foot of Libby's bed, channel surfing with the sound off while Libby finished talking on the phone to her friend Charlotte. She had *finally* come crashing down from the high she'd been on since 2:20 this afternoon, after she'd blasted that last cross-court forehand winner past The Hulk. Then, as if she'd needed to get any more jacked up, the Big Surprise had put her over the top. Papi and her so-called mother hanging out and chowing down on Beef Wellington with the Shavers! It was a lot to wrap her mind around, especially after the day she'd already had.

By the end of dinner she'd felt as if someone had yanked her plug right out of the socket. Physical exhaustion from the three hardest hours of tennis she'd ever played combined with the emotional exhaustion of pretending to get along with Isabel to totally wipe her out. When Libby had said her good nights and headed upstairs, Terry had been right behind her. Tired as she was, she'd still wanted to end the day the same way they had since coming to London, watching the Wimbledon news and gossip on the TV in Libby's bedroom, Libby propped against her mound of pillows with Terry stretched out in front of her, both of them usually falling asleep before the late news came on.

Terry paused on a channel with Jemma being interviewed. She

wanted to turn the sound on, but Libby was still on the phone. No matter, Terry could guess what she was saying. Jemma was famously diplomatic when she spoke about other players, always being fair and giving proper credit but somehow still managing to sound like she believed she was above everyone else. No doubt she was praising Terry for having some great wins and getting to the Final, but making it obvious at the same time that there was really no question who would be holding up the Venus Rosewater Dish during the awards presentation. Jemma was in for quite a shock.

"…All right Char, see you then," Libby said, "And don't forget, I always collect on my winnings!" Laughing at Charlotte's reply, she said good-bye and tossed the phone onto the pile of magazines beside her.

"What's that about?" Terry rolled over facing Libby, whose slightly flushed cheeks and glittery eyes made her look healthier than she had in a long time. Terry was so relieved that she was feeling better. In fact, not just better, but good, judging by the way she'd been all night—chattering non-stop and playing hostess as if she'd never been sick at all.

"A friendly wager on the Terry Gomez-Jemma York match," Libby replied. "If Jemma wins I make a donation to the British Juvenile Diabetes Association, and if you win, Charlotte makes one to Court Kids."

"How much?" Terry asked. Court Kids was Libby's foundation for poor kids to learn tennis and she was always planning events for it and raising money for camps and workshops and asking other famous people to help, which they always did. Nobody could say no to Libby.

"Enough. Let's just say that if you beat Jemma, you'll send some lucky kid to camp next month."

"Cool. One more reason to kick some British butt."

"You bet, no pun intended," Libby said through a yawn. "Listen, kiddo, I'm fading fast, so before I zonk out, let me say *one more time*—at the risk of being boring—how impressed I've been with you today..."

Terry faked a yawn of her own. "Ahh, you're boring me..."

"Seriously, and not only with how you played and behaved during the match. I'm sure you have mixed feelings about Isabel being here, but you made a great effort tonight to make things go smoothly. I realize a lot of it's for your grandfather's benefit, and probably some of it's for mine, since you know how thrilled I'd be for you and your mom to get back on track. But I also can't help hoping that some of it's because you know—deep down—how much Isabel loves you, otherwise she wouldn't be here."

"Uhh, I guess," Terry mumbled, rolling to the edge of the bed and sitting up, ready to escape. She didn't know what else to say because she couldn't say the truth. Sure, she didn't want to upset Papi or Libby by treating Isabel the way she deserved, but that had never stopped her before. And Libby was wrong. Isabel wasn't here because she loved her. You don't leave a daughter you love. No, she was here only because her daughter was sort of famous now and she wanted to be part of it. She couldn't tell Libby the main reason she was acting like things were cool was so Isabel would be sitting just where she was supposed to be on Saturday afternoon, court-side at the Final. When Terry was planning to let the world know she didn't *have* a mother anymore.

Of course, Libby would be totally disappointed, or worse, when that happened, but it was a risk Terry had to take in order to get the revenge she'd dreamed about for so long. Between now and then she needed to keep up the act.

"Look, Lib, thanks for bringing them here and trying so hard for us and all," Terry said. She got up and moved to the head of the bed. "I know you just want everyone to be happy. And I will be, I promise." She leaned over and planted a loud smacking kiss on top of Libby's head. "G' night," she said and walked across the room.

"Good night, sweetheart," Libby called after her, "...And don't think I won't hold you to that promise. Deal?"

"Deal," Terry replied and softly closed the door.

After Terry left, Libby turned off the TV and the bedside lamp and snuggled contentedly under the down comforter. She was deliciously exhausted, but it looked as if her efforts were going to be rewarded. If Terry kept her promise and decided being happy was better than being angry, then Libby could finally relax and let nature take it's course. She closed her eyes and drifted, her last waking thought of a photograph on the coffee table in Alberto's house. Terry and Isabel at the beach, identical wet heads together, beaming into the sun.

Libby's lips lifted into a smile on her way to sleep.

♀ 23

Saturday morning...

Pete peered at the newsprint in front of him. It was so blurry, he was having trouble reading it through his tears. But it didn't matter because he already knew what the words said on page four of the *London Times*:

"...Former tennis champion and philanthropist Elizabeth Staunton Shaver, 29, of Palm Beach, Florida and New York City, passed away in her sleep Thursday night...Ms. Shaver had been suffering from cardiomyopathy, a congenital heart disease, for the past eight months...Libby, as she was known to her family and countless friends, was a tireless supporter of many charities, especially her own Court Kids..."

The obituary went on and on, detailing what a wonderful, accomplished and generous person Libby had been and how many lives she had touched.

Pete let the paper drop to his lap and rubbed his eyes with his fists like a four-year-old. Why finish it? He knew all about Libby, had adored her since they were kids. To people who didn't know her, Libby may have seemed too good to be true. Beautiful. Smart. Talented. Kind. Rich. But it *was* true. *She* was true, with the purest heart of anyone he knew. And the irony that it was her heart that failed her weighed heavily on everyone who loved her.

It was the first thing he thought of when she'd told him last December, right before Christmas, about her diagnosis, that it was terminal, that the many specialists she'd consulted all agreed she had maybe six months to a year. She'd sworn him to secrecy. Other than him, her parents and Isabel and Alberto Gomez, nobody else knew. Not one among her army of friends, not even the closest ones who'd made her go to rehab.

And especially not Terry.

Libby had been adamant about that. She'd wanted the time she had left with Terry to be productive and positive, which would have been impossible if Terry had known the truth. And don't think for one minute it hadn't been hard on him, on *all* of them, acting for Terry's sake that Libby was simply sick. But it had been worth it. The kid had made monumental leaps forward.

Except...not knowing had placed Terry in a radically different emotional place than the other people in this house when they'd woken up yesterday morning to discover Libby had died during the night.

Pete, Glynn and Doug, and Alberto and Isabel, already dreading the inevitable, had been abruptly jolted to a new level of the grieving process they'd started months before.

Terry had gone into a functioning state of shock, or at least that's how Pete would describe the behavior of someone who'd reacted the way Terry had when he found her out in the garden and told her Libby was gone.

She hadn't cried out in denial or despair. In fact, she hadn't cried at all.

Instead, she'd become so calm, almost detached, comforting him instead. It was just the way Libby had described her reaction when her grandmother died. She'd been the same all yesterday. When one of them had broken down, she was right there, handing over tissues and giving hugs, but in a weird, robotic way. When Glynn, Doug and Pete had talked her into going ahead and playing the final today because it was what Libby would have wanted, she'd just nodded her head in quiet agreement, then asked if anyone wanted tea.

Pete didn't like it. It wasn't natural. Now he realized why it had always upset Libby so much that Terry never cried. And this seemed worse, how she was acting like a zombie with a brain. Something was far more wrong than a lack of tears.

It was time to give her the letter.

Pete reached into the back pocket of his jeans and pulled out a thick, cream-colored envelope with Terry's name written on the front in Libby's loopy oversized scrawl. Since the beginning of the year, Libby had given him a similar envelope, then asked for it back and given him another one, three different times. She'd handed him this latest one almost a month ago, right before they left for England. He knew it was a letter, and he had a pretty good idea about what it said. Yesterday—with the initial shock and arrangements and phone calls and people coming and going—had seemed too chaotic to hand it over. But now he realized that Terry needed something to plug her back into the world.

If Libby couldn't do it, no one could.

After breakfast, which she barely ate, Terry sat at the desk in her bedroom staring at the envelope propped against her laptop. The letter inside smelled faintly of White Linen, Libby's perfume. She'd started reading it but couldn't get past the first sentence, "*Hi Terry. If you're reading this it means I'm gone...*" before stuffing the letter back in the envelope and shoving it away. She wasn't ready to deal with it yet. Not now. Maybe not ever.

It didn't belong in The Zone.

Ever since yesterday morning, when Pete told her about Libby, she'd been in some kind of *Twilight Zone*, where she knew what was happening around her, and could hear what people were saying and answer their questions—only it seemed like it was all incredibly far away. In one way, it was strange, worse than the bad movie she'd been trapped in when Bria died. But in another way, it wasn't so bad.

Because here in The Zone, she didn't feel sad, or angry, or scared. She didn't feel *anything*.

The Zone was a Big Bubble of No Trouble, where she wasn't bothered by everyone else's crying, where it didn't matter that Libby was dead because nothing mattered. Safe in The Zone, she took comfort in the fact that she just didn't care anymore. She sure as hell didn't care what happened this afternoon. Here in The Zone, her Wimbledon Fantasy seemed ridiculous. Her determination to beat Jemma was gone. Her desire to win Wimbledon—buh-bye. Her thirst for revenge against Isabel—adios. As long as she floated in the tranquil waters of The Zone, nothing could touch her. She liked it here.

She was planning to stay for a long time. Maybe forever.

⚲ 24

Saturday Afternoon...The Wimbledon Ladies' Final

Pete searched the darkening sky over Centre Court, desperate to see a hint of rain. At this point it was the only chance Terry had to get a grip on herself while they closed the roof and try to claw her way back into this match. Ahh, but he was forgetting. The girl sitting courtside, staring off into space during the change-over, down 0-6, 0-1, wasn't the same Terry Gomez who loved the thrill of battle and fought for every point. That Terry had "left the building" as the saying went, on Friday morning and hadn't been seen since. Obviously, Libby's letter hadn't been able to reach her as he'd hoped.

"Are you thinking the same thing I am?" Isabel asked him, looking across the court at Terry with a mixture of sadness and frustration.

"If you're praying for rain and wondering if Terry is going to make an appearance today, then the answer is yes," Pete replied.

"If it does rain, are you allowed to see her, to coach her, while the roof thing happens?"

"Sure, but honestly, with the way she is..." Pete shook his head, totally discouraged. "I don't think all the coaching in the world could save her from herself. And right now, *she's* a much tougher opponent than Jemma."

Isabel nodded in agreement. She didn't know much about the game of tennis, but she knew her daughter. Terry had added a whole new level to the wall she hid behind—and added spikes on top—since yesterday. "I hear you loud and clear," she replied, never taking her eyes off Terry, who was directly in her sight line.

Pete stood and stretched, trying to get Terry's attention and give her some silent encouragement, for all the good it would do. She hadn't looked over at them once, though they were in the very first row above the court. At Wimbledon, the family and friends of the players traditionally sat together in the official "Friends Box". But Pete, Isabel, and Alberto had decided to sit in the Shaver's box instead. Somehow it had seemed more appropriate today, even though there was a terribly sad absence of Shavers. Doug and Glynn had arrangements to make and people to deal with in addition to the crushing grief over losing their beloved only child. They were still trying to decide when and where to hold a memorial, which Pete couldn't even bear to think about right now.

Wrenching his mind from that dark place back to the pathetic state of affairs here at Centre Court, Pete joined the crowd in applauding the players as they walked back out to resume the match, if that's what you wanted to call the embarrassingly one-sided destruction they'd witnessed so far. During the first set, only two games had gone to deuce, and Jemma had won the first game of the second set at love. It was so bad that this madly pro-Jemma hometown crowd had started cheering for Terry, trying to fire her up.

Good luck, Pete thought grimly, watching her plod back out to the court when normally she jogged out. You could set off fireworks that spelled her name across the sky and fail to get a rise out of her.

As Terry served for the first point of the second game, Pete felt the first drop of rain.

Four points later, at deuce, the Tournament Referee came out onto the court and ordered play to be suspended for the half hour roof closing process.

"Thank God for grass courts!" Pete exclaimed.

"But it's only a light sprinkle," Alberto said. "Why are they stopping so soon?"

"Because this grass gets slippery immediately. It's too dangerous. And since a sprinkle usually means more rain really soon, they have to get the court covered before that happens." Pete replied.

Sure enough, the grounds staff was running out with their giant green tarpaulin, which they could secure into position in under a minute.

"Now what?" Isabel asked. "Does Terry have to stay in the locker room?"

"Yeah, I'll head over there now." Pete rose from his seat and reached into his pocket. "Here's the Clubhouse Guest Pass. If you folks want to go on up, I'll join you as soon as I'm done trying to jump start Terry."

"Wait, Pete," Isabel grabbed him by the arm.

Terry sat on the floor, back against the wall, in the most remote corner of the cavernous locker-room. She had her iPod earbuds in, but no music playing. She just didn't want anyone trying to talk to her. Besides, she wasn't into listening to music anymore.

She knew it took around thirty minutes for the roof, not that it mattered. She was in no hurry to get back on the court and go through the motions. It was all so pointless. To think she had once dreamed about the thrill of walking out on Centre Court, holding her bouquet of flowers, waving to the cheering crowd. But when she'd actually done it earlier, she felt nothing but tired by the prospect of running around a square of grass hitting a fuzzy ball with a metal object. How stupid was that? How could she have *ever* put so much time and thought and energy into something so absurd? Well, you wouldn't catch her doing it again after today.

She heard a burst of laughter coming from another part of the locker-room. Jemma and her entourage, no doubt. Sounded like they were doing a little early celebrating. She could hardly blame them. There wasn't any question what would happen after they returned to the court. Jemma had come up to her before the match, saying how sorry she was about Libby, and how she hadn't known her well, but could see what a lovely person she was, blah-blahblah. Terry had just mumbled, "Ummm, thanks" and turned away because, really, what else could she say? There'd been a bunch of times during the match when she could see Jemma was feeling sorry for her. Before, when she lived outside The Zone, that would have made her want to smack the pity right off her face. Now, she couldn't care less.

Likewise, *before*, she would have gone ballistic over seeing who had just come around the corner, headed straight for her.

Now, she just said, "Hi."

"Hi," Isabel said. "Mind if I sit a minute?"

Terry shrugged and motioned at the bench beside her. "Go ahead. Where's Pete?"

Isabel perched on the edge of the bench as if to emphasize the temporary nature of her visit. "He'll be down in a minute. I told him I needed a private moment with you."

Terry sighed. "For what?"

"To tell you a few things I think you need to hear."

"No offense, but if you're going to tell me what I'm doing wrong out there, I suggest you get Pete instead."

"There!" Isabel exclaimed. "A spark of sarcasm. I never thought I'd be happy to hear it, but I am. It means Terry Gomez is in there somewhere."

"What are you talking about?"

"I don't care if you go back out there and never win another point. I just want to see you try."

"It doesn't matter," Terry said, wishing Isabel would can her pep talk and disappear.

"Listen, Terry, I know—better than anyone, believe me—how much Libby meant to you. Sometimes, I'm ashamed to say, I resented how much you loved her. And how much she loved you. How do you think it would make her feel, knowing you've apparently decided to give up on everything because of her? You should be playing this match in honor of Libby and instead you're not out there at all. And you're wrong. It *does* matter if you try. It's the *only* thing that matters, and you know I'm not talking just about tennis."

Isabel leaned forward, her eyes burning into Terry's. "Libby fought so hard to stay alive as long as she could. It would make her sick to see you with no fighting spirit. Where did it go, Terry? I know you had it once, because you got it from me. After your father died, I had to fight for my sanity, and I've had to fight my way through a lot of dark times since then. I've been fighting for *you*, whether you want to believe it or not, for the past two years, and I'm not going to stop until our family is whole again."

"I don't know what you want me to say," Terry said.

Isabel stood and looked down at her. "It's not what you say. It's what you do and what you feel in your heart. If Libby were here, she'd tell you the same thing. Maybe you'd listen to it coming from her." Isabel turned and began walking away. "I'll send Pete down now," she said.

"No, wait," Terry called as Isabel was turning the corner. "Tell him he doesn't need to come. I'm okay."

As soon as Isabel disappeared, Terry scrabbled in her tennis bag and came up with the envelope she hadn't opened since Pete gave it to her this morning. Removing Libby's letter she took a deep breath and read:

> *Hi Terry,*
>
> *If you're reading this it means I'm gone. I hope you're not angry that I didn't tell you back in December about the "fatal" part. Surely you can understand how I wanted our time together to be as wonderful as it turned out to be.*
>
> *In fact, I have you to thank for helping me stick around as long as I did. I've had a fantastic, privileged life which I wouldn't have traded for a different but longer one.*
>
> *My only regret is that I'm not going to be around to see what you choose to do with YOUR life. That's right, T, YOUR choice.*

*In earlier versions of this letter I used a lot of ink telling
you how proud I am of you and giving advice about goals
and college and boys, etc., until I realized two things.
I've said it all before. And ALL I've said before won't
amount to ANYTHING if you insist on embracing hate
and anger and revenge as your only friends. Thriving on
negativity is the saddest way to live that I can imagine.*

*Let it go, Terry. Let yourself love and be loved. Let
yourself be happy.*

*Let me tell you, kiddo, this business of dying is hard
work. I'm exhausted, and I'd gladly lie down and never
get back up, if only I knew that you were going be okay.
If there's just ONE piece of my advice you ever follow,
please let it be this. Open up and let the world back in.
Start now. I love you, sweetheart. You made my life
richer for knowing you.*

Libby

*P.S. You and Pretty Boy came to me at the same time,
so it's only fitting that you stay together. He always liked
you best anyway, but he's officially your dog now. I know
you'll take good care of him.*

Terry couldn't figure out why the ink on the paper was smearing in spots until she realized she was crying. She. Was. Crying.

The trickle of tears became a torrent until she was sobbing, her face buried in the letter. She cried for Libby. And for Bria. And for Margie, Irene and Tia—and all the other friends she pushed away. And for the father she never knew. And for her mother who she missed so much.

Glorious, salty, cleansing tears washed away the grimy filter of anger and resentment and hate that Terry had been seeing the world through. The heaving of her chest as she wailed cracked open the wall protecting her heart. Here on the floor of the All England Club locker room, using Libby's letter as a map, Terry

Gomez found the way back to her true self, the old Terry who had fun and friends and a mother who loved her.

The rain delay was over. Terry and Jemma walked down the hallway toward the entrance to Centre Court.

"Umm, Jemma, sorry if I seemed kind of rude to you before," Terry said. "You were just being nice about Libby, and I appreciate it. I just didn't know what else to say."

"Oh, please Terry, no offense taken. This must be so hard for you, and I really am very sorry," Jemma replied, thinking, poor kid. When she and her coach heard Terry sobbing in the locker room, Jemma wanted to check on her, but her coach wisely said to leave her be. It was true. She *did* feel sorry for Terry. But it wasn't going to stop her from going out and winning the next five games as quickly as possible.

Jemma had no idea yet that she was going to be facing a different player—and a different girl than the one who started the match.

Terry drank in the applause as they entered the stadium. Everything looked and sounded different now. The crowd was bigger and louder. The grass on the court was greener. The yellow balls and the purple and green clothing of the line judges were brighter. The lights were on now that the roof was closed. It reminded Terry of the moment in *The Wizard of Oz* when Dorothy throws open the door of her house to find the world had gone from black and white to color. She felt like dashing across the court and leaping into the box where Isabel, Papi and Pete stood clapping along with everyone else. Instead, when she reached her chair she waved at them, smiled as far as her lips would stretch and gave a thumbs up.

"Unless my eyes are deceiving me," Pete said to Isabel. "I do believe Terry has arrived to play the Final. Whatever you did worked like a charm."

"Somehow I think it was a lot more than that," Isabel replied.

What had begun as a pitiful spectacle turned into a highly

competitive contest as Terry and Jemma treated the crowd to two more sets of pounding serves, dazzling shot-making, amazing gets and brilliant winners. Oooohhs and aaahhhs and thunderous applause rippled through the stadium seats. The rabid cheering for *both* players was continuous. When Terry took the second set 6-4, anyone would have thought she was the British darling judging by the wild reaction of the fans.

And fifty minutes later, when Terry served an ace at 6-5, 40-30, to win the Wimbledon Championship, a nuclear explosion could have gone off on the Club grounds and no one would have been able to hear it.

Terry stood in the middle of Centre Court, holding the famous Venus Rosewater Dish, grinning and squinting in the glare of flashbulbs from the army of photographers in front of her. She was the Wimbledon Champion! As many times as she had imagined this moment, she'd never guessed it would feel like this. She was incredibly happy and terribly sad and overwhelmingly excited all at the same time.

Libby, wherever you are, I hope you can see me, she thought, tears spilling from her eyes once again. I hope you're satisfied that I've turned into a big crybaby. I hope you're pleased with how I played. But mostly I hope you know how much I love and miss you, and I hope you can see that I took your advice. You were right. Happy feels so much better. I'll never forget everything you did for me and you'll always be with me in my heart.

By the time she was handed the microphone after the trophy presentation, Terry had pulled herself together enough to give a very different acceptance speech than the one in her old Wimbledon Fantasy.

She'd watched enough of these to know about thanking all the tournament officials and sponsors, which is how she began. Then she praised Jemma (who would have thought!) for playing a tremendous match and saying she felt honored to be on the court with such a great champion (and she meant it!). *Then* she got to the real stuff.

Gripping the microphone and swallowing hard she continued, "I want to thank Jennifer Van de Veer and Charlie Swenson for giving me so much of their time, playing for hours in the hot Florida sun. There aren't enough words to properly thank my coach and friend, Pete May. Petey, you're the best. I couldn't have done this without you. I want to thank my family, my grandfather, Alberto and my mom, Isabel, who are sitting right over there. I love you both so much and I'm sorry I've been away so long. And there are two people who couldn't be here today in body, but I know they're here in spirit, so I want to thank them both and tell them I love them. My grandmother, Maria, who I miss every day and my friend and mentor, Libby Shaver, who saved me from myself, changed my life and showed me how to be a better person. This is for you, Libby."

Terry held the Venus Rosewater Dish as high as she could with one hand and looked skyward, face wet, eyes shining.

She swore she heard Libby say, "Thanks kiddo."

www.ingramcontent.com/pod-product-compliance
Lightning Source LLC
Chambersburg PA
CBHW071159260626
47162CB00003B/1100